Someone wants to crash Stone Barrington's party in Stuart Woods's bestselling series

Stone Barrington is in Bel-Air, overseeing the grand opening of ultraluxe hotel The Arrington, built on the grounds of the mansion belonging to his late wife, Arrington Carter.

The star-studded gala will be attended by socialites, royalty, and billionaires from overseas . . . and according to phone conversations intercepted by the NSA, it may also have attracted the attention of international terrorists. To ensure the safety of his guests—and the city of Los Angeles—Stone may have to call in a few favors from his friends at the CIA . . .

Praise for the Novels of Stuart Woods

Indecent Exposure

"Another entertaining episode."　　　—Associated Press

Fast & Loose

"[Woods] fascinates us with the lifestyle of the wealthy, sometimes beautiful, people. . . . The battle of wits and resources makes for a suspenseful series of high-flying episodes filled with action."　　　—*Florida Weekly*

Below the Belt

"Woods is a formidable storyteller who knows the art of monopolizing your attention. You may find *Below the Belt* his best novel."　　　—*The Washington Book Review*

Sex, Lies & Serious Money

"[An] irresistible, luxury-soaked soap opera."
　　　—*Publishers Weekly*

Dishonorable Intentions

"Diverting."　　　—*Publishers Weekly*

Family Jewels

"A master of dialogue, action and atmosphere, the Key West resident has added one more jewel of a thriller-mystery to his ever-growing collection." —Fort Myers *Florida Weekly*

Scandalous Behavior

"Woods offers another wild ride with his hero, bringing readers back into a world of action-packed adventure, murder and mayhem, steamy romance, and a twist you don't see coming."
—*Booklist*

Foreign Affairs

"Purrs like a well-tuned dream machine . . . Enjoy this slick thriller by a thoroughly satisfying professional."
—*Florida Weekly*

Hot Pursuit

"Fans will enjoy the vicarious luxury ride."
—*Publishers Weekly*

Insatiable Appetites

"Multiple exciting storylines . . . Readers of the series will enjoy the return of the dangerous Dolce."
—*Booklist*

Paris Match

"Plenty of fast-paced action and deluxe experiences that keep the pages turning. Woods is masterful with his use of dialogue and creates natural and vivid scenes for his readers to enjoy."
—Myrtle Beach *Sun News*

Cut and Thrust

"Goes down as smoothly as a glass of Knob Creek."
—*Publishers Weekly*

Carnal Curiosity

"Stone Barrington shows he's one of the smoothest operators around."
—*Publishers Weekly*

Standup Guy

"Stuart Woods still owns an imagination that simply won't quit. . . . This is yet another edge-of-your-seat adventure."
—*Suspense Magazine*

Doing Hard Time

"High escapist suspense."
—*Mystery Scene*

Collateral Damage

"Undoubtedly a hit. It starts off strong and never lets up, building to an exciting showdown." —*Booklist*

Severe Clear

"Stuart Woods has proven time and time again that he's a master of suspense who keeps his readers frantically turning the pages." —*Bookreporter*

Unnatural Acts

"[It] makes you covet the fast-paced, charmed life of Woods's characters from the safety of your favorite chair." —*Code451*

D.C. Dead

"Engaging . . . The story line is fast-paced." —*Midwest Book Review*

Son of Stone

"Woods's vast and loyal audience will be thrilled with a second-generation Barrington charmer." —*Booklist*

Bel-Air Dead

"A fast-paced mystery with an inside look into Hollywood and the motion picture business. Barrington fans will enjoy it." —*The Oklahoman*

Strategic Moves

"The action never slows from the start." —*Midwest Book Review*

Praise for Stuart Woods's Other Novels

Smooth Operator (with Parnell Hall)

"Fans are sure to welcome this action-packed start to a separate series within the larger Stone Barrington story arc." —*Publishers Weekly*

Barely Legal (with Parnell Hall)

"A fast-moving tale with a light touch . . . Crime fiction doesn't get much more entertaining than this." —*Booklist* (starred review)

BOOKS BY STUART WOODS

FICTION

Quick & Dirty[†]

Indecent Exposure[†]

Fast & Loose[†]

Below the Belt[†]

Sex, Lies & Serious Money[†]

Dishonorable Intentions[†]

Family Jewels[†]

Scandalous Behavior[†]

Foreign Affairs[†]

Naked Greed[†]

Hot Pursuit[†]

Insatiable Appetites[†]

Paris Match[†]

Cut and Thrust[†]

Carnal Curiosity[†]

Standup Guy[†]

Doing Hard Time[†]

Unintended Consequences[†]

Collateral Damage[†]

Severe Clear[†]

Unnatural Acts[†]

D.C. Dead[†]

Son of Stone[†]

Bel-Air Dead[†]

Strategic Moves[†]

Santa Fe Edge[§]

Lucid Intervals[†]

Kisser[†]

Hothouse Orchid[*]

Loitering with Intent[†]

Mounting Fears[‡]

Hot Mahogany[†]

Santa Fe Dead[§]

Beverly Hills Dead

Shoot Him If He Runs[†]

Fresh Disasters[†]

Short Straw[§]

Dark Harbor[†]

Iron Orchid[*]

Two-Dollar Bill[†]

The Prince of Beverly Hills

Reckless Abandon[†]

Capital Crimes[‡]

Dirty Work[†]

Blood Orchid[*]

The Short Forever[†]

Orchid Blues[*]

Cold Paradise[†]

L.A. Dead[†]

The Run[‡]

Worst Fears Realized[†]

Orchid Beach[*]

Swimming to Catalina[†]

Dead in the Water[†]

Dirt[†]

Choke

Imperfect Strangers

Heat

Dead Eyes

L.A. Times

Santa Fe Rules[§]

New York Dead[†]

Palindrome

Grass Roots[‡]

White Cargo

Deep Lie[‡]

Under the Lake

Run Before the Wind[‡]

Chiefs[‡]

COAUTHORED BOOKS

Barely Legal[††]
(with Parnell Hall)

Smooth Operator[**]
(with Parnell Hall)

TRAVEL

A Romantic's Guide to the Country Inns of Britain and Ireland (1979)

MEMOIR

Blue Water, Green Skipper

[*]A Holly Barker Novel
[†]A Stone Barrington Novel
[‡]A Will Lee Novel

[§]An Ed Eagle Novel
[**]A Teddy Fay Novel
[††]A Herbie Fisher Novel

SEVERE CLEAR

A STONE BARRINGTON NOVEL

Stuart Woods

G. P. Putnam's Sons
New York

PUTNAM

G. P. PUTNAM'S SONS
Publishers Since 1838
An imprint of Penguin Random House LLC
375 Hudson Street
New York, New York 10014

First G. P. Putnam's Sons hardcover edition / September 2012
First Signet premium edition / April 2013
First G. P. Putnam's Sons premium edition / December 2017
G. P. Putnam's Sons premium edition ISBN: 9780451414373

Printed in the United States of America

This book is for Jeanmarie Cooper.

1

Scott Hipp turned off I-295 South in Fort Meade, Maryland, at the dedicated exit entitled "NSA Employees Only" and drove to the mirrored black building that is the headquarters of the National Security Agency. The NSA was that part of the United States intelligence community responsible for communications surveillance and code breaking, and Hipp was its deputy director for cryptology, so he could park in the underground garage instead of in one of the eighteen thousand parking spaces surrounding the building.

Feeling smug that he would return to a cool automobile instead of one baking outside, he inserted his ID badge in the elevator panel and rode up to his office on the top floor, which he entered at the stroke of eight a.m., as he did every day. Four people awaited him at his conference table, drinking his coffee.

Hipp set his briefcase on the conference table and sat down. "Tell me something I don't know," he said without preamble.

The four exchanged some glances and shuffled through their papers.

Hipp watched them with satisfaction, since he knew they knew there was not much he didn't know.

"How about a cryptology joke?" asked one of them, removing a sheet of paper from a stack.

"Amuse me," Hipp said.

"Overnight down at Fort Gordon, one of our computers picked up a twenty-two-second cell phone conversation between someone in Afghanistan and someone in Yemen. The conversation was too brief to pinpoint locations, and much of it was garbled. The funny part is that, in the middle of the conversation, two English words were clearly spoken: 'the' and 'Arrington.'"

"That is terribly amusing," Hipp said with a straight face. "It's also very common, since English is a worldwide language, and foreigners often use phrases from or fragments of English."

"Yes, sir."

"Does anyone at Fort Gordon, or for that matter, anyone here, have any thoughts on what the words mean?"

"Well," the man said, "I Googled it and there

were essentially four hits, among a lot of duplication: first, there's some techie businessman named Arrington who's apparently famous in that world; second, there's an old Virginia family by that name; third, there's an Arrington vineyard; and fourth, there's a new hotel opening in Los Angeles called The Arrington. I like that one best because it has the 'The' in front of it."

"Tell me about the hotel," Hipp said.

"You remember the movie star Vance Calder, who was murdered some years back? The hotel is being built on the grounds of his former home, something like twenty acres, in Bel-Air, a top-scale residential community in L.A."

"Home of the Bel-Air Hotel, I believe," Hipp replied.

"Right," the man said. "The hotel is being named for his widow, née Arrington Carter, who herself was murdered early last year. Curiously, both Mr. and Mrs. Calder were murdered by former lovers."

"Any apparent significance there?" Hipp asked.

"Not really, just a coincidence. The hotel is having a grand opening soon—apparently it's a hot ticket out there."

"If it's a hot ticket in L.A.," Hipp observed, "there are probably not many invitations circulating in either Afghanistan or Yemen."

"That occurred to me, sir."

"In what language did the cell phone conversation take place?"

"A combination of Urdu and Arabic. Not enough was captured to make any sense of it."

"All right," Hipp said. "Put 'The Arrington' on the phraseology watch list and let's see if anything pops up. I don't think a single mention of the name is grounds for any sort of alert at this point."

"Yes, sir," the man said, scribbling a note on the message and setting it aside.

The meeting went on for another hour, five men trying to find some evil intent in the overnight traffic. At nine thirty, Hipp closed his briefcase and stood up. "I'm due at the White House at eleven," he said. "You people finish up somewhere else. I need the office."

The four men shuffled out, and Hipp spent a few minutes going over calls and correspondence with his secretary.

Hipp arrived at the White House at ten forty-five and was admitted to the cabinet room in the West Wing. By eleven there were eight representatives of other intelligence and security agencies present, and the president of the United States entered the room on time. Everyone stood, and he told them to sit, and the meeting began.

An hour and twenty minutes later, the meeting broke, and Hipp went down to the White House

Mess to get some lunch before driving back to Fort Meade. He chose a table by himself, but a moment later, the president's chief of staff, Tim Coleman, walked up. "Hi, Scott. Mind if I join you?"

"Not even a little bit," Hipp replied.

"How'd your meeting go?"

"Like most meetings—nothing monumental was decided. Sometimes I think all this Agency cross-talk has gone too far."

"I know how you feel," Coleman said. "That's why I wasn't there."

A Filipino waiter came with menus, and they ordered.

A discussion of the troubles of Tiger Woods ensued, and the two men agreed that all the man had to do was to win a couple of tournaments and he'd be back on track. They were on coffee when Hipp, trying to keep the conversation going, told Coleman about the capture of two English words in a foreign telephone conversation.

"What words?" Coleman asked.

" 'The Arrington.' "

Coleman looked at Hipp. "What do you think it means?"

"Could be a new hotel about to open in L.A.," Hipp said. "I put it on the phraseology watch list, and we'll see if it comes up again."

Coleman stood up. "I gotta get back to work, Scott. Good to see you."

"Same here, Tim."

Coleman turned to go, then stopped. "Say, let me know if your watch list catches that phrase again, will you?"

Hipp was about to ask why, but Coleman was already striding across the room.

Tim Coleman went back to his office, and on the way in he said to one of his secretaries, "Get me the director of the Secret Service, please. Right now."

2

Stone Barrington arrived at the offices of Strategic Services, his most important legal client, and was shown to a large conference room. A large object under a sheet dominated the table, and half a dozen men and women stood, chatting idly and drinking coffee.

At the stroke of three p.m. Michael Freeman, chairman and CEO of Strategic Services, the world's second-largest security firm, entered. "Ladies and gentlemen," he said, "please be seated." Everyone found a chair.

"I know most of you have already met, but let me take a moment to review. To my immediate right is Stone Barrington, legal counsel to Strategic Services, and the largest individual investor in the hotel. Strategic Services is, of course, a significant investor, as is Superlative Hotel Management, or Super, as we like to call it, and they are represented here by David Connor, CEO, to Stone's right, and by Morton Kaplan, to my left, who is serving as the executive director of our hotel. At the other end of the table are Katie Rogers, Super's marketing director, and Caroline Hugenot, the director of design for the hotel, and finally, Dick Trevor, who leads the architectural team for us.

"I have one more introduction to make. Ladies and gentlemen, The Arrington." Freeman took hold of the sheet covering the object on the table and, with a flourish, whipped it off, revealing a large model of the hotel. Everyone applauded.

"I know you've all seen the place at some stage of the construction, but this will be the first bird's-eye view that any of us has seen, unless someone owns a helicopter I don't know about." Freeman produced a laser pointer and switched it on.

"The front gate is here, of course, and the drive takes arrivals up the hill to the reception building, which is an expansion of the Vance Calder house and contains the reception desk, concierge staff, phone exchange, bell captain's office with adjacent luggage storage space, and the executive offices. Behind that building, where the Calder pool once was, is the house built for Arrington Carter Barrington and her husband, Stone Barrington, and next to that is the former Calder guest house, now Cottage One."

Freeman continued to point out the new pool, the par-three, nine-hole golf course, the tennis courts, gymnasium, cottages, and buildings containing rooms for both guests and their traveling staffs. "Most of the parking is underground, leaving the roads and paths free for the electric carts that will transport guests and their luggage to their accommodations.

"We have an indoor theater seating three hundred people and an outdoor amphitheater built into the hillside that seats fifteen hundred. There is a mini-mall here, containing a spa, hair salon, and eight top-end shops and boutiques. A guest who arrives having lost all his luggage can reequip himself or herself there in an hour or less."

Freeman pointed to two large cottages in a secluded corner of the property. "These are our two presidential cottages, and after weeks of diplomacy, negotiation, and security planning, I can finally divulge what most of you do not know: two days before our grand opening, the presidents of the United States and Mexico will meet to conduct final negotiations and the signing of a new trade and immigration treaty between the two countries, covering all sorts of things that you will read about in the newspapers. Additionally, both presidents will attend our grand opening celebration.

"The Arrington is an ideal location for such a meeting, especially since it will not yet have any guests except Stone Barrington and his party, and I can assure you that between the United States Secret Service and the people of Strategic Services, there will be security rivaling that of the White House."

More applause and happy smiles.

"There are two hundred suites, fifty rooms, three restaurants, and everything else a guest's heart could desire. As you may know, Centurion Studios has underwritten the grand opening celebration, and they have taken twenty-five suites for that night. Many of their out-of-town guests will be staying on for some days. Centurion has also seen that the crowd attending the celebration will be a star-studded one. One thousand invitations were sent out all over this country and the world, and I'm told that there have been more than nine hundred acceptances. Before you ask, the invitation list is now closed, but then you all had the opportunity of inviting guests.

"Now, I'd like to ask Mort Kaplan to take us through the schedule of events on opening day."

Kaplan stood up. He was a tall, slender, handsome man of around fifty in a Savile Row suit and a tan. "Good morning, ladies and gentlemen." Kaplan took them, step by step, through the schedule of the opening day and gave them their suite assignments. "Since all of our guests will be arriving on the same day, I would be grateful if you could check into the hotel with your luggage the previous day. The Secret Service will have your names at the gate. We've rented a fleet of golf carts, which will bear our logo, to supplement our own fleet of electric vehicles, so that will help us deal with the rush. We will also have a dozen check-in stations at the front desk, instead of the usual four. Each guest will receive a rather expensive gift box and a packet of information, including a map of the property, table assignment for dinner, and other amenities."

Kaplan continued for most of an hour, then thanked everyone and sat down.

"Thank you, Mort," Freeman said. "That was very impressive, and I'm sure everything will go smoothly. Ladies and gentlemen, that concludes our meeting. I'm sure I'll see you all at the grand opening."

The group chatted among themselves for a few minutes, then filed out and headed for the elevators. Mike Freeman tugged at Stone's sleeve. "Stick around for a minute, will you?"

"Sure, Mike."

Freeman closed the conference room door and waved Stone to a seat.

"You're looking very serious, Mike."

"I'm feeling very serious," he replied.

"What's going on?"

"I had a phone call this morning, a conference call, actually, with the director of the Secret Service, Howard Carroll, and the president's chief of staff, Tim Coleman, whom I believe you know."

"I know Coleman, but not Carroll."

"They told me that an NSA computer recorded a cell phone conversation between someone in Afghanistan and someone in Yemen. Most of it was garbled, but the words 'The Arrington' in English were discernible."

"That's disturbing," Stone said, and he felt it.

"Both the White House and the Secret Service feel that a single mention of the hotel's name is not necessarily significant, and they've put the name on a kind of electronic watch list to see if there's any further chat about it. In the meantime, nobody is panicking—yet—but we've agreed that our security for the grand opening should be stepped up even above the present level. We've twenty-five of our people assigned to the event, and I've told them I would speak with you and request that another twenty-five of our agents be assigned, plus half a dozen more to serve in the security center, monitoring the hundred and fifty high-definition cameras we have installed around the property."

"I'm certainly agreeable to that and anything else you feel we need," Stone said. "And I think we're fortunate to have you as a principal in the hotel."

"Thank you, Stone, I'll see to it. When I told the others that our security at the hotel is nearly at White House levels, I wasn't kidding, and now we're ratcheting it up a couple of notches. We've already made the perimeter of the property highly secure, and there are only four access points, which will be beefed up with concrete barriers. The Secret Service is now going to increase their number of agents, many of them armed with automatic weaponry, and they're bringing in shoulder-fired Stinger ground-to-air missiles and distributing them at high points around the property, in case of an attack from the air. Every airport in Southern California will be alerted to the possibility of airplane rentals by foreign nationals. And every flight plan filed in the area will be checked against the watch lists."

"It sounds as though you've got it covered," Stone said.

"Tim Coleman has told me that Kate Rule at the CIA is sending out orders to every station to question all informants."

"I can't think of anything you haven't done," Stone said.

"Neither can I," Mike said, "but I'm going to worry about it every day until this event is behind us."

"So am I," Stone said.

3

Stone returned from his meeting at Strategic Services to find Kelli Keane waiting for him. He had completely forgotten the appointment.

"Hello, Kelli," he said, shaking her hand. "I'm sorry I'm late. A board meeting ran on a bit." Kelli Keane was a former reporter with the *Post* who had quit to write magazine pieces. And a biography of Arrington. Stone was uneasy about talking to her, but she had made the point that he could help her be sure that what she had to say in the book was accurate.

He seated her on the sofa and took a chair opposite, while Joan brought in a bottle of mineral water and two glasses. He certainly wasn't going to drink while talking to her.

"Lunch will be ready in a few minutes," Joan said.

Stone had also forgotten that their appointment was for lunch. "How can I help you?" he asked.

"To begin with, I'd like to run through some chronology," Kelli replied, "to get events in their proper order."

"All right."

"You met Arrington when?"

"Oh, many years ago, at a cocktail party. Her first words on being introduced to me were 'We must never marry.'"

Kelli laughed. "Oh, yes, 'Arrington Barrington.' How did you ever resolve that point?"

"We ran through the options, and it seemed to her that 'Arrington Carter Barrington' worked, separating the two names just enough. This was after she had accepted my proposal."

"Why did it take you so long to marry?"

"Pretty simple—she married someone else."

"And how did that happen?"

"It was winter. We had planned a vacation bareboating in the Caribbean, on the island of St. Marks. We were to meet at the airport. I arrived first, it had begun to snow, and I was concerned that she might have trouble getting there. Finally, she called and said that the *New Yorker* had asked her to write a profile of the movie star Vance Calder, and that she had to meet with him, since he was returning to L.A. the following day. She promised to get a flight to St. Marks the next day.

"I went ahead to the island, but my flight was the last one out before they closed the airport. Turns out, Arrington was snowed in in New York for several days, and so was Vance Calder. We were communicating by fax, this being before e-mail was prevalent and before St. Marks got good cellular service, and after a few days, I got a fax saying that she was going back to L.A. with Vance, and that it was over between us."

"Pity."

"Yes, I had bought a ring and was going to pop the question."

"Oh, dear."

"Well, yes. Took me a while to get over that."

"And by that time, Arrington was pregnant?"

Stone froze; she had boxed him in, and this was a question he did not want to address. "It happens to married people."

"It also happens to unmarried people," Kelli said, "and to people who have not yet decided to marry."

"Yes, of course."

"And it happened to you and Arrington." It wasn't a question.

"We had been living together."

"So how did she know whose son she was carrying?"

"She didn't," Stone replied. "I think it was many

years later that it became clear to her, when the child was growing up."

"No paternity test?"

"Not until much later, and that was nearly by accident."

"And when did she tell you?"

"After Vance's death. She felt she owed it to him to maintain the status quo while he was alive, and she did."

"So why didn't you marry immediately after his death?"

"By this time we had very different lives, on opposite coasts, and they seemed incompatible. Then she decided to take Peter back to Virginia, her home state, and build a house there. I invited them both to come to New York for Christmas, and after that, things developed very quickly. Peter and I got along immediately, and he quickly guessed that I was his father. There's a photograph of my father in my study, and Peter resembles him closely. When he saw it—that was all he needed. I had promised Arrington I wouldn't tell him without her approval, and I didn't. But Peter is a very bright young man."

"I saw that in him when we met in Virginia," Kelli said. She had come down for the housewarming of Arrington's new house with her boyfriend, James Rutledge, who was photographing the place for *Architectural Digest*.

Joan came into the room. "Lunch is served in the kitchen," she said.

Stone led Kelli from his office through the exercise room to the kitchen, where his housekeeper, Helene, had laid the table for two, and he seated his guest.

Stone poured them glasses of Chardonnay, and they dug into a seafood risotto.

"May we talk about money for a minute?" she asked.

Stone sighed. "Must we?"

"I don't want details, just an overview. Vance Calder was very rich, wasn't he?"

"Vance, who was much older than Arrington but looked wonderful, had had a fifty-year career in Hollywood, and he was, financially, very astute. From his first film he waived salary in favor of a percentage of the gross receipts of his films, and he invested in Centurion stock. Sometimes, when the studio was having cash flow problems, he took stock in lieu of his percentage. Over the years, he became the largest single stockholder in Centurion Studios, and he also invested in California real estate, which brought him handsome returns."

"I've heard that his estate was worth something in the region of two billion dollars?"

"You said you didn't want details."

"Sorry. It was during those years that Vance acquired the land in Bel-Air where the new hotel is being built?"

"Yes. First, he bought an old house there and redid it; then, as his neighbors aged or just moved, he acquired adjoining properties."

"So Arrington inherited Vance's estate, and you inherited Arrington's estate? Thus avoiding inheritance taxes in both cases?"

"I made it clear to Arrington that I was uninterested in her money," Stone said. "In fact, I declined to participate in any of her decisions about her bequests. She worked with another attorney to draw up her will, and I was given a sealed copy, which was not opened until after her death. She left the great bulk of her estate to Peter, in trust, and a lesser share to me. Arrington died in a year during which, due to some congressional anomaly, estate taxes were suspended. I have made it a rule not to spend any of her money on myself, and I have willed my estate to Peter in its entirety, except for a few bequests."

"That's abstemious of you."

"I have funds of my own that are sufficient to my needs."

"And now The Arrington is about to open. Did you name it that?"

"Arrington had thought of calling it Casa Calder, after Vance, but after her death, the new name was suggested to me, and it seemed to fit. I understand you're covering the grand opening for *Vanity Fair*?"

"Yes, I'll be there with a team of photographers. It will be well covered."

"Centurion is doing a lot of filming, too. It should all be very exciting."

"You don't really sound very excited about it," Kelli said.

"I have mixed emotions," Stone said, "and I expect they will remain mixed."

"Stone, do you feel any guilt about your inheritance from Arrington?"

Stone shrugged. "I didn't do anything to deserve it."

"From what I've learned during my research, you did very well by Arrington after Vance's death: after you became her attorney, you helped her save Centurion from a rapacious property developer. You and your law firm took over her affairs and increased her wealth, and you saved her millions on the purchase of the Virginia land where she built her house. Surely it was natural of her to want to leave you a part of her estate, even if you hadn't married, and as her husband, there was nothing out of the ordinary about inheriting from her."

Stone shrugged again. "That's all very logical, and I suppose it should make me feel better about it, but . . ."

"I'm sorry," Kelli said, "I won't go any further with that."

"Thank you."

"There is a rumor I'd like you to address, though."

"What sort of rumor?"

"That you were married previously to a woman who has now been hospitalized for some years, but somehow, the marriage records went away."

"Funny, I hadn't heard that," Stone replied. He knew it, but he hadn't heard it.

"So you deny that?"

"Unless you have something more than a rumor for evidence, why should I bother?"

"One other thing," Kelli said, "and then I'll leave you alone."

"What's that?"

"There appears to be some discrepancy about your and Arrington's son's date of birth."

Stone frowned. He hadn't expected this, and he needed to make this go away immediately. "Peter has a birth certificate, like everybody else, and that's a public record."

"I know, I've seen it, and you are listed as the father. How did Vance Calder feel about that?"

"I wasn't privy to conversations between Arrington and Vance, so I've no idea what he felt."

"How does Peter feel about Vance?"

"He seems to have nothing but fond memories of him."

"Do you mind if I talk to Peter?"

"I certainly do, and if you pursue that line of questioning, my cooperation will end. Is that perfectly clear?"

"Perfectly," she said. She glanced at her watch. "Well, that's all I have at this time. May I call you if I think of anything further?"

"This has all been painful, and I would prefer not to discuss any of it any further. I think you have enough for your book."

"I understand," she said. "Thank you for your cooperation." She excused herself and left.

Stone was left staring into his wineglass.

4

Three months before Stone's conversation with Kelli Keane, three men sat in a dentist's reception room in Leipzig, Germany. There were no other patients waiting, and they did not seem to know one another.

From behind the two-way glass separating the reception room from the rest of the suite of offices, another man observed them. The three looked fit, but otherwise unremarkable; all appeared to be Anglo-Saxon, between twenty-five and thirty-five, and neatly dressed in casual clothing. Two of them leafed through magazines; the other stared at the mirrored glass, as if he could see through it, which the viewer found a little unsettling.

The observer pressed a button on the reception-ist's desk and the outside door to the reception room locked with a distinct click. The two reading magazines both looked at the door; the one staring into the mirror did not. The observer found that interesting. He leaned toward the microphone on the desk and spoke.

"The one farthest from the door, open the drawer in the magazine table next to you."

They all became alert. The man opened the drawer.

"There are three pairs of cotton gloves in the drawer," the observer continued. "Each of you put on a pair, and wipe clean any surface or magazine you may have touched."

They did so. When they had finished, the observer continued. "You, on the right, tell us your first name and something about yourself."

The starer wiped the brass pull on the drawer clean and looked back at the mirrored glass. "I am Hans," he said, in unaccented American English. "I work as a test driver at the Porsche factory in Leipzig, where the Cayenne and Panamera models are assembled. I was born in Monterey, California, to a German father and an American mother. They moved to Berlin when I was sixteen, so that my father could take over an automobile repair shop owned by my grandfather."

"Good," the observer said. "Now, you on the left."

"My name is Mike," the man said. "I was born

in New York City, but my parents soon moved to California, where my father opened a restaurant in the San Fernando Valley, which he still operates. I currently work as a bartender at the Beverly Hills Hotel, in Los Angeles."

"Good. Now you, the third."

"My name is Richard, called Rick. I was born and raised in Santa Monica, California. I attended a technical college in Burbank and studied computer science. I work for a large security company in their Los Angeles office, designing and building prototypes for large-scale alarm systems."

"Good," the observer said. "You may all call me Algernon. You all know that a short time ago an American SEAL team located our beloved Osama bin Laden in Pakistan and murdered him there. Our purpose—yours and mine—will be to wreak a vengeance on the United States for that despicable act from which that country may never recover."

There were excited murmurs from the three men, and they exchanged happy glances.

"Take a good look at each other, because you will not meet again for some time, but when you do, you must recognize each other on sight. Hans, we know why you are in Leipzig. Rick, how did you travel here?"

"I took a flight from Los Angeles to London, then spent a week touring southwest England in a rental car. After that I took a flight from Heathrow to Paris and from there to Leipzig. I am picking up another rental car tomorrow, with which I will tour Eastern Europe for another ten days, before returning to Los Angeles from Paris."

"Mike?"

"I flew from Los Angeles to Rome and spent five days there, before traveling by train to Leipzig on a passport supplied to me. Tonight, I will return to Rome and spend another three days there before returning to Los Angeles."

"You all belong to mosques, under Muslim names. Has any of you visited a mosque in Europe during the past two years?"

Hans raised his hand. "I was not told I couldn't."

"Does anyone at your mosque know your German name?"

"No. I was told not to give it to anyone."

"Good. Now, here are your instructions: Hans, you are a certified Porsche mechanic, are you not?"

"Yes," Hans replied.

"You are to resign from your job at the factory, saying that you wish to return to the United States. You will ask for a letter of recommendation to a Porsche dealer in Los Angeles and apply for a job there by e-mail. There is an envelope in the drawer with an e-mail address to the service manager at the dealership. You will apply by e-mail, sending as attachments your résumé and your letter of recommendation. The dealership will arrange your work permit. Later, you will leave this job for another, which you will be told about at a later date."

Hans opened the drawer, found the envelope, and put it into his jacket pocket.

"Mike," Algernon said, "you subscribe to a restaurant services magazine. When you return you will see an advertisement for kitchen and bar staff at a new hotel called The Arrington. You will apply for a bartender's job there as soon as you return."

Mike nodded.

"Rick," Algernon said, "you are currently working on alarm systems for The Arrington. Your employer is furnishing security personnel to The Arrington, and when you return, you will apply to your boss for a position as a security systems operator and repairman in The Arrington's security monitoring center, which is operated by your employer."

Rick said, "Yes, sir."

"You all have excellent backgrounds for the jobs to which you will apply, and you must do everything possible to see that you are hired. When you return to the United States, you must obtain throwaway cell phones, set up e-mail in your code names, then send your e-mail addresses to the following Web site." Algernon gave them the name, then repeated it. "When you have been hired at the hotel, you will send an e-mail to that address saying, 'All is well. I am fine,' signing it with your code name. I will contact you at those e-mail addresses and give you further instructions at a later date. When you go to work at the hotel, you will not give any sign that you recognize each other. Rick, your code name will be Wynken. Hans, your code name will be Blynken. Mike, your code name will be Nod. Everybody understand?"

The three men nodded.

"You may receive further instructions from me directly or by phone. I sign my e-mails with the name 'Algernon.'"

The three men nodded.

"Now leave, one at a time; five minutes apart. Don't leave any fingerprints on the doorknob. Throw the gloves into a public trash bin at least two blocks away from here. Hans, you first, then Rick, then Mike."

Algernon sat and waited until all three men had left, then he took out his cell phone and sent an e-mail message to someone who was waiting for it. Two minutes later, he received a reply: "All is well. I am fine."

Algernon left the office, locking the door behind him. A few blocks away he discarded the office key and the gloves he had been wearing.

5

Stone and Dino met for dinner at Patroon, a restaurant on East Forty-sixth Street. It was the first time they had dined there, and they were still looking for a replacement for Elaine's. Stone and Dino had been detectives and partners at the 19th Precinct many years before; Dino was now running the detective squad there.

They settled into a corner table in the handsome, paneled dining room, hung with photographs from the collection of the owner, Ken Aretsky.

"What do you think?" Dino asked.

Stone seemed distracted. "Huh?"

"Of the restaurant."

"Oh. I like the look and feel of it." He opened a menu. "More expensive than Elaine's, though."

A waiter materialized before them and set down

two drinks. "Knob Creek for you, Mr. Barrington. Johnnie Walker Black for you, Lieutenant Bacchetti."

Stone thanked the man. "That's a good start," he said, sipping the drink.

"How did he know?" Dino asked.

"Beats me. Did you get famous all of a sudden?"

A man appeared at the table and introduced himself as the owner.

"How do you do, Ken?" Stone asked. "Please pull up a chair."

Aretsky did so.

"Your waiter is gifted with second sight," Stone said, raising his drink.

"Not really," Aretsky replied. "Elaine told me to expect you two, though I didn't think it would take so long." The waiter brought him a drink.

"When did this happen?"

"About a month before she died," Aretsky replied. "I think she knew she didn't have long. Elaine said that the restaurant might not make it without her, and that you two were her most loyal customers. She said you'd turn up here eventually, and she told me what you drink."

Dino raised his glass. "Elaine," he said.

Stone and Ken raised their glasses and drank. They talked for a few minutes about the photographs on the walls, then Ken excused himself to greet another customer.

"She's still taking care of us," Stone said.

"How about that?" Dino took another sip of his scotch and looked searchingly at Stone. "Something's going on with you, pal. You depressed about something?"

"Nothing in particular," Stone replied. "I had lunch with Kelli Keane today."

"The redhead from the *Post*?"

"Not anymore. She quit to write a biography of Arrington. She had a lot of questions."

Dino looked surprised. "And you answered them?"

"Most of them. She seems to be doing a conscientious job of research, and I'd rather she had accurate information to work from instead of rumors."

"And you trust her?"

"It's not necessary to trust her. I don't think she'll lie outright, and if she does, I have a recording of the conversation." He patted his breast pocket.

"Smart move. Is she going to let you read it before publication?"

"I didn't ask."

"If a client of yours was talking to a former *Post* reporter for publication, what advice would you give him?"

"I'd tell him to record the conversation."

"Yeah, and you'd tell him to demand to see the manuscript before publication."

"I don't want to read it when it's published, and

I don't want to read it now. There won't be anything in it that I don't already know."

"I hope you're right," Dino said. "So this lunch depressed you?"

"It forced me to relive things."

"Speaking of 'things,' how are they with you and Marla Rocker?"

"Okay, I guess. She's going to direct Peter's play, and she's casting now. She won't be able to make it to the hotel opening." Stone and Arrington's son was a student at the Yale School of Drama, and he had written the play the year before. Dino's son, Ben, also a student there, had produced it, and now it was being readied for Broadway.

"You going to take somebody else?" Dino asked.

"Who? I'm not seeing anybody else."

"I've never known that condition to last very long," Dino said.

Stone sighed. "I don't know, everything is just kind of . . . flat."

"You've got the grand opening to look forward to. The kids and their girls are going to be there, and I'm bringing Viv." Dino had been seeing another detective, Vivian DeCarlo, who had worked for him at the 19th, and whom he had had transferred when he couldn't stand not going out with her.

"I'm happy for you," Stone said.

"The event sounds like it's going to be a hell of a lot of fun," Dino pointed out.

"Oh, there's something new," Stone said. He told Dino about the NSA intercept of a mention of the hotel.

"That's kind of creepy," Dino said.

"It's more than creepy. We're going to have Will Lee and the president of Mexico there, you know."

"I know. I can see how there might be a little concern."

"A *little* concern? Both the Secret Service and Strategic Services have doubled their manning for those days. Mike Freeman is taking it very seriously, and if he's worried, I'm worried."

Dino picked up a menu. "Let the pros sweat it," he said. "You and I are out of our depth with that sort of thing."

"Yeah," Stone said, picking up his menu, "and I don't like being out of my depth. That's how you drown."

They ordered dinner, and after it came, they liked it.

6

J. Herbert Fisher, formerly a loser of the Olympic class, but now an ace young attorney at Stone Barrington's firm, Woodman & Weld, stood at the bar of P. J. Clarke's, sipped his bourbon, and gazed at his prospects.

There was a pair of attractive brunettes a couple of barstools away, but they were both wearing wedding rings, and that made them out of bounds. Herbie, as he had been known formerly, until he had advised those who knew him that he preferred and insisted on being called Herb, had had a semi-long-term relationship with a beautiful associate at his firm, but she had finally told him that she didn't think an in-house pairing would be helpful to either of their careers. Since that time, it had been catch-as-catch-can, which hadn't been all bad, but he had had to start seduction from scratch about twice a week, on average, and the experience was wearing thin.

Herbie caught an elbow in a rib and surmised that someone behind him was trying to nail down a space at the bar. He considered elbowing back but decided that the elbower might outweigh him. He peered over his shoulder and found empty space, until he ratcheted his gaze down a few inches and located the top of a blond, female head. Herbie didn't exactly mind tall women, but he wasn't all that tall himself, and he found it comforting when he could look slightly down at a female.

"Pardon me," he said, "are my ribs crowding your elbow?"

She looked up at him, revealing a strikingly pretty face. "Not anymore."

"Pretty good elbow," Herbie said to her. "Did you play high school football?"

"Oddly enough I did," she said. "I was an ace kicker: thirty-two extra points and eighteen field goals my senior year. Would you like to experience my field goal attempt?" She waved frantically at a bartender who was busy being busy elsewhere.

"Maybe later," Herbie said. "May I get you a drink? I have influence here."

She shot him a withering glance. "If you can produce a Laphroaig on the rocks right here"—she tapped the bar in front of her—"within sixty seconds, I'll give you . . . the benefit of the doubt."

Herbie made sure his gaze did not leave hers. He raised his right index finger and made a twirling motion.

A bartender materialized. "What can I get you, Herb?"

"Sean, this lady would like a Laphroaig on the rocks, my tab."

"Sure thing." There was the sound of ice hitting a glass, then of glass hitting the bar, then liquid striking ice. The result was set down in front of the young woman.

"I reckon that took about twenty seconds," Herbie said. "That should get me more than the benefit of the doubt."

"You're right," she said. "You can ask me two questions."

"One: May I have the sixty-second version of your biography? Two: Will you have dinner with me?" He watched her expression, which did not change. "I am reliably informed that there is a restaurant at the rear of this establishment."

"Okay," she said, "here goes." She took a deep breath: "Born in New York City twenty-nine years and two months ago, educated in the public schools and at Columbia University, followed by one year of Columbia Law School: boring. Joined the NYPD as a patrol officer, served four years, quit when I didn't make detective, went to work for a security company called Strategic Services for three years, then quit to become a PI. That's the twenty-second version—you'll have to pry the rest out of me over dinner." She raised her glass, then took a long, grateful swig of the single-malt scotch. "I'm hungry. How long will it take you to get a table?"

"Follow me," Herbie said, tossing two twenties on the bar and leading the way aft. A moment later they were wedged into a corner of the crowded dining room. She polished off her drink and raised her glass. "Join me in another?"

Herbie instructed a waiter, and the drinks appeared. He raised his glass. "I know that single-malt scotch is delicious," he said, "but it will eventually eat your liver."

"You worry about your liver, I'll worry about mine," she replied. "What else do you want to know?"

"Let's start with your name."

"Harp O'Connor," she said. "Call me Harpie or Harpo and I'll show you that kick of mine in a painful place."

"I perceive that you are Irish."

"You are very perceptive. Both sides. I'm first generation. My mother is a nurse, my father, a bartender who owns the bar."

"Why aren't you drinking in his place?"

"The surveillance there is intrusive, and the old

man won't let me have more than one drink. And he'll eighty-six any man I talk to."

"All good reasons for drinking somewhere else," Herbie said.

"Your turn, Herb."

"Fisher, and I don't like extensions of my first name, either. Born in Brooklyn thirtyish years ago, played hooky from the public schools, followed by NYU Law School."

"What happened to college?" she asked.

"I finessed that."

"How'd you get into law school without pre-law?"

"I passed the bar. That impressed the admissions committee enough to allow me to enter. I finished in two years with a three-point-nine GPA."

"Okay, so you're smart. Are you employed?"

"I'm a senior associate at the firm of Woodman & Weld."

"Do they give you anything responsible to do there?"

"One of my clients is your former employer, Strategic Services, whose CEO, Michael Freeman, gave me the business."

"Mike Freeman is a smart guy," Harp said. "One of the reasons I left was that I couldn't get anywhere near him."

"You seem to have a history of quitting when

your employers won't give you responsibility quickly enough."

"Well put. I decided I'd be happier if I had *all* the responsibility. That's what being self-employed is all about."

"Why a PI?"

"Because that's what people were willing to pay me to do. One of Strategic's clients asked me to investigate a couple of his employees in my spare time. As a result, both employees were fired, and I was hired. Word about me somehow got around that hiring me more than paid for itself, and other work appeared. Now I'm well afloat."

"Admirable," Herbie said.

They both ordered steaks and onion rings, and Herbie picked out a good red from the list.

"**W**ell," Harp said, when they had finished dinner and reduced the bottle to half a glass. "I'm not tired, are you?"

"Nope."

"Show me where you live," she said.

"That's direct."

"Saves time. One of the ways I judge people is by how they occupy the spaces they live in. If you live in a rat hole, tell me now, and I'll be on my way."

Herbie signed the check and pulled the table out for her. "Come with me," he said.

They took a cab over to Park Avenue, to Herbie's building. They took the elevator up, and when they walked into his apartment she didn't take her coat off until she had had a look around. Finally, she handed him her coat. "You'll do, Herb," she said.

7

Herbie was awakened by the smell of bacon frying. He pried open an eye, stumbled into the bathroom, brushed his teeth and hair, and got into a robe.

He was salivating as he arrived in the kitchen and found her setting the table by the window. "Good morning," he said.

"First kitchen I've seen in New York that has a window that doesn't overlook an air shaft," she said, raking eggs out of a skillet onto the plates as two English muffins popped out of the toaster.

"It's a penthouse," Herbie said. "The air shaft surrounds the apartment."

She recovered the bacon from the microwave, buttered the muffins, poured orange juice, set the coffeepot on the table, and sat down. "Join me?"

"Don't mind if I do." Herbie sat down and tasted the eggs. "Wow," he said. "What's your secret?"

"If I told you my secrets, they wouldn't be secret."

Herbie was eating too fast to talk.

"I know what you're thinking," she said.

"Mmmmf?"

"You're thinking, as my father would put it, 'How did I fall into this pot of jam? How could I meet such a beautiful woman, experience the best sex of my life, and have the best breakfast ever, all in such a short time and with so little effort?'"

Herbie swallowed. "You're a witch," he said, then filled his mouth again.

Harp smiled. "There you have it. Tell me, how did you get rich enough at the age of thirtyish to live like this? Inherited wealth?"

"I inherited it from the New York State Lottery."

Her mouth fell open.

"I kid you not."

"So, you blew it on fast living, the way lottery winners always seem to?"

Herbie shook his head. "I got smart before it was all gone. Now I actually make more than I spend."

"A good practice," she replied, sipping her coffee. "I'm there, myself, and I like it."

"Are you getting interesting work?" Herbie asked.

"I am. I like investigation, especially when people are trying to hide things, which they usually are. I'm a whiz on the computer, and that helps. I'm an urban girl, and I don't really like fresh air all that much." She cocked her head. "Ever been married?"

"Once," Herbie said.

"How long?"

"Let's say it was counted in months, not years. She and her brother ran off with a huge sum of money stolen from their father's business and moved to a safe haven in the Pacific."

"Didn't she invite you?"

"Yes, but I have this thing: I can be sneaky, but I'm not dishonest. I wouldn't live on money stolen from somebody else. Mind you, I got a very nice divorce settlement, and I don't mind having that in the bank."

"How do you get a divorce settlement after being married only a few months?"

"By getting it before no-fault divorce was signed into law in New York State. She didn't really mind signing the money away, since it had already been sequestered by the feds, pending settlement of the firm's losses. My attorney managed to get it unsequestered. You ever been married?"

"Yeah. I married a guy I met when we were both

at the Police Academy. Lasted a little over two years. We were working different shifts in different precincts and hardly ever saw each other. He was a sweet guy, but not smart. He was on the take a week after he got his shield, and I couldn't live with that."

"You were smart to get out."

She shrugged. "I guess. He's doing time now, along with a dozen other guys who got caught when Internal Affairs busted them. I had to loan him money for a lawyer."

"I'm sorry you had to go through that," Herbie said.

Harp shrugged. "I just chalked it up as life experience. I decided to make more objective judgments of people, instead of being hooked on charm."

"I noticed that last night," Herbie said. "I didn't have time to be charming."

She smiled. "You were more charming than you realized. Honesty is charming. Beats bullshit every time."

Not far away, Dino Bacchetti and Vivian DeCarlo were sitting up in bed, naked, eating toast and drinking coffee.

"Viv," Dino said, "how many nights have you spent here in the past three months?"

She smiled. "Most of them, I guess."

"Just about all of them, and yet you haven't moved any clothes here. Not to speak of."

Viv brushed crumbs off her breasts. "I've got a little problem, Dino."

"Let me help you solve it."

"There's something I can't figure out."

"Cough it up. You'll feel better."

"I've always thought you were an honest cop, and I admired that. But this apartment—how can you afford the rent on a lieutenant's salary? It's gotta be ten grand a month."

"I don't rent; I own. The maintenance is two grand a month. I can afford that."

"Your father ran a candy store. Where'd you get the money to buy it?"

"Honestly," he replied.

"Honestly, how? Come on, help me out here."

"Here's the short version: I was married to a rich woman who had a rich father. She also made a lot of money in investments while we were married. When she walked, her old man insisted that she make a settlement, and I got a very nice check. Everybody was happy, and since it was a division of marital property, there was no tax. I spent a chunk of it on this apartment."

She heaved a sigh of relief. "I'm so glad to hear that."

"Good, now why don't you move in with me?"

"Well, Rosie couldn't pay our rent all by herself. She'd need time to get another roommate."

"Tell you what: I'll pay your share until she finds somebody," Dino suggested.

Viv brightened. "Yeah, that would work."

Dino dug in his bedside drawer and came up with a card. "This is a guy from my old neighborhood who has a carting business. Pack up your stuff and call him. Tell him to send me the bill."

Viv leaned over and kissed him on the ear. "I'll do it this weekend."

"Then we'll both feel better," Dino said. He set down his coffee cup and got a leg over. "Let's celebrate," he said.

So they celebrated.

8

Mike arrived at The Arrington's front gate, where a security guard checked his driver's license photo and gave him directions to the executive offices.

"Don't stop anywhere along the way," the guard told him. "They expect you at the office in three minutes."

Mike nodded, then put his car in gear and drove up the hill. He found a parking space next to a Dumpster overflowing with building material scrap and went inside. A woman at a makeshift desk in the hallway pointed at a door. "In there," she said, checking his name off a list and noting the time.

There was a Sharpie-lettered sign on the door: "Director of Food and Beverages." Mike knocked and walked into an unfurnished reception room.

"Back here!" a voice called out.

Mike walked through the room to an office and found a man in a work shirt sitting behind a desk. "Mike Gennaro?"

"Yes, sir," Mike replied.

"Take a seat."

Mike took the only option, a paint-stained wooden chair with some of the caning missing from the seat.

"Sorry for the mess here," the man said. "It'll look more like a real office in a couple of weeks. The emphasis here is on finishing the cottages and suites first. I'm Tim Duggan, the food and service director for the hotel."

"How do you do," Mike said, crossing his legs and folding his hands in his lap. He was wearing his best suit.

"I expect you've heard about this place," Duggan said.

"Hasn't everybody? I think every hotel manager in L.A. is convinced it's going to cost him half his business."

"We should be so lucky," Duggan said. He picked up a sheet of paper and glanced at it. "I liked your résumé," he said. "Only two jobs in your whole life."

"I'm nothing if not loyal," Mike said.

"I've had dinner a couple of times at Franco's, in Studio City. That's your dad's place, is it?"

"It is."

"Tell me about your experience there."

"I started as a dishwasher when I was twelve," Mike said, "and over the next ten years I worked just about every job in the place, up to and including sous-chef. On my twenty-first birthday, I started tending bar."

"So why didn't you make a career of the family business?"

"I have two older brothers who had that idea, and they're still there. When the time came for them to take over, I'd still be tending bar."

"And how long at the Beverly Hills Hotel?"

"Six years. The tips are better than at Franco's."

"I would imagine. So you want to make a move here as a bartender? You think the tips would be better here than at the Beverly Hills?"

"I understand you're going to have four bars here," Mike said. "What I'd like is to be your head bartender, to manage all four and to fill in when somebody's out or the traffic is heavy."

"We haven't budgeted for a head bartender," Duggan said.

"So, you're going to run four bars yourself, in addition to all the restaurants? The bartenders will steal you blind."

Duggan sat back and regarded the applicant with an appraising eye. "We're instituting a computer system to regulate that."

"Yeah? And every time a guest pays cash, half of it will go into the bartender's pocket."

"And how would you stop that? What's your system?"

Mike tapped his temple with a finger. "It's right in here. I can look at the empties and tell you what a bar took in that night and what the bartender got in tips. Remember, I'm one of them, not one of you."

"How many bartenders should I hire?" Duggan asked.

"For three restaurants and the pool? Fourteen, plus me. That will cover all the bars for a five-day week and the occasional sick day. Remember, I can always fill in."

"I had reckoned on sixteen," Duggan said.

"Count me as two," Mike said, "and I'd expect to be paid both salaries. I'll divvy up the tips, and I'll make up the booze orders every week, saving you the trouble. I'll deal with the wholesalers, too, if you like. I already know all the salespeople and most of the managers."

"You're an ambitious guy," Duggan said.

"I am. By the time you retire and move on, I'll want your job. I know the restaurant side, too, and I'm good on wine."

"Double a bartender's wages sounds low for all of that," Duggan said.

"I'd rather be a bargain at first. Pretty soon, you'll know what I'm worth to you."

Duggan was impressed. His source at the Beverly Hills had already told him that Mike Gennaro was highly regarded there; the man had an outstanding work record, plenty of charm, and a good ear for a customer's story. Duggan handed him a sheet of paper. "Here's the rundown on benefits: health insurance, retirement package, etcetera. This will be the kind of place that will repay loyalty and hard work over the long run. I'm aiming for a very low turnover among employees."

Mike looked it over. "This is good. Have you hired any bartenders yet?"

"This is the first day I've interviewed."

"If you'll let me hire them, I'll have you half a dozen by the end of the day and all of them by the end of the week."

"I like your style, Mike, but I'll want to meet your choices."

"Of course."

"How soon can you start?"

"I'll go to work today on the hiring, but I'll need to work my shift at the Beverly Hills for the next two weeks. They've been good to me, and I don't want to stiff them, especially since I'll be taking a couple of their guys with me—assuming you approve."

"All right," Duggan said, "you'll go on salary as of today. You can work days here and nights at the Beverly Hills until your time is up there." He handed Mike a file folder. "Here are all the personnel and tax forms you need to fill out. I'll have a written contract for you to sign in a day or two." Duggan stood up and offered his hand. "Welcome aboard, Mike."

Mike stood and took the hand. "I'm looking forward to it, Mr. Duggan."

"Call me Tim. We're going to be working together closely."

"Tim it is. If I can have a fruit crate for a desk and a phone, I'll start calling bartenders."

Duggan handed him another file folder. "Here's the list of those who answered the ad, along with their résumés." He led Mike to the office next door. "Use this for a while," he said.

Mike took off his jacket and tossed it onto a file cabinet. He loosened his tie, sat down, and looked at the list in the folder. His first call was on his new cell phone, a text to the e-mail address he had been given in Leipzig: "All is well. I am fine," it read. He signed it "Nod."

9

Mike Freeman arrived in Los Angeles aboard Strategic Services' Cessna Citation jet 4, which he piloted himself. He landed the light jet at Santa Monica, then left the airplane in the care of his copilot and got into the waiting Mercedes.

"To the hotel, sir?" the young driver asked.

"No, to the office. I'll do some business before I go to the hotel."

The Los Angeles offices of Strategic Services were located in a five-story, wholly owned office building on Santa Monica Boulevard. In addition to the five stories of the building, two of which were rented out pending expansion plans, there were two underground levels, and Mike went directly there. His operations manager received Mike in his office.

"Good morning, Mr. Freeman," he said.

"Good morning, Harvey," Mike replied.

"I thought you'd be going to the hotel today. I didn't expect to see you until tomorrow."

"It's not the first time I've caught you off guard, is it?"

Harvey laughed. "I know to be ready for you at any time, sir."

"What have you got for me?"

"I think it won't be necessary to hire a supervisor for the watch room at The Arrington. One of our better people here has applied for the job, and he's qualified."

"Tell me about him."

"His name is Richard Indrisie—we call him Rick. Rick is young but smart. He's a tech-school graduate with a broad and firm grounding in computer science, and he's been with us for a little over two years. We've trained him for design and repair work, and he's as good as guys who've been here a lot longer."

"You said young—how young?"

"Twenty-eight."

"Would you describe him as mature?"

"More than that, he's a very cool customer, quick to grasp a situation and quick to deal with it."

"Let's talk to him."

Harvey picked up a phone. "Send Rick in."

Rick Indrisie knocked on the door and entered.

"Rick," Harvey said, "this is our CEO, Michael Freeman." The two shook hands.

"Sit down, Rick, and tell me something about yourself."

Rick sat down, looking very much at ease. "I was born out in the valley," he said. "Public schools and technical college. I've loved computers since the first time I saw one. I built my first one when I was fourteen, and I've never seen a broken one I couldn't fix."

"What do you do in your spare time?"

"I've got a little business on the side," Rick said. "I buy vintage small appliances, restore them to perfect working order, make them look new, and sell them, mostly on eBay."

"That's enterprising," Mike said.

Harvey interrupted. "I should tell you that Rick has a gift for catching anomalies on-screen," he said. "He seems to know when a movement or a gesture picked up by a surveillance camera is a threat. He's nipped crimes in the bud more than a dozen times since we put him on monitoring a year ago. And he can repair any piece of equipment in the watch room. He's great with software, too."

"Thank you, Rick," Mike said. "We'll let you know later."

Rick shook hands and left.

"I like him," Mike said. "Hire him when you're ready."

"That will be today," Harvey said. "All of the wiring at The Arrington is complete, and equipment installation starts tomorrow. I'd like Rick to be there to supervise as everything is connected and tested."

"Go right ahead," Mike said. "I'll be in my office if you need me." He left the lower level and took the elevator to the top floor, then walked to his corner office. It was smaller and less luxurious than his New York office, but it had everything he needed. He spent a few minutes returning phone calls, then met with the engineers who were working on the fire plan for The Arrington.

"We're up and running," said the team leader. "All the automatic fire extinguishers are installed, sixty-one of them, and we have video hookups to every area where fire could be a problem."

"What about explosions?" Mike asked.

"I don't have to tell you that all bets are off if we get a significant explosion," the man said. "What we get is complete chaos while we marshal forces and get them to the scene. We're likely to lose our cameras in such a scenario. Everything is in the hands of the response team. The local fire department will be there in five minutes or less, of course."

Mike nodded. "Are you satisfied that our response teams are trained and ready?"

The team leader nodded. "They're assigned sectors, and the plan is for them to be on scene in no more than ninety seconds, usually less."

"Have the Secret Service people vetted the plan for the presidential cottages?"

"Yes, sir, and they were pleased. They're also relieved that they won't have to be the first responders to an event, allowing them to concentrate on body protection."

"Very good," Mike said. He dismissed the men, made a few more phone calls, then called his car for the trip to The Arrington.

From the front gate he noted the drill of every one of his people. He found them businesslike, but polite. His site commander was waiting outside his suite, and another man dealt with his luggage.

"Welcome to The Arrington," the commander said. "You'll be the first overnight guest."

"Your people looked good at every point," Mike said. "Spread the word that I want more smiling when guests start arriving. A smile doesn't make a man any less alert, and it puts the guest at ease. I want to give an impression of a welcoming committee, rather than a private police force."

"I agree, sir. Smiling will start immediately."

Mike laughed. "I appreciate your confidence in your men," he said. "As you know, installation of the watch room starts tomorrow. We've appointed a supervisor for the room, and he will appoint deputies. His name is Richard Indrisie, known as Rick. Young guy, late twenties, but very good."

"I'll look forward to meeting him," the commander said.

"The fire and explosion plan is well set up. I had a briefing an hour ago. As soon as the watch room is up and running, start the drills."

"Will do."

"And tell your people that when an alarm goes off, they're not to look alarmed."

"Shall I tell them to smile?"

"That and not to knock any guests down when they're rushing to a scene."

"Yes, sir. You're having dinner with the Secret Service detail commander at seven, as requested."

"Where?"

"Here in your suite's dining room. I'm afraid you're the first guinea pigs for the room service kitchen."

Mike laughed. "I brought Alka-Seltzer."

Rick Indrisie left work at six that evening. As soon as he had cleared the indoor parking lot, he pulled into the drive-by line at a McDonald's, and while waiting his turn he dug out his throwaway cell phone and sent an e-mail. "All is well. I am fine." He signed it "Wynken."

10

Hans was replacing a defective alternator on an elderly Porsche 911 when his supervisor tapped him on the shoulder. Hans looked up at him.

"There's a visitor to see you in the showroom."

"Can you send him here?" Hans asked.

The supervisor looked around the shop, then turned back to Hans. "All right, we are not so busy. Next time, meet your friends in the showroom on your break."

Hans nodded and went back to work, tightening the last bolts. When he looked up again, a man in a sports jacket, no tie, was watching him closely. "Yes?" Hans said, straightening from his work.

"My name is Carl Webber," the man said, offering his hand. "From The Arrington."

Hans shook the hand. "I thought you might like to see the shop."

"Yes," Webber said, looking around. "It's very clean, isn't it?"

"Always the mark of a well-run shop—any kind of shop."

"Is there somewhere we can talk?"

"The break room," Hans said. "This way." He led Webber off the shop floor and into a room containing food-and-drink dispensing machines and a few tables and chairs. It was after eleven, between coffee break and lunch. "I don't think we'll be disturbed here," Hans said.

They took seats. "Your résumé is very interesting," Webber said. "You had Mercedes training?"

"Right out of gymnasium—that's German high school," Hans replied. "Then I worked in a dealership for four years, while I raced sports cars on weekends."

"Why did you change to Porsche?"

"They had a better racing program, and I liked the cars better. Besides, there were no openings for drivers at Mercedes. At Porsche, one could do race driving, then, between races, give buyers who were taking delivery of their vehicles at the factory a few rides around the race track and, if they were buying the Cayenne, around the off-road park. Before I went to work there, they sent me to the mechanics' school, and I became a certified Porsche technician on all models."

"Good, good," Webber said. "Your references were excellent, too. Let me tell you about the job."

"I would like very much to hear this," Hans said.

"Most of the car parking will be underground at The Arrington, a feature that will make the grounds more beautiful."

"I've heard that."

"We will also maintain an underground repair facility for on-site hotel vehicles, among which will be a dozen Porsche Cayennes with the hybrid engines, and a dozen Bentley Mulsannes. Have you ever worked on Bentleys?"

"I had a private job dealing with the Flying Spur model, but never have I worked on the Mulsanne."

"We have obtained a six-hour training course on DVD that Bentley produced for the training of foreign mechanics. I think you will find it adequate to familiarize you with the Mulsanne."

Hans nodded. "Good."

"We will stock a range of parts for both types of vehicles, and, of course, any other necessary parts will be available from a dealer. Since the cars will be in continuous use by guests of the hotel, most of the work on them will be conducted at night, when the vehicles are more readily available. Should there be an emergency, like an accident, then of course some daytime work would be likely, too."

"I understand. I have worked a night shift before, at the Mercedes dealership, and I found I like it. Things were quieter."

"Exactly. There are other vehicles to be serviced, too. We have a fleet of electric cars—glorified golf carts, really—that will deliver arriving guests to their suites and cottages, and another fleet for the use of staff for delivering room service meals, plus laundry and dry cleaning."

"I've no experience at all with that kind of vehicle."

"Don't worry, we have two mechanics who will attend to them."

"Good."

"I wish to offer you the position of vehicle maintenance supervisor. You will have an assistant who will schedule the jobs and deal with the paperwork, plus a second mechanic trained in Bentleys. You will also supervise the electric car mechanics, and of course you will work on the Porsches and Bentleys as time allows." Webber handed Hans a folder.

"Here is our offer, along with terms, salary, and fringe benefits. I think you will find everything satisfactory."

Hans scanned the documents. "It's a good offer. I accept," he said.

"I'm pleased that you will be with us," Webber said. "Now, read the documents carefully overnight, then sign them and return them to me at the hotel. How much notice must you give here?"

"Two weeks, I suppose," Hans replied.

"That is satisfactory, though I wish you could come sooner. Perhaps if you will come to the hotel this weekend, I can familiarize you with the setup and see if you have any suggestions as to the arrangement of the shops."

"I can come tomorrow morning at nine," Hans replied. "And I will talk to my supervisor about giving notice."

The two men shook hands, and Webber left.

Hans sought out his supervisor. "I've had an offer to join the staff of the new hotel, The Arrington," he said, "and I've accepted."

His supervisor shrugged. "I'm sorry to lose you, Hans, but it's not such a bad time for me. I've got a new man starting on Monday. If you will spend that day orienting him and watching him work on cars, then you can start your new job on Tuesday."

"Thank you very much," Hans said, shaking his hand.

At the end of the day, Hans called Webber and gave him the good news.

"I'm delighted," Webber said, "but I'd still like

to see you tomorrow. We'll put you on salary from then."

Hans hung up and left for the day. In the employee parking lot, he sent an e-mail from his anonymous cell phone. "All is well. I am fine." He signed it "Blynken."

11

At seven p.m. sharp, the doorbell rang, and Mike Freeman went to the door. A Secret Service agent in his early forties, athletically built, with salt-and-pepper hair, stood there.

"I'm Steve Rifkin," the man said, offering his hand.

Mike shook it and pulled the man through the door, closing it behind him. "I'm Mike Freeman, Steve. It's good to meet you at last. I've heard about you. Would you like a drink?"

"Well, since I'm not protecting anyone early tomorrow, I'd love a scotch on the rocks. How could you have heard of me?"

Mike mixed two drinks and handed his guest one. "We draw a lot of our people from various federal agencies, including the Secret Service. It's part of my job to know who many of them are. I'll tell you, I was very impressed that you were given this assignment. You've been in the protection end only a couple of years, haven't you?"

"That's correct," Rifkin said. "I was doing investigative work before, but when I was assigned to the White House detail I took to it right away."

"And the right people noticed," Mike said, "including the president."

"That's the best reference I could have," Rifkin said, "since it's his life he's putting in my hands."

"Come outside and let's enjoy the California evening," Mike said, leading the way to a walled patio off the living room.

"I smell orange blossoms," Rifkin said.

"Were you based in Florida for a time?"

"Oh, yes, Miami, working on counterfeiting cases. Funny how scents can be so evocative of times and places."

"I hope you don't mind, I've ordered onion soup and steaks for us. I'm told you like yours rare."

"You've done your homework," Rifkin replied. "That's fine with me."

The two men chatted idly for a few minutes, then Mike got down to business. "I hope my people have kept you sufficiently briefed on our end of this."

"They've done a very good job of that," Rifkin said.

"I'm afraid your people haven't done all that good a job of briefing mine."

"You'll have to forgive us, Mike, we're unaccustomed to sharing with outsiders, even those from other federal agencies. The more people who know our methods, the more leaks there could be."

"I assume you've run your own checks on our people."

"On your people and on every person who will be employed by this hotel or who will be a guest while the two presidents are here. By the way, I'm impressed with the backgrounds of your people, Mike."

"But not sufficiently to be open with them."

"The way I see it is you and I are running parallel but separate operations here. Your concern is for the safety of The Arrington's guests and property, and ours is for the safety of the president of the United States and his guest, the president of Mexico. Where those operations overlap, we'll be as helpful as we can, but it's part of our standard operating procedure to see that our duties overlap with others' as little as possible. It's true of local police departments when the president travels, and it's true of your people in this particular situation."

"I understand that, believe me, and I'll do my best to respect that view, as long as my people can do their jobs efficiently."

"Of course. Two people have been hired in the

past couple of days that I'd like to ask you about. One of them belongs to you."

"Let me guess: Rick Indrisie."

"Good guess. Can you guess why I'm concerned about him?" Jeff Rifkin asked.

"Because he's to be right at the nerve center of our surveillance security, and because he's so young."

"Correct on both counts," Rifkin conceded.

"You'll have to take our word for it that Rick is qualified for his job," Mike said. "We screen our people just as carefully as you do yours, and he has met or exceeded every qualification we've assigned to that task. As for his youth, I think that someone who has risen through a government bureaucracy sometimes has difficulty perceiving how a privately owned company can bring someone up through the ranks so quickly."

"I take your point," Rifkin said.

"From our point of view, Rick's education and work experience make him a seasoned professional at twenty-eight, while in your operation, someone of that age might be thought of as green."

"There's truth in what you say, Mike. I myself managed to move up more quickly than is common in the Service."

"I'm sure you've seen our file on Rick."

"I have."

"Then you'll have to take our word that he's the

right man for the job—at least until your investigation of him turns up something to contradict that."

"Fair enough," Rifkin said.

"And I think the other man you're worried about would be the German national, Hans Hoffman."

"Once again, you're ahead of me. Even though he's not your employee, I'm sure that you've verified his educational and employment history," Rifkin said, "but I wonder: have you investigated his political history?"

"One of the items on his employment application questioned that history, and Hoffman denied ever having been a member of any organization, not even a political party. In interviewing the people he's worked for over the years, none of them has said anything to indicate that he's not telling the truth. But the Secret Service should have access to various databases that we don't, including the German intelligence services."

"We do to some extent," Rifkin agreed, "but we don't always get the answers to our questions as quickly as we would like."

"Then you should have a chat with somebody at Langley, to see if there's anything about him in their databases."

Rifkin smiled ruefully. "Of course, though we don't always get from Langley even as much cooperation as we get from some foreign services."

"Ah, yes: interagency rivalry rears its ugly head. Is there anything in particular that troubles you?"

"If anything, it's because he is so outstandingly clean. There's very little meat on that bone."

"Well, I think you have to accept that there are outstandingly clean people in the world, Steve. Tell you what, I'll see what our Berlin office can discover about Herr Hoffman."

"That would be very helpful, Mike."

The doorbell rang. "That will be our dinner, I think," Mike said. "Shall we dine outside?"

"A little chilly for me."

"Then let's do it inside." Mike led the way.

When they had finished dinner and Rifkin had left, Mike looked at his wristwatch. It was nine hours later in Germany, so, using his cell phone, he dialed the direct line for the head of his Berlin office.

"Peter von Enzberg," a voice said.

"Peter, it's Mike Freeman."

"Good morning, Mike."

"I have something I'd like for you to do, and as quickly as possible."

12

Scott Hipp returned to his office at the National Security Agency after a lunch in Washington and found one of his code section supervisors waiting for him. Hipp hung his jacket in a cupboard and sat down at his desk. "Good afternoon, Fritz. You look puzzled. What can I do for you?"

"I'm not even sure why I'm here," Fritz replied, "and I don't know what you can do for me."

"Then get out of my office," Hipp said jovially. "You're wasting our time." Fritz always needed a touch of the cattle prod to get him moving.

"We picked up an e-mail transmission from a cell phone in California to a Web site we have a continuous watch on."

"What was the text?"

"It was in English: 'All is well. I am fine.' We ran a decode on the phrase and got nothing."

"Sounds like a prearranged signal," Hipp pointed out.

"That's what we think, but there is a further wrinkle."

"What's that?"

"It was signed 'Nod.'" He spelled the word.

Hipp leaned back in his chair and recited: "'And Cain went out from the presence of the Lord and dwelt in the land of Nod, on the east of Eden.' Genesis four, verse sixteen."

"I figured you'd come up with something a little off the wall," Fritz said.

"Such flattery," Hipp replied.

"What do you make of it?"

"Read all of chapter four—hell, read all of Genesis. Run Abel against it, run Enoch."

"Who is Enoch?"

"The son of Cain."

"I wasn't raised religious," Fritz said.

"Then you are at a disadvantage in the world," Hipp said. "Reading assignment for you: the King James Bible."

"The whole thing?"

"Be good for you. It's the basis of so much of the Christian world, and the translation is very beautiful."

"I know about Cain and Abel," Fritz said. "I read Steinbeck's novel *East of Eden*."

"Maybe that's the reference, instead of Genesis. Run names from that, too, Cal's brother, father, and mother. Cast a wide net."

"Okay," Fritz said, rising to go.

"Wait a minute," Hipp said.

Fritz sat down again.

"Give me a minute," Hipp said. He stared dreamily out the window, then he began to recite:

> "*Wynken, Blynken, and Nod one night*
> *Sailed off in a wooden shoe—*
> *Sailed on a river of crystal light,*
> *Into a sea of dew.*
> *'Where are you going, and what do you wish,'*
> *The old moon asked the three.*
> *'We have come to fish for the herring fish*
> *That live in this beautiful sea;*
> *Nets of silver and gold have we!'*
> *Said Wynken,*
> *Blynken,*
> *And Nod.*"

Hipp raised his eyebrows and looked at Fritz questioningly.

"I haven't read that, either," Fritz said.

"Then read it. It's by Eugene Field, who wrote

children's poetry in the late nineteenth century. There are four stanzas. I don't have time to recite the whole thing for you, so Google it, print it, and go through it carefully. Give some thought to the wooden shoe and the nets of silver and gold. There could be other meanings, who knows? Now beat it."

Fritz left Hipp's office, went back to his cubicle, found the poem, and printed it, while two of his colleagues looked over his shoulder. "What is it?"

"A poem that Hipp said to take a look at," Fritz replied. He printed two more copies and handed them to the two young men, who read it.

"Check out the last stanza," one of them said.

Fritz read aloud:

"Wynken and Blynken are two little eyes,
And Nod is a little head.
And the wooden shoe that sailed the skies
Is a wee one's trundle bed."

The three looked at each other. Fritz was the first to speak. "So what the fuck does that mean?"

13

Holly Barker was working at her desk at CIA headquarters in Langley, Virginia, when her boss, Lance Cabot, the Agency's deputy director for operations, walked into her office and sat down across the desk from her.

"Good morning," he said.

This was odd, Holly thought; she had met with him two hours before, at eight a.m., as was their daily custom. "Good morning again," she replied.

Lance looked at her thoughtfully but said nothing.

"What?" Holly asked.

"It appears that you will no longer be working for me," he said finally.

Holly sat back in her chair. "Are you firing me, Lance?"

"There are signs you might be moving from under my wing."

"Come on, Lance, spit it out."

"Are you saying you don't know what I'm talking about?"

"Finally, you understand me. First of all, there's nowhere to promote me. I've gone as far as I can in operations, so unless you are resigning or being promoted, where would I go?"

"Only the director knows," he said.

Holly shook her head. "I'm baffled." Her phone rang.

"Answer it," Lance said.

Holly picked up the phone. "Holly Barker."

"This is Grace, in the director's office," a voice said. Grace was the director's secretary.

"Good morning, Grace."

"Good morning, Holly. The director would like to see you."

"Certainly. What time?"

"Now."

"I'll be right up," Holly said, then hung up.

"Are things a little clearer for you now?" Lance asked.

"Not in the least," Holly replied. "Now please tell me what this is all about."

"Do you swear you don't know?"

"Bring me a Bible and I'll take an oath on it."

"Holly, if this is some sort of power play . . ."

"Lance, something is eating your brain," she said. "I don't have any power, except through carrying out your instructions. I'm a worker bee around here."

"You know nearly everything I know," Lance said.

Holly thought about that. "I know only what you have chosen to tell me, and, Lance, you *never* tell anybody *everything*."

"Well, I've told you very nearly everything."

Holly stood up. "I've been asked to come to the director's office right now. Please tell me whatever you can before I go up there and get my head handed to me."

"You know nearly everything I know," Lance said, then he got up and went back into his office.

Holly took a compact from her desk drawer, ran her hand through her hair and made sure nothing was stuck to her teeth, then she took the elevator upstairs and presented herself to Grace.

"Good morning, Holly."

"Good morning, Grace." God, she was getting sick of saying good morning.

"Have a seat. The director will be free shortly."

Holly sat down and picked up a three-month-old copy of *Proceedings*, the magazine of the U.S. Naval Institute, and flipped through it nervously. She heard a door close, and when she looked up Stewart Graves was standing in front of her. Graves was the assistant deputy director of intelligence, the Agency's analysis division; it was the same job that Holly held in operations. "Good morning, Stewart," she said.

"Did you have anything to do with this?" he asked. His tone was vaguely hostile.

"To do with what?" Holly asked. Everybody seemed to think she knew more than she did.

"I've been posted to London," he said. "Deputy for analysis to the station chief."

"Congratulations," Holly said. "That sounds great." As great as it sounded, Holly knew, it wasn't as great as his current job.

Graves turned and walked toward the elevators.

Holly looked at Grace. "What was that all about?" she asked.

"The director will see you now," Grace said. She placed her hand on the button under her desk that unlocked the director's office door and waited for Holly to move.

Holly walked to the door, heard the click, then opened the door and walked in. "Good morning, Director," Holly said.

Katharine Rule Lee looked up from her desk. It had taken an act of Congress to make her director, because, although she was a career CIA officer, she was also married to the president of the United States. "Good morning, Holly, have a seat." She pointed at a chair at a seating area by the window, then she got up and walked in that direction.

She isn't smiling, Holly thought. *She usually smiles a lot. What the hell is going on?* She walked over and sat in the chair indicated.

The director settled into a chair on the other side of the coffee table and opened a thick file in her lap.

Holly knew it was a personnel file, and she feared it was hers.

"You've been with us for a little over eight years, now," the director said.

"Yes, ma'am."

The director ran her finger down a page. "You've had an unusual career for the Agency—retired from the army as a major after twenty years' service. You should have made colonel. Why didn't you?"

Surely she knew all about this, Holly thought, but she told her story anyway. "I was serving under a colonel as his exec. He blocked my promotion."

"For what reason?"

"He made repeated sexual advances toward me, which I rebuffed, so he gave me a less favorable fitness report than I had every reason to expect. After that, he tried to rape me, and I fought him off and turned him in."

The director looked at the file. "It says here you struck him."

"I broke his nose rather badly," Holly said. "He was court-martialed for the attack on me. It turned out he had actually raped another female officer, a lieutenant."

"And he was acquitted," the director said.

"He was, ma'am. He had friends on the court, and two of them were in a position to see that I was never promoted again. I had put in my twenty, so I took retirement."

The director consulted the file again. "And you became the chief of police in Orchid Beach, Florida?"

"The deputy chief, Director. The chief who hired me was murdered the day before my arrival, and the city council shortly voted for me to succeed him."

"And you had quite a career there," the director said.

Holly didn't know how to respond to that.

"And then you impressed someone here and we recruited you."

Holly just nodded.

The director closed the personnel file. "And you have done nothing less than splendid work for us since the day you arrived."

Holly blinked. "Thank you, Director."

"Holly, as you know, my husband is in the last year of his second term."

"Yes, ma'am." The entire planet knew that.

"And when he leaves the White House, I will leave the Agency and retire with him."

"Yes, ma'am."

"As you might imagine, there has been a great deal of speculation within the Agency about who my successor will be. What you may not know is that there has been a cabal at work here which has been plotting to see that a particular someone from the Agency succeeds me, rather than someone from the outside. Or someone from elsewhere in the Agency."

"Really, ma'am?" Holly knew about this, because Lance had told her.

"From what I can determine, the cabal wishes to see Frank Hellman, the deputy director for intelligence, have this job."

Holly nodded.

"You probably saw his assistant, Stewart Graves, leave my office before you came in."

"Yes, ma'am. He said he was being posted to the London station."

"That is correct. I thought I would toss a little grenade into the hierarchy here as a way of expressing my displeasure about all this. As a result, Mr. Graves is going to London, and since you hold the same job in operations, you are being moved out of there, as well."

"Out of Langley, ma'am?" Holly knew that she was held in some measure of disdain by those higher-ups in the Agency who knew she had never held a foreign station post.

"No, Holly," the director said. She pointed at an open door across the room. "You are being moved into that office. I've posted my assistant, Greg Barton, to Rome. I'd like you to replace him here."

Holly stared blankly at her. All sorts of things had run through her mind on the way up there, but this was the one thing she had not anticipated.

"Holly," the director said, "are you still with me?"

"Yes, ma'am," Holly replied, though she was not sure about that. Now she knew what was meant by the mind reeling.

"I chose you for two reasons," the director said. "First, because of your outstanding record, and second, because you are the least political person I know at your level."

"Thank you, ma'am."

"I also chose you because of my high personal regard for you."

"Thank you, ma'am. I'm very grateful to you for the opportunity."

"Then you accept?"

"Oh, yes, ma'am!" Holly said.

"Good," the director said. "I wasn't sure there for a minute."

"I'm just a little bowled over."

"All right, you go down to your office and spend the rest of the day getting ready to hand off to your successor, who will be appointed shortly. And you start here tomorrow morning." She stood up and offered her hand.

Holly stood and took the hand.

"Grace will issue you new credentials before the day is out. Your new title will be—well, I'm a little torn about that. Greg was assistant to the director, but that might make you sound like a secretary, and that's Grace's job. I think assistant director is better. You'll be the only person in the Agency with that title. Oh, and you'll get a better parking space, too, right next to mine." She made a shooing motion with her hand.

Holly went back to her office in a daze. She stopped at Lance's open door and looked in.

"I heard everything," Lance said. "This is the best possible thing that could have happened. We're in a new ball game now."

Holly took that to mean that Lance felt his chances of succeeding Kate Lee had improved. "In that case, congratulations, Lance," she said.

"Yeah, yeah. Now get out of here. I'm reviewing candidates for your job."

Holly turned to go.

Lance called after her, "And, Holly?"

She looked back. "Yes?"

"Congratulations to you, too." Lance actually smiled.

14

Mike Freeman picked up his phone at the L.A. offices of Strategic Services. "Yes?"

"Mike, it's Scott Hipp."

"Hello, Scott, how's life?"

"Interesting," Hipp replied.

"Uh-oh."

Hipp laughed. "You have a point: when it's interesting here, it's often hairy elsewhere."

"That has been my experience," Mike replied. "What is it this time? Any more mentions of The Arrington in your traffic?"

"No, but . . . You still have a scrambler on that phone?"

The scrambler was one manufactured by the electronics division of Strategic Services, and Hipp had been given one. Mike pressed a button. "Go," he said.

"My people picked up an e-mail sent from a cell phone in California to a Middle Eastern Web site we keep a watch on. It read: 'All is well. I am fine.'"

"Did you run it through decoding?"

"Yes, and it appears to have been sent in the clear."

"Sounds like someone has completed a task," Mike said.

"Right. It was signed 'Nod.'"

"As in land of Nod?"

"Correct. We're running references on that now."

"So the only connection to The Arrington is that it came from California?"

"So far. That and the fact that it was transmitted via a cell tower at the top of Stone Canyon, in L.A."

"I know the one—it would cover The Arrington's location."

"Yes, but because of the tower's elevation, it would cover a big chunk of Beverly Hills and the San Fernando Valley, as well."

"You have a point."

"A rather blunt point, I'm afraid."

"Right now, that's the way I like it," Mike said. "If it were any sharper, I'd be worried."

"Are you worried enough for me to pass this on to the Secret Service?"

"If it were my call, no," Mike said. "But that's your call."

"I think I'll hold off until I have more, if we should actually get more, which I doubt."

"I think that's wise."

There was a brief silence, then Hipp said, "You know Holly Barker, don't you?"

"Sure," Mike said. "I sold our air transport company to the Agency a few years back, and Holly ran it for a few months, until they could hire somebody who could get through the vetting."

"Well, Holly got promoted to assistant director at the Agency."

"Assistant director? I didn't know they had those. I thought it was deputy director."

"That's the way it was, until Holly got the title. She's replacing Greg Whatshisname, who was assistant to the director. Greg got shipped off to Rome, and Stewart Graves, who was ADDI, was packed off to London."

"Sounds like a shake-up," Mike said.

"Sounds to me like Kate is paving the way for Lance Cabot to replace her when she goes."

"That's interesting, if she can pull it off," Mike said. "But for that to happen, the Democrat would have to get elected to replace Will Lee, and it would have to be a Democrat whose ear Kate has."

"I think our beloved veep, Stanton, has the inside track for the nomination, don't you?"

"Well, yes, because he's veep. There'll be some competition, though."

"Lance has done some major cultivation in the garden of the Senate Select Committee on Intelligence," Hipp said. "Lance might get it, even if a Republican is elected."

"Well, if anybody could work both sides of the street, it's Lance. I wouldn't be upset if he got it."

"Neither would I," Hipp said. "I can't say I'm fond of Lance, but I don't hate him, and that's something."

"I'm fond of him on some days, and I hate him on others," Mike said. "But I'm fond of Holly all the time."

"I don't know her all that well, but I hear good things."

"She's gotten some of the credit for the way Lance has smoothed out operations."

"You think that if Lance gets the job, he might pick her to replace him at ops?"

"Nobody's closer to Lance than Holly."

"Well, we'll see what we shall see, won't we? Gotta run."

"See you, Scott. Keep me in the loop, will you?"

"Sure." Hipp hung up.

Mike switched off his scrambler and called Stone Barrington.

"Hey, Mike."

"Just got some news, Stone: shake-up at the Agency. Stewart Graves and Greg Barton are out."

"I know the names, but not the people," Stone replied.

"The big news is that Holly is replacing Barton in Kate's office, with the title of assistant director."

Stone made a whistling sound. "Big jump!"

"I read the changes as Kate's paving the way for Lance."

"I'm sure Lance would like nothing better."

"And if he gets it, Holly could be the next DDO."

"You know," Stone said, "if Holly ever leaves the Agency, you should pounce on her."

"I've thought that ever since I saw the way she ran the air transport company. She made me wish we still owned it."

"Well, if Lance doesn't get Kate's job, Holly will be at a dead end at the Agency. That's when you should go after her."

"That's good advice."

"She still has a New York apartment from when she did that thing for Lance here a few years back."

"I didn't know that."

"Nice place, on Park."

"No relocation costs!" Mike laughed.

"Where are you?" Stone asked.

"In L.A. I had dinner last night with Rifkin, the Secret Service detail honcho."

"Any news from him?"

"If he had any news, he wouldn't share it. They're like that."

Mike told him about the cell call from L.A. to the watch-listed Web site. "That's why I'm not telling him about that, or anything else. They've already doubled their efforts at The Arrington, and that's all I want from them. At the moment."

"Does this cell call from California worry you?"

"Not at the moment. Time will tell."

"Thanks for the news about Holly. I'll drop her a note—she'll be impressed that I know."

"You do that, and congratulate her for me."

Stone hung up, called Dino, and told him the news.

15

Holly Barker spent the morning unpacking her things, hanging a couple of pictures, and registering the Agency desktop to her identity. Her new office was more than three times the size of her previous one and contained a small conference table, a sofa, and a pair of comfortable chairs and more bookcases. She had indeed been given a prime parking spot, one that would cause envy among the Agency's hierarchy, and she liked it.

"Getting settled in?" Kate Lee said from behind her.

Holly turned to find her boss standing in her doorway. "Yes, ma'am," Holly said. "I'm ready to go to work."

"That's good, because you're headed to London tonight."

"I am?" Lance rarely sent her anywhere.

Kate made herself comfortable on Holly's sofa, and Holly joined her, bringing along a pad.

"We have an operative in Europe that you and Lance don't know about. He has always communicated with me through what is now your office. I've sent him a message to expect you tomorrow, and he'll call you on your cell phone after you've landed."

"All right. Who is he?"

"His birth name was Ari Shazaz," Kate said, "but his passport is British, in the name of Hamish McCallister. He was born in Syria to an Algerian father and a Scottish mother. He's in his early forties, and you will find him to be impeccably British— Eton, Oxford, White's, the Garrick Club, etcetera. At school and university he was known as McCallister, his mother's maiden name. His father died when he was eight or nine, and she took him to London to bring up. She's from landed gentry— they own an island off the west coast of Scotland, appropriately called Murk.

"Hamish is fluent in Arabic and Urdu along with French and Italian. After university, he worked in a family-owned bank, doing business in the Middle East and on the continent. He has earned his living for the past ten years as a weekly columnist for the *Guardsman*, a leftish London paper, and he writes the occasional penetrating article for some magazine or other on things like Arab-Israeli relations."

Grace appeared in the doorway. "Excuse me, Mrs. Lee, but I have Ms. Barker's new credentials."

"Come in, Grace," Kate said.

Grace opened a large envelope and shook out the contents onto the coffee table. "First, may I have your old credentials, please? Your Agency ID, your passport, your gate and building pass, and your iPhone and BlackBerry."

Holly fetched her purse and produced those items.

Grace handed her a new Agency ID and a plastic card that would allow entry through both the main gate and the Agency's front entrance. "That card will also work at any American embassy or consulate abroad. You now have a full diplomatic passport," she said, handing over the document. "Please sign here." She held the passport in place while Holly signed it. "Here's another card to keep with you," she said, handing over another piece of plastic. "It states that you are a federal agent and licensed to carry firearms anywhere in the United States and its territories and possessions. It can also be useful with foreign police, though it carries no official weight abroad. Here are your new American Express card and Visa and MasterCards. You may use them for all official expenditures and you may withdraw funds from any ATM in the world with no daily limit. Your PIN number is the last four digits of your Agency employee number."

Holly picked up the American Express card, which was black. "It seems to be made of titanium," she said.

"Yes, it's called the Centurion card. Here's a packet listing the various benefits and services accruing to it, including a travel agent. Here's something else made of titanium," she said, handing Holly a small, light semiautomatic pistol. "It was designed and developed by the Agency and is currently in use by only high-level officers. It will later be issued to all those expected to travel armed." Grace handed her a box. "Here is a shoulder holster and a belt holster for your use, as well as a box of nine-millimeter ammunition, four magazines, and a small but very effective silencer. You should familiarize yourself with the pistol on the range as soon as possible."

Grace also handed her two new phones. "This iPhone and this BlackBerry already contain all the information in your old phones. They contain a GPS chip not found in commercial phones, which allows the Agency to track you anywhere in the world to a distance of one meter."

"I'll never be alone again," Holly said.

"Removing the SIM chip will disable the GPS function. If you don't want to be tracked, pull out the chip. If you lose a phone, there will be hell to pay." Grace raked all of Holly's old credentials and equipment into her envelope and left the room.

"Where was I?" Kate asked.

"Ari Shazaz, or Hamish McCallister."

"We'll always refer to him as Hamish, since it is important that his Arab name remain unknown, except where he needs to use it."

"Understood. Why am I seeing him in London?"

"Two reasons: First, since you will be his main contact here, you should know each other. Second, I want you to speak with him about an upcoming event, about which you may have heard—the grand opening of a hotel, The Arrington, in California in a couple of weeks."

"I've read about it," Holly said.

"And of course, you know its namesake through Stone Barrington."

"No, we never met, but I certainly know about her."

"I've received word that an NSA computer picked up a cell phone conversation between someone in Afghanistan and someone in Yemen, during which the words 'The Arrington' were spoken. This is of concern to us because, as you may know, the president and the president of Mexico will be in residence at the hotel just prior to and during the grand opening."

"I can see how that would cause concern."

"I've also heard that an e-mail was sent from somewhere in California to a Web site that the NSA keeps watch on. The message was, 'All is well. I am fine,' and it was signed 'Nod.' I want you to instruct Hamish to take whatever contacts are available to him to learn if anyone else anywhere has heard anything at all concerning the hotel or anything about the Nod message."

"How long will I be in London?"

"Long enough to meet Hamish and get a first report from him after he has made his contacts. After that, he will phone or send encrypted e-mails to you, using equipment we have supplied to him."

"Should I make travel arrangements?"

"Not necessary. You will be flying in an Agency aircraft, along with Stewart Graves, who is taking up his post as deputy station chief at the London embassy. Greg Barton will be along, too, and after dropping off you and Stewart, the plane will continue to Rome to deliver him there. The aircraft will then return and collect you as soon as your business is done. If it's needed elsewhere, we'll send another aircraft or have you fly home commercial. Be at our facility at Dulles at eleven p.m. tonight, and pack for a week, just in case. You'll be staying at the Connaught Hotel, which is near the embassy. By the way, Stewart is aware of Hamish's existence, but make no mention of him."

"I understand."

"No need to contact me while you're gone, unless it's urgent. In that case use the communication facilities at the London station. Oh, by the way, one of your jobs will be to travel with me, so you and I will be attending the opening of The Arrington with my husband, and we'll travel on Air Force One."

Kate shook her hand and went back to her office, closing the connecting door behind her.

Holly continued putting her things away, then she noticed her iPhone vibrating on the coffee table. She picked it up and found an e-mail waiting.

"Congratulations on the new job," it said. "Stone."

"Now, how the hell did he know so soon?" she asked herself. She e-mailed him back: "Thanks, see you in L.A. for the opening of The Arrington."

16

Holly arrived at Dulles half an hour before flight time, parked in a reserved spot, and unloaded her luggage. The facility looked like any other Fixed Base Operator, or FBO, on the field, though the reception area was smaller than most. Her pass card allowed her through the door.

"Good evening," said a young woman behind the front desk. "Your name, please?"

"Holly Barker." She produced her Agency ID.

"Your flight is the Gulfstream 450 parked on the ramp. You may board whenever you like, and your luggage will be loaded into the cabin."

"Thank you," Holly said. She left her two bags and took her briefcase and purse with her.

A stewardess greeted her at the door of the airplane. "We've made up three seats as bunks, Ms.

Barker," the woman said. "You may choose any other seat, and when you're ready to sleep, a bunk. May I get you anything to drink?"

"Thank you, I'll have some fizzy water, please." Holly found a seat at the rear of the airplane and checked her e-mail. There was one from Kate Lee, announcing her appointment to a list of Agency executives. She forwarded that to her father, Ham, in Florida. "Thought you'd like to see this," she wrote. "Kiss Daisy for me." Her workload had been so heavy that she had left her Doberman pinscher with her father and his wife, where there was room for her to run. She missed Daisy but knew she was in good hands.

Stewart Graves and Greg Barton arrived together, chatting like old friends. She got a perfunctory greeting from both, then they sat down and buckled in. The stewardess closed the cabin door, and the engines started. At the stroke of eleven the airplane began to taxi, and five minutes later they were roaring down the runway.

When they had been climbing for fifteen minutes the pilot's voice was heard. "Good evening; we're now at flight level 450, and we have a ninety-knot tailwind. We should arrive at Biggin Hill Airport, in Kent, at five thirty a.m., Dulles time, ten thirty London time."

The stewardess appeared again. "Would you like dinner?" she asked.

"No, thank you," Holly said.

"Breakfast will be served an hour before we land. What would you like? We have cereals, pastries, or scrambled eggs with bacon."

"I'll have the eggs," Holly said. She settled in to read the Agency's handbooks for her two phones and discovered that both could send and receive encrypted messages. Forward of where she sat Graves and Barton were in earnest conversation. Holly chose the aftermost bunk, set her watch forward five hours, and was soon sound asleep.

The stewardess woke her at nine o'clock, and she went to the toilet and freshened up. When she returned she raised the shade of her window and got an eyeful of bright sunshine. There was an undercast far below. She switched on the screen at her seat and found the moving map. They would make their landfall south of Land's End soon, and their arrival time had not changed. The breakfast was much better than she had expected.

They touched down at Biggin Hill three minutes early, and her luggage was taken into an FBO, where a customs and immigration official awaited them. She was unimpressed by Holly's brand-new diplomatic passport and gave it its first stamp.

"There's a van waiting for us," Stewart Graves

said. He had eight or nine pieces of luggage; this was a move across the Atlantic for him.

Greg Barton shook her hand. "Good luck in the new post," she said to him.

"Thanks. You, too." Those were the only words he had spoken to her since they had boarded the airplane. Holly thought he might have given her a few pointers on her new job, since she was replacing him, but apparently he was not anxious for her to succeed. Stewart Graves was similarly tight-lipped. After a hideously long drive through the south London suburbs, the van stopped at the Connaught, and the doorman unloaded her bags.

"Good luck," she said to Graves, and he nodded. "You, too." Then he was gone.

Holly checked in and was walked upstairs by a young woman. She was delighted to find that a suite had been booked for her, a first since she had joined the Agency. She showered, then dried her hair and had a light lunch. She was dozing on her sitting room sofa when her iPhone rang.

"Yes?"

"This is Hamish. Seven p.m. at a pub called the Grenadier, in Wilton Row. Any cabdriver will know it." He hung up.

"Okay," she said into the dead line. She watched a cricket match for an hour, trying to figure it out, then gave up and watched an old movie.

17

The cab dropped Holly at the doorstep of the Grenadier, which was located in a pretty mews behind Wilton Crescent, in upper-upper-class Belgravia.

She walked up the front stairs and into a cozy barroom. A fire crackled in a hearth to her left, and the room was crowded with expensively dressed young people. Holly ordered a scotch over ice and found a spot to sit near the fire. She had begun sizing up the young men in the room, when somebody stepped in front of her. She looked up to see a trim figure in clothes that were clearly bespoke. He had a bald head with a fringe of dark hair and he had, of all unexpected things in London, a suntan.

"Holly Barker?" he asked.

Holly stood up and found that the top of his head came to about the tip of her nose. "Hamish?"

They shook hands, and Hamish guided her into an adjoining dining room, where a single table had been set for two. "Please," he said, pulling out the table so that she could get behind it and sit on the banquette. He set his own drink on the table and waved at a waitress. "May I have a large Lagavulin with a single ice cube, please?" He had dark, almost black eyes and perfect teeth.

"Lagavulin?" Holly asked.

"It's a single-malt scotch from the island of Islay," he replied.

"It's hard to keep up with single malts."

"Don't even try," he said, smiling. "Kate didn't make it clear that you were beautiful, as well as smart. I particularly like the red hair. Tell me, is it from a bottle?" His English was entirely upper class, reflecting his Eton and Oxford education.

"It's from a salon," Holly replied. What would he want to know next, her bra size?

He moved a hand up and down. "It's all a very pleasing combination. You chose exactly the right things to wear to a fashionable pub."

Holly had chosen tweed slacks and a jacket and a cashmere sweater, all covered by a trench coat, which she now struggled out of. "Thank you, Hamish."

A young woman brought them menus and a wine list. "The food here is very good, for a pub, and they have some decent wines. What did Kate do with Greg Barton?" he asked, as his eyes roamed the wine list. "Take him out and shoot him?"

"On the contrary," Holly said, "Greg was rewarded with a very nice job in Rome. He's already there."

"I heard Stewart Graves will be coming to London."

"We were all on the same aircraft coming over."

"Did Greg fill your ears with descriptions of my exploits?"

"Neither of them had anything to say, so I got some sleep."

"Ah, yes, the woman thing. I don't think either of them liked working for Kate, then to have yet another woman inserted between them and Kate must have been a blow."

"As I said, they didn't share. What I know of you came from Kate."

Hamish nodded. "I'm sure she was objective and fair."

"Always, in my experience."

"What job were you in before?"

"Assistant DDO."

"And now you are assistant director! A great leap. I'm sure Kate was very deliberate in leaving out the 'to' between 'assistant' and 'director.'"

Holly smiled. "She's always deliberate."

"Yes! Not a hothead, our Kate."

"Not in my experience."

"I expect her cool confidence comes from the proximity of the man who appointed her."

"I think it comes from her core, and I think being married to Will Lee has as many pitfalls as advantages."

"I can't keep up with American politics."

"Don't even try."

He laughed. "And soon she will be gone, with her husband. What then for the ambitious at Langley?"

"Anxiety, I should think."

"And it's already begun, hasn't it? The removal of Stewart and Greg must have got their attention!"

"I left the country only hours after I was appointed, so I wasn't around to hear the chatter. I hear you roam far and wide, Hamish. What brings you to London?"

"Why, the pleasure of meeting you, Holly," he replied smoothly, "and also my curiosity about what message Kate has sent me. She has sent me a message, hasn't she?"

"She has."

"Well, let's order first to get the waitress out of our hair—pardon me, *your* hair," he said, stroking his bald pate.

"I'll have the steak-and-kidney pie," Holly said, "and whatever wine you're ordering."

Hamish crooked a finger at the waitress, who came over. "Each of us will have the steak-and-kidney pie, with chips," he said to her, "and a bottle of the Corton '99."

The woman jotted down the items and left.

"And now," Hamish said, "I can't wait to hear from Kate."

"Have you ever heard of a hotel in Los Angeles called The Arrington?"

"Of course. Opening soon, isn't it?"

"Quite soon, and with a big splash. The presidents of the United States and Mexico will be in attendance, which, as you might imagine, has cranked up the Secret Service and the hotel's security operation."

"I can imagine."

The waitress delivered their food and wine, and they spent a few minutes eating and chatting idly.

Later, as they were finishing the wine, Holly got back to business. "Something troubling happened recently. The NSA intercepted a cell phone call from Afghanistan to Yemen, in which the words 'The Arrington' stood out."

"Well, I don't imagine that the hotel's public relations people had reached as far as Afghanistan."

"Apparently, neither did anyone else imagine that," Holly said.

"So what would Kate like me to do?"

"She'd like you to canvass your contacts in Europe and the Middle East for anything pointing to a possible planned attack on the hotel. There could be mischief afoot."

"I suppose I could do that," Hamish said, "but if I start calling around, then the NSA would suddenly be picking up mentions of The Arrington all over Europe and the Middle East, which would disturb them even more."

"You have a point," Holly said. "Let's not get them any more excited than they already are."

"Then I will need to speak to some people face-to-face, if we wish not to provoke a red alert in American intelligence circles."

"A wise suggestion, I think. How long will it take you to manage it?"

"I think that, if I leave tomorrow morning in a small jet, I could do it in four or five stops: say, a week?"

"Are you contemplating chartering a jet aircraft on our nickel?"

Hamish smiled. "That is exactly the question Kate would ask, were she here. Fortunately, I have access to a Citation Mustang belonging to a friend. All it will cost Kate is the fuel."

"What about the pilot?"

"Oh, I am the pilot," Hamish said, "and I am already bought and paid for."

"I have a friend in New York who flies that airplane," Holly said, thinking of Stone, something she had been doing a lot lately.

"How fortunate for him," Hamish said. "Do you fly?"

"A Piper Malibu," Holly replied. "No jet time, as yet."

"Lovely airplane. Of course, there will be the usual attendant expenses: airport handling, hotels, etcetera."

"Within reason," Holly said, imagining Hamish in a huge suite in a fabulous hotel.

"Always," Hamish replied. "Would you care to come with me? It should be an enlightening and pleasant trip."

Holly thought that traveling to exotic places in a jet with Hamish McCallister at the controls would not be unpleasant. "I'm required elsewhere," she said.

"Perhaps another time," Hamish said, locking his eyes on hers.

Holly felt a blush coming on and coughed into her napkin. "There's one other thing to look for: any mention of the word 'Nod.'"

Hamish frowned. "In what context?"

"Any context you might come across. It appears to be the code name of an operative. It was sent in an e-mail from California to a suspected al Qaeda Web site that is being watched."

"Was the message translated?"

"It read, in its entirety, 'All is well. I am fine. Nod.'"

"I see. Sounds like someone has accomplished some task."

"That's how it seems to us, too. We need to know more."

Hamish handed her a card. "These are all my contact numbers and e-mail addresses, should you ever need to reach me."

"Thank you."

Hamish glanced at his watch. "Now, if you will excuse me, I have some flight planning and other preparations to make, so that I can get an early start tomorrow." He tossed off the remainder of his wine. "Would you mind getting the bill? It should be easier for you to reclaim expenses than I."

"Not at all."

Hamish stood and offered his hand. "A great pleasure. Must run. Will you be in London when I get back?"

"Maybe, I'm not sure. In any event, you know how to reach me."

"Of course. Must run." And he did.

18

Stone cooked dinner for himself and Marla Rocker, whom he had been seeing for many weeks. After dinner, they repaired to his bed and did what they usually did after dinner.

When they were finished, Marla said, "I'm sorry I can't come to California with you for the hotel opening, but I'm beginning to get very busy with Peter's play."

"I'm sorry, too, though I understand your reasons."

"In fact, when you get back, it's going to be difficult for me to see much of you."

That set off a little *ping* in Stone's frontal lobe; he read it as the first evidence of a dump to come. "Oh?"

"I have a musical that will fall hot on the heels

of Peter's play, and an actor I've been close to will be starring."

So an old boyfriend was back in the picture. "I think I can see where this is headed," Stone said.

"It's not you, Stone. You're a lovely man, and I've enjoyed our time together. I hope . . ."

"That we'll always be friends? Of course."

"I'm glad you understand," she said, sounding relieved. She put her feet on the floor and started reaching for clothes. "I can't stay over—early start tomorrow, and I have to be fresh."

A moment later, after a quick hug and kiss, she was gone.

Really gone, Stone thought. He looked at the bedside clock. Nine thirty, and he wasn't even sleepy. He reached for the TV remote control.

When Stone awoke, it was nearly seven a.m. and *Morning Joe* was on the TV. His phone rang. "Hello?"

"Are you really awake?" an English-accented voice inquired.

"I really am," he replied. "Good morning, Felicity." Felicity Devonshire was an old friend and lover who, after a long career in British intelligence, had risen to be the head of MI-6, the foreign arm of their intel services, code name: architect.

"It appears that I will be attending the opening of your new hotel, The Arrington, in Bel-Air."

"Then I'm looking forward to seeing you. Business or pleasure?"

"I'm anticipating a bit of both," she said.

"I'll do what I can to help out with the pleasure side."

"I knew you would, Stone."

"What else is new in your life, Felicity?"

"Everything is always new in my line of work, except when it's old."

"I'm curious as to what business would bring you to The Arrington. Is there something I should know about? I am, after all, an investor and a director."

"Nothing I can mention at the moment," she said. "Not on this line. Perhaps later."

"I'll be all ears," Stone replied.

"And I'll be tugging them."

Stone remembered on what occasions and in what position she liked to tug his ears. He laughed. "What day are you arriving?"

"The same day as President Lee."

"Perhaps you'd like to come to New York a day or two earlier and lay over with me?"

"If I can lay over with you, I shall certainly come earlier," she said with a low chuckle.

"I and my party are flying to L.A. on a Gulfstream 550, supplied by Strategic Services. You can travel with us, if you like."

"A fetching thought," she said. "I'll try and do

that. I must go now. I'll be in touch." She hung up without further ado.

Stone hung up, too, his spirits lifted by the sound of her voice. Then he remembered that Holly Barker would be in Bel-Air, too. *This might get hairy,* he thought.

19

Holly hung around London for another three days without hearing anything from Hamish McCallister. Finally, after having toured the National Gallery and the National Portrait Gallery and seeing the Degas exhibit at the Royal Academy of Art, and having gained two pounds on Connaught room service, she called the pilot who had flown her to London.

"Hello?"

"It's Holly Barker. Are you still on this side of the Atlantic?"

"We are," the man replied, "in Zurich. Are you ready to return to D.C.?"

"I am."

"Will tomorrow morning be good enough?"

"That will be fine."

"We'll be ready to depart Biggin Hill at noon."

"I'll be there. See you then." She hung up and called her office. Grace answered her phone, since Holly hadn't had time to choose her own secretary.

"Ms. Barker's office."

"It's Holly, Grace."

"Good morning, Ms. Barker."

"You're going to have to get used to calling me Holly, Grace, since I hardly know who Ms. Barker is."

"I'll try, Ms. . . . . Holly."

"I'm departing London at noon tomorrow, and I expect to be in the office between three and four."

"Would you like me to arrange ground transportation?"

"No, my car is at Dulles. Has anything of importance come up?"

"The director is anxious to hear your report."

"Tell her I haven't heard anything yet. My friend is out of town."

"I'll tell her."

"See you tomorrow." Holly ended the call. Almost immediately, the phone rang.

"Hello?"

"Encrypt," a man's voice said.

Holly entered the code. "Encrypted."

"It's your jet-setting colleague." The transmission was scratchy. "Can you hear me all right?"

"You break up now and then, but I can make you out."

"I have something for you."

"Go ahead."

"The Nod reference is to a nursery rhyme: 'Wynken, Blynken, and Nod.' Do you know it?"

"I was a child, once," Holly replied.

Hamish chuckled. "My information is that there are three operatives somewhere on the West Coast of the United States. I couldn't learn where or how long they've been there or what they are planning. Did you get that?"

"I got it," Holly said. "I don't like it, but I got it. Is there any connection with the hotel?"

"I think that's a reasonable inference," Hamish said, "but I couldn't learn anything specific to support it. I'll keep contacting people for another day or two, though."

"Where did you get this information?"

"I can't talk about my sources."

"Not who—where?"

"I got that much in Lebanon, but I couldn't trace it further back than that."

"All right; I'll be in London until ten tomorrow, then I'm headed back to my office. You can contact me here or there."

"If I come up with anything else, I'll be in touch," Hamish said. "If I hear nothing, you won't hear from me at all."

"Got it. Thanks for dinner. I look forward to working with you."

"Thank *you* for dinner," Hamish said, "and same here. Good-bye." He ended the call.

The G-450 landed at Dulles ahead of schedule, encountering only light headwinds. Holly walked into the director's suite at three thirty.

"Welcome home," Grace said. "The director asked that you see her as soon as you get in."

"Right now is good for me," Holly said. She put her briefcase on her desk and knocked on the door between her office and the director's.

"Come in, Holly!" Kate Lee called.

Holly came in and took the seat across the desk from her boss.

"Good trip, I hope."

"I hope so, too," Holly replied. "I saw Hamish as planned, the evening of my arrival."

"What did you think of him?"

"Smart and charming. I asked him to find out what he could about The Arrington and Nod, and we agreed he shouldn't do it on the phone, so he borrowed an airplane and took off the following morning for parts unknown to me. I heard nothing from him for three days, then he called late yesterday afternoon."

"And what did he have to say?"

"He said that, from what he was told by his

sources, there are three al Qaeda operatives on the West Coast. Their code names are Wynken, Blynken, and Nod. He couldn't find out where they are or how long they've been there or what they were there for."

"That's it?"

"That's it. Although he wouldn't reveal his sources, I asked him where he got the information, and he said in Lebanon."

"He said he went to Lebanon?"

"He said over dinner that he wanted to speak to his sources face-to-face, so I took him to mean that he was or had been in Lebanon. The reception on the call was not great."

"Did he say he was still in Lebanon?"

"No, but he said he would keep at it for another day or two, and that if he got anything more, he'd be in touch."

"Was the call from Hamish encrypted?"

"Yes."

"Interesting. Well, I heard not half an hour ago that an NSA computer had picked up two more messages from California, one signed 'Wynken,' the other, 'Blynken.'"

"So I might as well have stayed at home."

"Your trip wasn't for nothing. You got to know Hamish, and he got us confirmation on the three operatives. That's worth a lot. It will make Scott

Hipp at NSA very happy to know that his people's work was confirmed."

"Who is Scott Hipp?"

"A deputy director, in charge of electronic surveillance and cryptology. Very political. I expect to hear from the White House tonight that he has told them about Wynken, Blynken, and Nod."

"I expect the Secret Service will be interested in that information."

"Yes, they will," Kate replied. "One thing troubles me, though."

"What's that?"

"Remember when Grace issued you your credentials and the two phones?"

"Yes?"

"Remember that we have constant GPS tracking on some of our phones?"

"Yes."

"Hamish has one of those phones, one of those with the facility of encrypting, and the tracking on that phone indicates that he never left London."

Holly stared at her boss blankly.

"Also, that Citation Mustang that he occasionally borrows from his friend, a London entrepreneur, has not been out of its hangar at Blackbushe Airport for the past ten days."

"So Hamish lied to me?"

"Exactly," Kate replied. "Now I want to see if

he claims reimbursement for the airplane's fuel usage. He can always say that he found another way to contact his sources and changed his mind about flying, but if he claims for the fuel, I'll have his head."

"But what about the information he said he got from his sources? Can we trust that?"

"Yes, because it has already been confirmed by the NSA—also, because Hamish has always been very careful not to overstate the quality of the information he passes to us, and he has never been wrong."

"Somehow, I feel had," Holly said.

"You haven't been had, Hamish has just blown in your ear, that's all. Now, don't you have secretaries to interview?"

Holly stood up. "Yes, ma'am." She went to her office, where the first candidate awaited her.

20

Mike Freeman answered his suite door at The Arrington to find a messenger standing there with a package. He signed for it, tipped the man, and took it inside. He unwrapped a large cardboard tube and found a note attached to it.

"Call me when you receive this," it said, and it was signed by Scott Hipp.

Mike opened the tube and shook out an enlarged photograph, a satellite view of the Los Angeles area. He flattened the photo and weighted the corners, then he called Hipp on his direct line.

"Scott Hipp."

"It's Mike Freeman, Scott. What have you sent me?"

"First, a little preamble," Hipp said. "Yesterday

one of my people was going through data collected on an automated computer, and he found two more messages with the text 'All is well. I am fine.' One was signed 'Wynken,' the other, 'Blynken.'"

"Uh-oh."

"Exactly."

"What does the satshot you sent me have to do with them?"

"Are you looking at the photo?"

"I am."

"Then you'll see three straight lines emanating from a point on the high ground, just above the Stone Canyon Reservoir, which is the cell tower that received and transmitted the e-mails."

"I see the lines."

"They're fairly close together, you will observe. Through some technology I'm not allowed to tell you about, we've gone back to the computer record of the three e-mails, which were all sent from cell phones, and determined the radials from the tower on which each caller was located when the e-mails were sent. This is not definitive, of course, because we can't determine the distance of the sender from the tower. In theory, they could be standing anywhere on those lines, out to infinity. In practice, they were probably all within five miles of the tower."

"I understand."

"As you will no doubt note, one of the lines—the message signed 'Nod'—passes through the grounds of The Arrington, so Nod could have been on the property when it was sent. Of course, he could have been north or south of The Arrington, too, or it could simply be a coincidence, but you get my drift."

"I do."

"That's all I've got for you," Hipp said. "I thought you'd find it interesting."

"I find it fascinating, Scott. One more thing: do you have the dates on which the e-mails were sent?"

"Nod transmitted a week ago yesterday, the twelfth, Wynken, the fourteenth, and Blynken, the fifteenth."

"Thank you again, Scott. Very much."

"Take care." Hipp hung up.

Mike stared at the map a little longer, then he got up and walked down the hill to the old Calder House, now the site of The Arrington's executive offices. The building was nearly finished, now, and all the offices were occupied. He stopped at the reception desk.

"Good afternoon," he said. "My name is Michael Freeman, of Strategic Services. We're supplying all the security personnel for the hotel."

"Yes, Mr. Freeman, I've seen you before."

"Who is in charge of hiring for the hotel?"

"Well, each department head hires his own people: Food and Beverages hires the kitchen and restaurant staff, Domestic hires the maids, Landscaping, the outdoor workers, and so on."

"Is there a director of personnel, who presides over the entire hotel?"

"No, sir. Each department has a budget and hiring conforms to that."

"Who's in charge of the overall budget?"

"Why, Carol, I suppose."

"And who is he?"

"She. It's Carol Pressler. Her office is just down the hall." She pointed.

"Thank you." Mike continued down the hallway and found a door labeled "Comptroller." He knocked, and a woman's voice yelled, "Come in." He opened the door to find an attractive woman in her forties seated at a computer, her desk stacked with printouts. "Mrs. Pressler?"

"It's Ms., and I'm Carol," she said, holding out her hand. "You're our security guy, aren't you?"

"Mike Freeman, of Strategic Services."

"Have a seat, Mike. What can I do for you?"

"I've just been told that there is no personnel director, as such, and that each department head is in charge of his own budget. Is that correct?"

"It is. The philosophy is that each department

head will be much better acquainted with the qualifications of hirees in his department than an overall director of personnel."

"But your department pays everybody?"

"Correct."

"So you have a computer record of all employees?"

"Correct."

"Can you tell from your records the date on
which each was hired?"

"I can, otherwise I wouldn't know when to start
paying them."

"I would be very grateful if you could give me a
list of all the people hired on the twelfth, fourteenth, and fifteenth of this month."

"Overall, or by department?"

"By department would be helpful."

"Can you give me a few minutes?" she asked.

"Of course." Mike rose to go.

"Oh, not that many minutes. Just wait."

Mike sat down again.

Carol Pressler turned to her computer and began typing. As she typed, her printer began to dis-
gorge paper. A few minutes later, she got up,
retrieved the paper from the printer, and handed
it to Mike. "A total of a hundred and thirty-five
workers were hired during those three days."

Mike took the stack of paper from her. "So
many?"

"We'll have a little over one employee for every guest," she said.

"I mean, so many in just three days?"

"Peak hiring time," she said. "The hotel wants to hire people only shortly before they are to begin working. Interviewing has been going on for weeks, of course, but we want to hire personnel just in time to train them and put them to work, so the actual hiring is compressed into just a few days."

"I see," Mike said. "And did the Secret Service review the records of each hiree?"

"Yep. First time I've ever dealt with them, but given the importance of the guests, it's understandable."

"And did the Secret Service decline to clear any of them?"

"Only two, and they were Mexican-Americans who had counterfeit green cards. Very good counterfeits, too. Fooled me."

"And they were not hired?"

"Nope. It's the policy of the board to hire only legal workers. You should know that, since you're on the board."

"Quite right." Mike stood up. "Thank you, Carol," he said.

"You're entirely welcome. I expect we'll meet again."

"I hope so," Mike said. He shook her hand and left the office.

Walking back to his suite, he reflected that if Wynken, Blynken, and Nod were hired on those days—and that was only an assumption—and each had undergone the extensive background check by the Secret Service, then he was going to have a hell of a time figuring out who they were.

21

Holly Barker looked across her desk at the young woman. Her name was Heather Scott, she was thirty-five, single, and had been at the Agency since her graduation from college. Holly liked her. She particularly liked that she had held responsible assistant's jobs in both analysis and operations, so she had an understanding of how both directorates worked.

"Heather?"

"Everybody has called me Scotty, since childhood."

"You were born and raised in a place called . . ." Holly checked her application. "Delano, Georgia?"

"That's right. Public schools, followed by the University of Georgia."

"And you were recruited where?"

"On campus at Georgia. A recruiter spent a few days there."

"What do you hate most about the Agency?"

Scotty erupted in laughter. "That's a tough one, since I like so many things about it. I like coming to work every day."

"Come on, what do you hate?"

"I hate it when I can see a piece of information as relevant, even critical, and it takes the Agency too long to come to the same conclusion."

Holly laughed. "I think we've all had that experience. No matter how exotic our work, we're still a bureaucracy."

"I've had to get used to that."

The two women talked on for another half hour, then Holly said, "I'll get back to you in a few days."

"Right," Scotty said. She stood up and shook hands with Holly. "If it's offered to me, I'll take it."

"Good to know." Holly watched her leave, then she got up and walked across the reception room to Grace's desk. "Okay, I've found my assistant. What next?"

"I'll send her name to our internal security people, and they'll do a fresh background check, from the ground up."

"How long will that take?"

"Yours took a week," Grace said, "but Heather Scott's is likely to take a lot less, since she's never been employed anywhere but here."

"Then go," Holly said, handing her Heather's personnel file. "The sooner she's cleared, the sooner you can wash your hands of me."

Grace smiled. "Oh, you're not so bad. You're a piece of cake, compared to the director."

Holly laughed and went back to her office, past the outer room where her assistant's desk was. Her phone buzzed: the director.

"Yes, ma'am?"

"Come in for a minute, Holly."

Holly opened the adjoining door and walked in. Kate Lee was sitting on a sofa by the window and waved her to a seat.

"How's the search for an assistant going?"

"I've found her, I think."

"Did you talk only to women?"

"I've seen half a dozen people. Two of them were women. The one I didn't choose was probably a good secretary, but I thought she would never be more than that. All the men were too nakedly ambitious, I thought."

"And the other woman was just right."

"I believe so. Grace is ordering the requisite recheck of her background, and if she passes, I'll offer her the job."

"Good. Now there's something else I want to ask you about. I'm reviewing a number of people who might be suitable to replace me, and one of them, of course, is Lance Cabot."

Holly nodded.

"I want to ask you some questions about Lance, and I want you to put aside personal loyalty for a moment and give me straight answers, the unvarnished truth. Is that clear?"

"Yes, ma'am."

"Forgive me if I cover territory you're already familiar with, but it's necessary."

"Yes, ma'am."

"Lance had a stellar career as an agent in Europe, but nobody he worked with liked him very much, including his boss in the London station, Dick Stone, whose untimely death allowed Lance to leapfrog into his position as DDO—at least, that's the way some people saw it at the time. Why do you think he's not very well liked?"

Holly thought about that for a moment. "A minute ago, you said you wanted the unvarnished truth."

"And I do."

"The unvarnished truth is what Lance offers, and he doesn't much care who the recipient is. He states his opinions flatly and backs up his hunches with facts, then he defends his positions very strongly."

"I think that's fair to say," Kate replied.

"It may be fair, but a lot of people don't find it attractive. Lance can be charming, when it suits him, or when it's required to get what he wants, but he doesn't employ charm a lot in intra-Agency relations. As a result, people always approach Lance with some trepidation."

"And what is the result of that trepidation?"

"People who know him walk into his office and present themselves concisely, and they're always ready to back up what they say. There's no shooting the breeze, there's no idle gossip. Everything has to be to the point when talking to Lance."

"That's very interesting," Kate said. "Of course, I look at Lance from the top down, not from below, so I don't see that side of him too much. However, I think the characteristic you describe would be an important asset in a director. I'm more easygoing than Lance, so people sometimes talk too much when reporting to me. Sometimes I wish I had Lance's gift for demanding that they get to the point. What do you think of Lance's attitude toward the women who work for him?"

"Lance has always—well, nearly always—treated me respectfully. He's been demanding, but fair."

"What about the other women who've had dealings with him?"

Holly thought some more. "I think when assigning important work, Lance tends to go to men first. He assigns women as women, not as agents. I mean, he'll assign a woman when the job calls for a woman, explicitly. I've nudged him about this from time to time, and he's responded to a degree, but I think he still shies away from putting a woman in charge of men."

Kate smiled. "That's an astute judgment. What do you think Lance will say when I ask him about you? Do you think he would be reluctant to put you in charge of men?"

"Well, when you ask him, I guess we'll find out how well I've trained him."

Kate burst out laughing.

"Seriously, I have no fear of what Lance might say about me, and I think you should consider his comments very carefully, because they will be just as unvarnished as his views on everything else."

"Do you think he's an honest man?"

Holly shrugged. "I'm not sure honesty is a desirable quality in a spymaster. Lance can certainly be devious and, like everyone else, self-serving, but if it matters, I would be happy to work in an Agency with Lance running it."

"You've been very helpful, Holly. Now get back to work." Kate opened a file and started reading.

Holly got out of there.

22

Herbie Fisher sat in his office, speed-reading files. His secretary buzzed. "Mark Hayes on line one for you."

Hayes was one of Herbie's clients, an important one. He ran High Cotton Ideas, a hot software company.

"Good morning, Mark."

"Good morning, Herb. I have a problem I haven't been faced with before, and when I have a problem like that, I always come to you."

"How can I help, Mark?"

"One of my top programmers has disappeared, and I'm concerned."

"Concerned for his safety or concerned about the work he did?"

"He didn't show up for work for a couple of

days, and he wasn't responding to phone calls or e-mails, so I sent somebody to his apartment to see if he was there. It was empty, and there were painters at work. Turned out that his lease had expired and he had moved out, but nobody knows where. This morning I got an e-mail from him. It reads: 'I resign. I'll let you know where to send my final paycheck.' That's it."

"You didn't respond to my question about the work he did. Are you afraid he might have gone to a competitor and taken your intellectual property with him?"

"That's a possibility."

"Did he have a contract?"

"Yes, I recently promoted him and gave him a big raise. You wrote his contract."

"What's his name?"

"Jimmy Chang. He's Chinese-American, born in this country."

"Hang on a second," Herbie said. He pressed the hold button and buzzed his secretary. "Please bring me the executed contract for a Jimmy Chang, at High Cotton." He pressed line one again. "How long did he work for you, Mark?"

"Nearly three years. He was one of the first dozen people I hired. At first, he was just writing code, but he moved up quickly."

"Did he have any company stock?" High Cotton was about to go public.

"He did, but like a lot of employees, not as much as he thought he was entitled to."

"What will his stock be worth at the opening of your IPO?"

"About a million and a half dollars, but who knows? It could double that day."

"How much was he being paid?"

"He started at seventy-five thousand. He was making half a million when he resigned."

Herbie's secretary walked in and handed him the contract.

"I've got the contract," Herbie said, leafing through it. "I remember this one. His attorney asked for some minor changes that you agreed to, but if he leaves the company, he has to give you three months' notice, and if he leaves during that time and you continue to pay him, he can't work for anyone else. He also has a nondisclosure clause that prevents him from divulging any of your proprietary information to a new employer. How do you pay him?"

"All salaries are electronically transferred to employees' bank accounts."

"Then continue to pay him, to hold up your end of the contract. I'll write to his lawyer and ask him to remind his client of his contractual obligations and to go and see you immediately. I think we should also start trying to locate him now."

"Do you know someone who can do that?" Mark asked.

"I do," Herbie said, "someone very good. I have to divulge to you that I have a personal relationship with this woman."

"I'm not troubled by that," Mark said.

"All right, I need you to e-mail me his original employment application and any letters of recommendation you received."

"It wasn't much of an application at that time, but you revised it, and I asked everybody to complete the new form, so I'll send you both."

"Was he married?"

"No, but he had a girlfriend who seemed to be living with him."

"Her name?"

"Jasmine. I can't remember a last name."

"Okay, shoot me the information I asked for, and I'll get the investigator on it right now. She may need to get in touch with you. Her name is Harp O'Connor, and don't call her Harpie or Harpo."

"Thanks, Herb."

"Glad to be of help. I'll get back to you as soon as I hear something." Herbie hung up and dialed Harp's cell number.

"Speak to me, Herb," she said.

"I've got you a skip tracer job for a very important client. Can you start right now?"

"I'll have to make a few calls, but I can start in half an hour. Give me the rundown."

Herbie described his conversation with Mark Hayes. "I'll e-mail you his employment application, any letters of recommendation, his contract, and the name and address of his attorney."

"What do you want me to do when I find him?"

Herbie liked it that she said, "when," and not "if." "If he's in town, I want to see him, face-to-face, at the earliest possible moment. If he's in Silicon Valley or anywhere else, I'll send you to talk with him. At the very least, I want to talk to him on the phone."

"Gotcha. As soon as I make my calls and get his documents, I'll hit the pavement. See you to-night?"

They had seen each other nearly every night since they had met, and she had slept at his apartment most of them. "You may be too busy," he said. "We'll talk. Bye."

"Bye."

They both hung up. *Now,* Herbie thought, *I'm going to find out whether she's as good as she says she is.*

23

Harp O'Connor looked through the two employment applications Jimmy Chang had filled out, one on joining the company, another two years later, when the document was expanded. The first told her little, except his current address. She would start with that, but first she read the later document.

This listed his parents' names and addresses, in two different California towns, San Mateo and San Rafael, both in the San Francisco area. It also listed his previous employers, but she didn't reckon they would have any idea where he was, and she didn't think that his parents were likely to rat him out; they would be a last resort. She phoned Chang's attorney's office, got the man on the phone, and requested Chang's current location and phone number. She was stonewalled, so she took a cab downtown to Chang's most recent address. She found a six-story apartment building with an "Apartment for Rent" sign outside. A man was standing on the doorstep, looking at his wristwatch.

Harp paid the cab and walked up the steps. "Good morning," she said.

"Hi. You here to see the apartment?"

"Sure," she said.

"Are you with John Trefford?"

"No, but I'm interested in the apartment."

"Well, he's late, so I'll show it to you." He unlocked the street-level door and they stepped inside and took the rickety elevator to the top floor. Some paint cans and folded drop cloths and a ladder were in the hallway outside the door.

"The painters will come back for that stuff," the man said. "They just finished yesterday." He opened the door for her, and they stepped inside. It was a very nice two-bedroom apartment with high ceilings, windows overlooking a planted garden, and a good kitchen. It was devoid of any evidence of the previous occupant. Even the wastebaskets were empty. The man told her the rent.

Harp sighed. "Too rich for my budget," she said, "but thanks for showing it to me."

"Maybe you've got a friend who's looking for a place?"

"I'll think about that." She accepted the man's card. "Say, did Jimmy Chang live here?"

"Yeah, that was the guy."

"He's a pal of mine. Do you know where he moved?"

"Nope. I just got an e-mail saying he was moving out at the end of his lease. That was three, four days ago."

"Where did you send his security deposit?"

The man produced a notebook. "To his mother, in San Mateo, California."

Harp already had that address. "Thanks again," she said, and took the elevator down. A young man was waiting on the front stoop. "He's up on the sixth floor," she said, holding the door open for him. She looked around the front of the building for trash bags, but none were in sight.

Harp walked slowly down the block, checking out the shops along the way, until she came to a small but invitingly decorated restaurant. It was getting on toward lunchtime, so she went in and took a seat at the bar. She ordered a club sandwich and a beer, and watched faces as the place started to fill up.

The bartender sidled over. "You new in the neighborhood?"

"Yeah," Harp replied. "I just looked at an apartment a few doors down."

"I'll bet that was Jimmy Chang's place," he said.

"That's how I heard about it," she said. "I got an e-mail from Jimmy."

"You know Jimmy?"

"Yeah, we went out a few times a while back. You know where he moved to?"

"Out of the neighborhood," the bartender said.

"How far outside the neighborhood?"

"About three thousand miles."

"Ah, West Coast. Silicon Valley?"

"How'd you guess?"

"That's where those computer geeks go, isn't it?"

"It sure is. Jimmy said he doubled his salary."

"No kidding? He was pulling down half a million at the old place—what's it called?"

"High Cotton Ideas. They're so damned hot, I'm surprised he walked."

"Who would pay Jimmy a million a year?"

"He told me," the bartender said, staring at the ceiling. "It'll come to me in a minute." Then he looked at Harp. "Hey, why do you want to know?"

Harp laughed. "Don't look at me like that, I'm not carrying his baby."

The bartender laughed. "Yeah, Jasmine wouldn't like that."

"Yeah, she's the new girlfriend, isn't she?"

"Right."

"What's her last name?"

"Shaz something or other—something like Shazam."

"Did you think of where he's working?"

"I got it: TIT."

"What?"

"Technology Investment Team. They're whatcha-callit . . . venture capitalists?"

"Right."

"A name like that should have been easier to remember. They're where that big college is."

"Stanford?"

"Right. And it's Shazaz—Jasmine's last name. The place is owned by her brother. She got Jimmy the deal. They're investing in his new start-up." The bartender moved along to help another customer.

Harp wrapped up her sandwich and put it in her purse. She left cash on the bar and headed out to look for a cab. While she was waiting, she called Herb.

"Yeah, baby?"

"Okay, I nailed the guy. The whole thing took less than an hour, including downtown." She related her conversation with the bartender. "So he's in Palo Alto. What's your pleasure?"

"Pay him a visit and get him back here," Herbie said. "You need an advance?"

"Yeah, put ten grand in my bank account." She read the account number from her checkbook. "I'll need to buy him a ticket home."

"Keep in touch," Herbie said.

"Will do." She hung up and threw herself in front of a cab. She gave the cabby the address of her apartment, then went on her iPhone and booked a flight to San Francisco, departing in two hours. When the cab arrived, she said, "Keep the meter running. I've got to grab a bag, then we're going to JFK." She ran to her apartment, grabbed her ready bag, and ran back to the cab.

"That was fast," the cabby said.

"I'm nothing if not fast," Harp replied. She got back on her iPhone and Googled TIT. An address in Palo Alto, a clip from some electronics trade magazine about a potential investment, and that was it. *Technology Investment Team must be very new,* she thought.

She booked a rental car and a hotel room on-line.

24

Her flight got into San Francisco International in the early evening. She walked quickly to the rental car desk, rolling her bag behind her. "Something with a navigator," she said to the woman manning the desk. She took the shuttle to the lot and found the car, got it cranked, and entered two addresses into the navigator.

The woman's voice got her successfully out of the airport and on the interstate to Palo Alto. An hour later, she sat in front of the address for TIT and took a good look at the building, then she got out and walked into the outer lobby and checked the building directory. Ninth floor of twelve. She noticed that two other companies occupied the ninth, and it wasn't that big a building. Then she got back into her car and pulled up her hotel's address in the navigator.

In her room, she ordered a steak from room service and had a double scotch from the minibar. After dinner, she watched an old movie on TV, until she fell asleep.

She woke up after nine, showered, dressed, and checked out of the hotel. Back at the office building, she took the elevator to the ninth floor and found the TIT door. She walked in and found a barely furnished reception area, no receptionist. From there, she could see into a small conference room, and she could hear the clicking of a computer keyboard. She followed the noise to an open door and found a young Asian man in an office containing only a steel desk and two chairs, working at a laptop.

"Hey, Jimmy," she said.

He looked up. "I'm sorry, do I know you?"

"My name's Harp, like the beer. Now you know me." She sat down in the other chair.

"Did Mo Shazaz send you?" he asked. "I'm anxious to meet him face-to-face."

"Not exactly," she said. "I'm here representing the firm you still work for."

"And who would that be?"

Harp opened her briefcase and held up a document. "High Cotton Ideas. I've got a copy of your signed contract right here."

"How the hell did you find me?" Jimmy asked.

"Everybody always asks me that," Harp replied. "It's just what I do, that's all."

"You find people for a living?"

"I do a lot of things—finding people is just one of them. Now listen carefully. I have some advice for you."

"I need advice from *you*?"

"Yes, and badly. You are in violation of the terms of your employment contract, stated very clearly in this document. I'm surprised your attorney didn't explain that to you."

"Yeah, well, contracts are made to be broken."

"I can tell you're a bright guy, Jimmy, but believe me, intelligence does not buy wisdom, and what you've done is very unwise. That little start-up you worked for back in New York is now a professionally run corporation, with all the legal safeguards in place to protect its property, which still includes you."

"They don't own me."

"Of course they do, Jimmy, you just haven't figured that out yet. Now, there's a legal and proper way to separate yourself from High Cotton, but you haven't followed that procedure. You need to come back to New York with me and talk with Mark Hayes and with Herb Fisher, his attorney."

"Yeah, I know Fisher, the legal shark."

"Finally you've said something smart, Jimmy.

Herb is certainly a shark, and he patrols the waters that High Cotton operates in, and he can make your life miserable."

"I've already got a new deal," Jimmy said.

"Look around you, Jimmy. Does this look like the offices of a legitimate venture capital firm?"

"The new furniture arrives next week," Jimmy said.

"No, it doesn't," Harp replied. "Mo Shazaz is scamming you. He wants something from you that you can't legally give him—the trade secrets of your employer. If you take his money, then you will spend the next decade in the courts. How much money have you saved?"

"Enough."

"Not enough. It will all go to your lawyers, and the wheels of justice grind exceedingly slowly. Are you beginning to get the picture?"

"I've already taken Mo's money."

"Have you cashed the check?"

"Not yet."

"Tear it in half and leave it on the desk with a very brief note saying the deal's off."

"Does Mark really want me back that bad?"

"Bad enough to send me out here to bring you back," Harp said.

"I'm not legally required to go with you."

"I can have a court order by midafternoon," she lied, "if that's the way you want to go, but believe me, this will be a much more pleasant experience if you just come with me now. We have a two p.m. airplane back to New York, and we'll have time for a nice lunch at the airport."

Jimmy looked confused. "I've got to call . . ."

"Call Jasmine from the airport," Harp suggested.

"How do you know about Jasmine?"

"Oh, Jasmine Shazaz is famous at a certain level of the tech world," Harp lied again. "You're not the first hotshot techie she's lured away from a great job with promises of billions. You don't want to see her again."

Jimmy stared forlornly at his keyboard.

"Just close the laptop, put it away, and come with me."

"I'll need to stop at the hotel and pick up my clothes."

Harp shook her head. "Time is of the essence, Jimmy. You have to be back in your office at High Cotton at nine tomorrow morning, if you're going to have a chance to make this right. I'll arrange for the hotel to ship your luggage back to New York, and I'll see that your bill is paid."

"I need to call Mo Shazaz," he said.

"He won't answer his phone. Has he ever answered his phone?" She was taking a chance here.

"No, now that you mention it. He always calls back the next day."

Harp stood up. "Come on, Jimmy, let's get out of here while you still can."

Jimmy stood up, closed his laptop, yanked the cord from the receptacle, and shoved it into a canvas briefcase.

They were in the car before Harp spoke again. "Let's use the time to the airport," she said. "Tell me what Mo wanted you to do for him." She listened while he talked for a while, then she spoke again. "Jimmy, you're well out of this. You were about to get mixed up in something that would have ended in disaster for you."

Jimmy took out his cell phone.

"Don't," she said. "Don't let *anyone* know where you are. I'll put you into a good hotel in New York, and then I'm going to get you the help you need to get out of this mess."

In the airline's VIP lounge, she waited for Jimmy to go to the men's room before she called Herb.

"Where are you?" he asked.

"On my way home," she said, "and with Jimmy in tow."

"How did you convince him to come back?"

"I lied some, but mostly I told him the truth. Then he told me what his new employer wanted him to do."

"What was that?"

"You mentioned to me your friend Stone Whatshisname . . ."

"Barrington."

"Yeah. You said he had some connections to the intelligence world."

"Yeah."

"Arrange a meeting with you, Jimmy, and Stone for tomorrow morning. Both of you will get an earful. Uh-oh, here comes Jimmy. Gotta go." She broke the connection.

"Who were you talking to?" Jimmy asked.

"To the guy who's going to get you out of this," she replied.

25

Stone was on the phone with Mike Freeman, hearing about Wynken, Blynken, and Nod, when Herbie's call came.

"He says it's urgent," Joan said.

"I've got to run," Stone said to Mike, and pushed the button for line two. "Herb?"

"Hey, Stone. I need to set up a meeting with you for first thing tomorrow morning."

"Okay, what's up?"

"It's to do with one of Mark Hayes's people at High Cotton. He's gotten himself into something that may involve American intelligence, and I'm out of my depth there."

"Okay, nine o'clock?"

"Good. I'll be bringing my investigator, too. Her name is Harp O'Connor."

"Okay. I'll help if I can. See you at nine." He hung up.

Nine came early for Stone; he wasn't usually at his desk much before ten. His housekeeper, Helene, made coffee and pastries and left them in his office.

Herbie arrived on time and sat down. "They'll be along shortly."

"What's this about?" Stone asked.

"It started with a High Cotton employee who disappeared. Mark Hayes called me and asked me to look into it. I put Harp on it, and she found the guy in Palo Alto, California, brought him back last night, and stashed him in some way-in hotel downtown."

"And how does this relate to intelligence?"

"Harp will have to explain that. By the way, I've been seeing a lot of her."

"Good for you."

"You still seeing Marla?"

"Not so much."

Joan walked two people into Stone's office, and Herbie made the introductions.

"Hi, Jimmy," Stone said, "we met once before at your big office party a while back." They shook hands.

"Okay, Harp, tell us what's going on."

"First, let Jimmy tell his story."

"Go ahead, Jimmy."

"About three weeks ago, I met this girl named Jasmine Shazaz," he said. "A real knockout. Almost immediately, she began telling me about her brother, Mo, who is a venture capitalist. She said he had heard about me and wanted to put me in a start-up that would make me a huge amount of money when it went public. I talked to Mo on the phone a couple of times, and he impressed me by immediately offering me twice what I was getting at High Cotton. He began pressing me to quit immediately and come to Palo Alto, where he had offices. The lease on my apartment was up, and I finally caved. I put my belongings into storage and went to Palo Alto. What I found was a rented space—one of those short-term things you see advertised in the tech magazines."

"Tell them what Shazaz wanted you to do," Harp said.

"The first thing he wanted me to do was to set up a chain of Web sites, where members could contact his company and each other while concealing their identities and whereabouts. He told me that this was part of a venture of his, and it would make it easier to set up a company for me. I didn't understand it, but I started to work in this empty office. Then Harp showed up and brought me back."

"Tell him about the messages," she said.

"There was an existing Web site that was part of this, and there were three messages left on it that hadn't been deleted. Each of them said the same thing: 'All is well. I am fine,' and they were signed 'Wynken, Blynken, and Nod.'"

Stone leaned forward and picked up a pen. "How do you spell 'Shazaz'?" he asked, and wrote it down.

"That's some kind of code or signal," Harp said. "I Googled Mo Shazaz: there wasn't much on him, but I found out that Mo is short for Mohammad. That worried me. I know enough about communication among cells—spies or terrorists—that the messages probably meant that agents were in place and ready to do something. This whole thing smells of fish: the way the girl recruited Jimmy, the lack of a written proposal, the big promises, and the empty offices. Mo may not even be in this country. He could be anywhere."

"I'm feeling pretty dumb," Jimmy said.

"You're going to be fine," Herbie said. "Don't worry, Mark wants you back at work."

"That's a relief," Jimmy said.

"So you never met Mo at all?" Stone asked.

"No."

"Where does his sister live?"

"She was pretty much living with me for a couple of weeks," Jimmy replied. "She said she had an apartment on the Upper East Side, but I never went there. All I had for contact was a cell number."

"And what is that number?" Stone asked, then wrote it down. "Something bothers me," he said.

"What's that?" Harp asked.

"Why would Mo want somebody at Jimmy's proficiency level to set up this chain of Web sites?" Stone asked. "I don't know all that much about it, but it sounds like the sort of thing that a bright college student could do."

"Well," Jimmy said, "not to get too technical on you, but he wanted a lot of safeguards against penetration. It was the sort of thing a high-tech security company might do for him. He said there were other things he wanted me to do, too, things that would lead to software products I could develop for the new company."

"I see," Stone said, though he didn't, really. "Is there anything else you can tell me about Mo and Jasmine?"

"No," Jimmy said.

"I can run down the cell number," Harp said. "Give me the day for that."

"All right," Stone said, "leave this with me, and I'll run it past some people I know. Jimmy, you'd better go talk to Mark and get back to work."

"I'll do that," Jimmy said.

"I'll run you down there," Harp said. "And, Stone, I'll get back to you with what I find on the cell number. I'd like to speak to Jasmine, myself."

"Maybe you shouldn't do that," Stone said. "Not until I've checked out some things."

"She and her brother will be wondering where Jimmy is," Harp said. "He doesn't have an apartment anymore, so it won't be easy to find him."

"Yeah. I just want to know as much as I can before Jimmy calls Jasmine again."

"I understand," Harp said. "Jimmy, you shouldn't answer your cell phone. In fact, give it to me, and I'll get you another one this morning."

Jimmy gave her the phone, and they all left.

Stone called Mike Freeman. "Mike," he said, "something weird has happened."

26

Mike Freeman hung up the phone and called his contact at the NSA.

"Scott Hipp."

"Scott, it's Mike Freeman. I just came by some information I thought you ought to have."

"I'm always happy to have more information, Mike."

"There's another report on Wynken, Blynken, and Nod."

"How so?"

"Have you ever heard of anyone called Mohammad Shazaz, who calls himself 'Mo'? Has a sister named Jasmine?"

"Hang on a sec."

Mike could hear the tapping of computer keys.

"That's interesting," Hipp said, when he came back on the line.

"What's interesting?"

"They're not in our database. Hardly anybody is not in our database. The name doesn't even register as Muslim. Sounds made-up to me."

"Could be, I guess."

"I got a couple of hits when I Googled Mo, but nothing of substance, and I think they must be very recent, because everything on Google migrates to our database pretty quickly."

Mike gave him the address of the office in Palo Alto. "It's a furnished, short-term let, Scott. I doubt if it will yield anything of value, but I can send one of my people from our Palo Alto office there to go over it, if that will be helpful."

"I think it would be more helpful to the FBI or CIA than to us, but I would appreciate it if you wouldn't mention this to them right away. I'd rather they get it from the White House."

"What about the Secret Service?"

"Okay, talk to them, if you think it's necessary. I've already alerted the White House to the first reports of the nursery trio, and they would, of course, alert the Secret Service."

"Okay, I'll wait a few days before taking this to one of my Agency contacts, and I probably won't give it to the FBI at all, since I don't think they're involved."

"Right. Why stir them up?"

"Will you let me know if anything else comes up in this regard?"

"Of course, Mike, and thanks for calling."

Mike called Agent Rifkin, who was based in a conference room attached to the presidential cottage, and invited him over.

They ordered lunch from room service; then Mike spread out his satshot of the L.A. area and showed Rifkin how the radials ran from the cell tower up the mountain. He held back the information about the office in Palo Alto. There was no point in swarming in there with Secret Service agents yet; it would only diffuse their efforts to protect the president at The Arrington, Mike reasoned.

"So they're all in L.A.," Rifkin said.

"Or were."

"I don't like it a bit."

"Neither do I," Mike said.

"I especially don't like it that this radial right here"—he tapped the photo with a finger—"runs right through where we're standing."

"That may be meaningless. The caller could have been anywhere on that line, up to about five miles from the cell tower."

Rifkin just looked worried.

"Look at it this way," Mike said, "there is no tangible, verifiable threat to the president or the hotel.

We're just taking this bit of intelligence and overlaying our fears on it. This might be an exercise in paranoia."

"Just because I'm a paranoiac doesn't mean that somebody doesn't want to harm the president. I'm paid to be a paranoiac."

"My very point," Mike said.

Rifkin went back to his warren, looking troubled.

27

Hamish McCallister, aka Ari Shazaz, got off an airplane at San Jose International and presented himself at an immigration window, handing the female agent his British passport, which contained a permanent visa. He was dressed in a Savile Row suit and a necktie, very probably a rare sight for the agent.

She looked him up and down, smiled slightly, compared his face to the photograph, then swiped the document and gazed at her computer screen. "Welcome to the United States, Mr. McCallister," she said, handing back his passport.

"Thank you," Hamish replied. "It's good to be back." He strolled through customs with his finely made Italian luggage on a cart, and caught a taxi at the curb, giving the man an address in Palo Alto.

He dozed as the taxi made its way south and came fully awake only when the driver announced his arrival.

He paid the fare, added a tip, and the driver set his bags on the curb and drove away. Hamish disliked carrying his own luggage, but he picked up the two bags and walked into the building.

He emerged from the elevator into an office suite that featured his younger half sister, Jasmine, as the receptionist.

She ran around the desk and kissed him. "Welcome to the USA!" she nearly shouted. "Mo? He's here!"

Mohammad Shazaz came out of an office and embraced his older half brother. "We've been anxiously awaiting your arrival," he said.

"Is Dr. Kharl here yet?"

"Arrived day before yesterday."

"And your computer genius?"

"I'm afraid there have been problems there, but nothing that can't be fixed. He bolted after three days of work, but he got an amazing amount done. I've hired a student at Stanford, a Saudi, to complete his work."

"That's what you should have done in the first place," Hamish said. "Now, there are two things to be done: first, find me a home."

"Already done. I've rented a large, furnished flat in a building near here. Dr. Kharl is there, already working."

"Have you given anyone the address?"

"Of course not."

"The second thing we have to do is to move out of these offices at once. Your bringing Chang from New York has compromised this address."

"Already done," Mo replied. "I'm just waiting for our computer man to finish his work. He says he'll have us up and running by the end of the day."

"All right. Where's the flat?"

"Jasmine will drive you there and get you settled. There's nothing for her to do here anyway."

Hamish shoved one of his bags toward her. "Let's go. Jet lag is already creeping up on me. I need to have a drink and some dinner and go to bed."

Jasmine picked up the heavy bag. She was well muscled from working out, and he suspected she might be stronger than he.

The flat was large, comfortably furnished, and commanded views east across the southern end of San Francisco Bay. Hamish immediately poured himself a scotch and found some sandwiches in the fridge, then Jasmine led him to the master bedroom, which featured a mirror over the bed. "My God," he said, "the mind boggles."

"Last time I was in Abu Dhabi, my room had one," she replied.

"Where's Kharl?"

"Dr. Kharl is sleeping. He's had a hard time with the jet lag, coming all the way from Dubai."

"Let him sleep. The way I feel, I wouldn't be able to understand anything he says." She left him alone. He unpacked, put on his pajamas, and crawled gratefully into bed. He was asleep almost immediately.

He awoke the following morning with sunlight streaming into the room, but he wasn't fully awake until he had showered. He dressed and went looking for the kitchen. He found Dr. Kharl eating cereal.

"Good morning, Dr. Kharl," Hamish said.

"Ah, Ari," the diminutive man said, rising.

They shook hands and embraced. "Please remember, I'm Hamish. No one must ever hear the other name."

"Of course, of course."

"What is that you're eating?" Hamish asked, nodding toward the cereal bowl.

"Sugar Puffs. Wonderful! Would you like some?"

"No, thank you, I'll forage." He found some English muffins and a toaster, then poured himself a cup of coffee and sat down. "So, my good doctor, how does it go?"

"Very well," the doctor replied. "I have everything I need, except the rare thing."

"That will arrive in due course."

"Mohammad found a very nice Louis Vuitton steamer trunk and two matching cases in a pawnshop, of all places."

"Even the affluent have been pressed hard during the recession," Hamish said. "Is it presentable?"

"They have the look of age and use. You may see for yourself," Dr. Kharl said, then had a second bowl of the cereal.

Half an hour later, Hamish regarded the trunk with approval. "That will pass muster, I believe," he said. He loved old trunks, but he had never traveled with one.

Mo came into the room bearing a laptop computer. "Our man finished his work and tested it around midnight last night," he said. "We are now up and running." He set the computer on a desk and plugged it in, then he showed Hamish how to find his way into the secret Web site.

"Good," Hamish said. He entered the three e-mail addresses of his operatives and typed a short message. "Arrived last evening," he typed. "Request a status report from each of you today. This address is your entry point." He signed it "Algernon," sent the message, then he walked across the room to Dr. Kharl's worktable and inspected the parts arrayed there.

Dr. Kharl entered the room. He had been near

the top of the Pakistani team that had created that country's arsenal and he had sold his talents to the highest bidders, which had turned out to be Iran and the People's Republic of North Korea. Now he lived in Dubai, mostly retired, but he was available to credible and discreet clients. He had been provided with a passport that allowed him into the United States. He took a roll of plans, weighted one end, and spread it out on the table.

"Did you bring this into the country?" Hamish asked, incredulous.

"On film secreted on my person," the doctor replied. "I had it printed at a photo shop. The operator hardly glanced at it. He thought it was a piece of refrigeration equipment."

Hamish breathed easier. "Will it actually fit into the trunk?"

"I am tailoring the dimensions to the trunk."

"I see, and it's a good idea," Hamish replied. "A very good idea." He thought he already knew how to get it into its final resting place. "Mo, where are the three smaller units?"

"They are being assembled from parts we imported by an agent in place," he said. "They will be delivered tomorrow, and you will be walked through their operation by Dr. Kharl, who will complete their assembly."

Hamish nodded. "I must set up a meeting in L.A.," Hamish said. "Do we have a suitable place?"

"I have rented a small hangar at Santa Monica Airport. Sorry, but I had to take it for three months. It wasn't cheap."

"At least it's convenient," Hamish replied.

"What transportation is available? I don't want my name to appear on any passenger lists."

"There is a Cessna Caravan available with a reliable pilot. It will carry anything we can stuff into it."

"Good." He sat down at the computer and sent a message to Wynken, Blynken, and Nod, summoning them to a rendezvous three days hence.

28

The following day Hamish was driven by Jasmine to a large storage facility outside Palo Alto, where a double garage had been rented. She opened the door with a remote control, drove inside, switched off the engine, and closed the door. The only objects in the garage were a large steel locker, a ratty-looking, chest-style freezer, and a folding table.

A young man awaited them. He had set three small suitcases on the table. "Good day," he said. No introductions were made.

"Let's see what you have for me," Hamish said.

The young man opened the three cases and exposed their contents. "I have followed the plans given me," he said. "What we have is simple, really: the necessary wiring, a space to contain a cube of plastic explosive, six inches on a side—about a kilo—and a kitchen timer, which can only be started or stopped with a key."

"Show me," Hamish said.

The young man took three identical objects from his pocket: each was a T-shaped piece of stainless steel with a hexagonal tip. He inserted one of them into a device and turned it to the right. The kitchen timer came on, set to thirty minutes, and began counting down. "At zero, the blasting cap will fire and set off the plastique." He turned the key back to vertical, then to the left. "If you turn it to the left, the cap will fire instantly."

"And the option requested?" Hamish asked.

The young man put a fingernail under a small flap and raised it, exposing a row of four tiny switches. "As you see, all the dip switches are in the up position." He flipped the left-hand switch down. "That's all you do, and the two firing positions— timer and instant—are reversed." He flipped the switch up again.

"And how will the plastique be connected?"

"In this space here," he said, unlatching a larger flap and lowering it. He took out a short length of wire dangling into the space. "You simply plug this into the blasting cap, then push the cap into the plastique, and you're good to go."

"Excellent," Hamish said. "I prefer things simple. Jasmine, pay the gentleman." He turned and walked toward the car.

Jasmine opened her purse, took out a small pistol with a silencer, and shot the young man in the head. He collapsed into a heap, and she shot him in the head once more. "Give me a hand," she said.

The two of them dragged the limp corpse to one side of the garage where the beat-up freezer chest hummed. She opened it, and they lifted the body into the chest, then closed and padlocked it.

Hamish closed the three small cases and put them into a steel locker next to the freezer, along with the keys.

"When you arrive at Santa Monica airport tomorrow," Jasmine said, "the explosive packs will be waiting for you." She locked the cabinet and handed Hamish the key.

"No, you keep it," he said. "I'll want you to pick up the three cases and the keys tomorrow and deliver them to the Cessna Caravan at the airport. I will be transporting my luggage."

They got back into the car, and she drove him to the flat.

"Everything go okay?" Mo asked as they came in.

"Perfectly," Hamish said. "Jasmine performed brilliantly."

29

Stone heard the front door slam upstairs. They had arrived. There were bumping sounds as Peter put his luggage into the elevator, then footsteps on the stairs, and then Peter came into Stone's office, followed by his girlfriend, Hattie Patrick, and Dino's son, Ben Bacchetti.

Stone embraced Peter and kissed him on the cheek, then Hattie, then had a manly handshake with Ben. "How are you all?"

"Everybody's fine," Peter said. "I've got to run Hattie and Ben home, then I'll be back for lunch, all right?"

"All right. Helene's in there cooking Greek food right now. You sure you won't all stay for lunch?"

They looked at each other.

"Okay, I'll put my car in the garage," Peter said.

* * *

They sat at the kitchen table and chattered as Helene served them moussaka.

"I've got an appointment with Marla Rocker tomorrow to see some of her casting choices," Peter said. "Is Marla coming to L.A. with us?"

"No, she's staying here to work on your play," Stone replied. "She's going to be very busy for a while, so I won't be seeing much of her."

"So, she dumped you, huh?" Peter asked.

Stone twitched. The kid was getting too smart. "We agreed to let it go."

"So you're going alone?"

"Don't worry, I'll have friends at the hotel. You're meeting one of them in a couple of days."

"Who's that?"

"Her name is Felicity Devonshire. She's British."

"Who is she? What does she do?"

"She's a civil servant in London."

"A civil servant?" Ben asked. "Does that mean she's in intelligence?"

"Don't ask," Stone said. "And when you meet her, don't start asking probing questions."

"Yeah," Peter said, "we'd only get lied to. You said a couple of friends. Who else?"

"Holly Barker will be there."

"The one at the CIA? Great! I finally get to meet her!"

"Holly has recently been promoted. She's now assistant director. In fact, she'll be traveling with the president and Mrs. Lee, who, you will remember, is her boss."

"Who will Felicity be traveling with?" Peter asked.

"With us, aboard the Strategic Services airplane."

"What kind of plane?" Ben asked.

"A Gulfstream 550."

"Wow! I guess there'll be room for us all—Dad, too."

"And Viv. Plenty of room for all."

"And where is Felicity sleeping?" Peter asked.

Stone looked at him sharply.

"Well, Dad, if Marla's dumped you . . . you need female companionship."

"It runs in the family," Hattie said.

"Felicity will have her own quarters. She'll be there to meet with the president and Mrs. Lee."

"So, she's a pretty high-up civil servant?" Peter asked.

"Pretty high up."

"This is going to be interesting," Peter said. "The three of us have made some L.A. arrangements of our own."

"Oh?" Stone asked, raising an eyebrow.

"Leo Goldman is going to give us all a tour of Centurion Studios."

"That sounds like a great idea."

"And I'm going to get to play with the studio orchestra, when they record a film score," Hattie said. Hattie was a brilliant young pianist, who was studying musical composition at Yale, while Peter and Ben were at the School of Drama.

"Good, then you can watch the movie on television for years to come."

"And we're going to get to meet some movie stars," Ben said.

"You'll meet lots of them at the hotel's opening festivities. Centurion has taken twenty-five suites for their people."

"Then there's the Immi Gotham concert," Peter said. Immi Gotham was Centurion's greatest star and a wonderful singer; critics had called her a combination of Meryl Streep and Barbra Streisand.

"Along with the Beverly Hills Philharmonic," Hattie said. "It's really going to be something!"

"The whole event is going to be something," Stone said. "Every suite and room is booked."

"If there are two hundred suites and rooms," Peter asked, "how are they going to fill up the fifteen hundred seats in the Arrington Bowl?"

"There's an invited audience," Stone said. "The Bowl has its own entrance and parking, separate from the hotel's. People have been fighting over the tickets for months. The *Times* says scalpers have been offering ten thousand dollars a ticket and getting no takers."

"There's never been anything like this, has there, Dad?"

"Not in my memory. Centurion is making a documentary film about it, and it'll be shown on TV at Christmas."

"Dad, can we rent a car while we're there?"

"You have to be twenty-five to rent a car these days. I'll arrange for you to go to Centurion in a hotel car, and Leo can send you back in one of his."

"Sounds good."

"You're going to have to get used to a lot of security at the hotel," Stone said, "what with two presidents and a lot of other VIPs. You'll be issued ID cards, and you can't get in or out of the hotel grounds without them."

"All the time, or just for this event?" Peter asked.

"Just for this event," Stone replied. "After the opening, it'll be just like any other hotel."

"Has there ever been another hotel like this one?" Ben asked.

"Well, there are some very fine hotels scattered around the world," Stone said. "But The Arrington will be unique, I think."

"You know, I think Mom would have liked all this," Peter said. "I mean, she had already given her permission to build the hotel on the property, but I really think she would have loved the way it's turning out."

"I think she would have, too," Stone said.

Then they all ate quietly for a while.

Finally, Peter asked, "When is Felicity arriving from London?"

"She arrived yesterday," Stone said, "but she's been resting."

"Is she staying with us?"

"No, she's staying at the residence of the British ambassador to the U.N. He has quite a nice house."

"Dad," Peter said gravely, "I want you to know that it's all right for you to have sleepovers when I'm here."

Stone didn't know whether to laugh or cry. "Thank you, Peter, that's very kind of you." And he meant it.

30

Stone hired a driver and picked up Felicity Devonshire at the ambassador's residence. "You look radiant, as always," he said, holding both her hands and looking her up and down.

"And you are a great flatterer, as always," she replied. "Where are we having dinner?"

"At a place that's new to me, called Patroon. It's not all that far away."

"Then why did you bring your car?"

"I would be nervous taking you out on the street, since the last time you were here someone was gunning for you. The car is armored, so you will be protected." He led her out and down the stairs.

"Oh, you have a new car, a Bentley?"

"Yes," Stone said. "My Mercedes came to a bad end last year. Mike Freeman at Strategic Services had this in his fleet and sold it to me. Their armoring division had done a lot of work on it."

"Why do you have armored cars?" Felicity asked, getting into the rear seat.

Stone got in beside her. "Accidental in both cases. I went into the Mercedes showroom to buy the first one, and they had it on the floor. It had been ordered by someone of shady reputation, and it arrived one day late. Somebody got to him, so I bought it from the widow. When I smashed it up, Mike was there to help."

"You are the most fortunate man," she said.

"If I were more fortunate I wouldn't have totaled the Mercedes. By the way, thank you for your kind note after Arrington's death."

"It was the least I could do," she said.

They arrived at the restaurant and were seated.

"This is very nice," she said, looking around.

Stone ordered them drinks, and they were visited by the owner, Ken Aretsky. They chatted briefly, then the drinks arrived and he moved on to another table.

"Is this your new Elaine's?" she asked.

"It's one of them. Dino and I have learned that Elaine's cannot be replaced—there is just no other place like it."

"To a better future," Felicity said, raising her glass.

"I'll drink to that."

"So you have a son now?"

"You're keeping up, aren't you?"

"What is the point of being in the intelligence game if you can't spy on your friends?"

Stone laughed. "You'll meet Peter and his girlfriend, Hattie, as well as Dino's son, Ben, and Dino's new girlfriend, Viv. They'll all be on the airplane."

"Why are you going out there in advance of the actual opening?" she asked.

"Well, I'm an investor and on the board, as is Mike Freeman. We both want to have an opportunity to look the place over before the guests swarm in."

"What with having two presidents in residence, you and Mike must have some security concerns." She didn't look directly at him when she said this.

Stone caught something in her statement; he wasn't sure what. "Yes, the Secret Service will be there in strength, and so will the Strategic Services people."

"Good," she said.

"Felicity, is there something you want to tell me?"

"Want to but can't," she replied, looking into her martini.

"Suppose something terrible happens, and you didn't warn me?"

"Then I would feel very guilty," she replied.

"Come on, unburden yourself." But the menus

arrived, and they took time to study them. "I'm not letting you off the hook," he said when the waiter had taken their orders and gone.

"Something did come across my desk," she said, "but I don't want to raise the alarm over what might be nothing."

"Do you recall that a couple of years ago you forced me to sign your Official Secrets Act?"

She brightened. "That's right, I did, didn't I? Prescient of me."

"Yes, it was. Now give, please."

"Oh, all right." She looked around to be sure no one was within earshot. "Our signals people have picked up a series of oddly signed messages," she said.

"Would the signatures be from a nursery rhyme?"

Felicity's jaw dropped. "Now you must tell me how you know that."

"No, I mustn't."

"I have to know if there was a leak on my end."

"There was no leak. Those messages were picked up by the NSA."

Her eyes widened. "And they circulated that information to *you*, a private citizen?"

"Actually, they probably don't know that I was in the loop. Let's just say they circulated it to someone I know."

"Someone at the CIA?"

"No."

"Well, if I were in charge around here, I'd have this person you know taken out and shot!"

"You may recall that I am still under contract to the Agency as a consultant," Stone said, "and I have the appropriate security clearance—in spite of my friendship with you."

"But do you have a need to know? I believe that's the phraseology they use."

"I have a very definite need to know," Stone said, "since a substantial chunk of my inheritance from my late wife and of my son's trust fund are invested in the hotel mentioned in the signals you referred to."

"Oh, all right, I suppose you're not a security risk."

Their dinner arrived, and the subject changed.

"How are you . . . coping since becoming a widower?" she asked.

"You needn't be so delicate," Stone replied. "I plan to take you home and ravish you as soon as you've finished your Dover sole."

She giggled. "Oh, good. But where is your son?"

"He occupies his own flat on the top floor of the house," Stone said, "and he's probably there, in the sack with his girlfriend, as we speak."

"Goodness, his generation starts young, don't they?"

"How old were you on the occasion of your first time?" Stone asked.

Felicity blushed deeply.

"Oh, come on, you can tell me. Official Secrets Act, remember?"

"Sixteen," she said. "With a young gamekeeper on my father's estate."

"Shades of Lady Chatterley!"

"It was only afterward that I read the novel," she said. "But he was very sweet. He was twenty-two, and he seemed like much the older man. What about you? When was your first time?"

Stone laughed. "I was sixteen, too, and she was nineteen. Much the older woman, and I was grateful to her for her experience."

"So we were both precocious."

"And will be again," Stone said. He waved at a waiter. "Check, please!"

31

There was sunlight filtering through the shutters in Stone's bedroom when he looked over and found Felicity next to him. Their hips were touching, and she had a wisp of her red hair across her face. Gingerly, he brushed it away, and she opened her eyes.

"My goodness," she said, turning toward him. "How long it's been since I awoke to find a man in my bed!"

"In actual fact," Stone said, "you awoke to find yourself in a man's bed."

"Even better," she said, placing a hand on his cheek and kissing him lightly.

"More, please," he said, and they did it again. From there it was but a short hop to an embrace and a joining of flesh.

When they had finished and lay panting in each other's arms, Felicity said, "What will your sleeping arrangements be at the hotel?"

"I'll be staying in a four-bedroom cottage with its own garden and pool that was part of the original deal for the building of the hotel. The master bedroom, where I will sleep, has a private, walled patio off the back garden, to which I will give you a key, so that you may steal in and out at will."

"What a lovely arrangement," she said.

"Of course, you may encounter a Secret Service agent or two along the way, since we're next door to the presidential cottage, but they are very discreet people."

She sighed. "From what you've told me, I won't be able to move without rubbing elbows with either the Secret Service, the Mexican protective detail, a team of Strategic Services guards, or all of the above."

"That's about the size of it, but as long as you don't come to me naked, there shouldn't be a problem."

"I suppose I can stand to wait until I'm in your bedroom before disrobing."

"A good policy. How many other Brits will be in residence?"

"I'm the only one, except for a few private citizens and one journalist," she said. "I'm meant to be consulting with Kate Lee on some security matters, among them the signals you and I talked about last night."

"I'm reliably informed that Kate already knows about the signal traffic. The NSA figure in charge of all that, Scott Hipp, is politically connected, and he just loves sending little items like that to the White House."

"To which Kate is well connected," Felicity said. "I wonder what it would be like if I were married to the prime minister."

"Does he interest you?"

"Oh, no, I was just talking about having that connection. I wonder if Kate and her husband talk about work in bed."

"You've got me there," Stone said. "Would you like some breakfast?"

"May I have a full English breakfast?" she asked. "Eggs over easy, sausage, bacon, grilled tomato, tomato juice, and very strong coffee?"

Stone picked up the phone, buzzed Helene in the kitchen, and placed their orders.

"May I have a bath while we're waiting?" Felicity asked.

"Of course. May I watch?"

"That might get dangerous," she said, getting out of bed and walking across the bedroom to her bath. "I won't be long."

Stone's phone rang. He looked at his watch:

seven thirty. Who the hell? He picked up the phone. "Hello?"

"It's Mike."

"Good morning, Mike. You're an early riser."

"I'm getting reports that someone has completed the computer work that High Cotton's Mr. Chang began, and that it's in use."

"Anything specific?"

"Someone called Algernon is communicating with the three men in a shoe or a boat, or whatever they're in."

"What sort of communications?"

"They're meeting—we don't know where."

"This is the first we've heard of an Algernon, isn't it?"

"It is. It sounds as though he's running the three, and I'll bet he's hot off a plane from the Middle East."

"Maybe you should speak with the Secret Service about this."

"I have already done so, directly to Rifkin, who's the AIC at The Arrington. Are you still on schedule to arrive tomorrow?"

"We're wheels up at ten o'clock Teterboro tomorrow morning."

"Good."

"Oh, one other thing," Stone said. "MI-6 is picking up the same traffic NSA is."

"And you know this because?"

"I had . . . dinner with Felicity Devonshire last night."

"Ah, Felicity!"

"She's flying out with us to take a meeting with Kate Lee."

"I wonder if she knows anything else of interest to us."

"I wonder, too. I'll press her on that subject."

"Never hurts to triangulate on something like this."

"I guess not." The bell rang that signaled the dumbwaiter was on the way up from the kitchen. "I gotta run," Stone said.

"I'll see you at the hotel." Mike hung up.

Felicity came out of the bathroom in a terry robe with a towel around her hair. "I smell sausage," she said.

Stone took the tray from the dumbwaiter, set it on the bed, and whisked away the covers.

"This is the best hotel I know," Felicity said, picking up a sausage with her fingers and biting into it.

"Mike Freeman just called," Stone said. "There's further news of Wynken, Blynken, and Nod."

"Do tell."

Stone told her about the defection of Chang from High Cotton and the work he did in Palo Alto. "His work has now been completed, and someone code-named Algernon is communicating with the trio, setting up a meeting. Mike thinks Algernon may have arrived in California to run the trio."

"I think that's a sensible conclusion to draw," she said. "I'll check with my people this morning to see if they have anything new to add."

"We would all appreciate that," Stone said.

She set the plate of eggs and bacon in her lap and started to work on it. "One way we might be able to help is to go back into our files and see if we've ever had an Algernon operating anywhere."

"Excellent idea. If we knew who he was it might be easier to track them all down."

"I think we can guess where they're heading," Felicity said.

32

When Hamish went to the kitchen for breakfast, Mo was looking very nervous. "What's wrong?" he asked.

"Nothing is wrong, it's just that the material has arrived, and I'm excited. The doctor has been working most of the night."

Hamish went into the dining room where Dr. Kharl was working and found him on his knees before the open Vuitton trunk, tightening some screws. He was wearing heavy gloves.

The doctor looked up. "Welcome back," he said.

"Is it finished?" he asked.

"All done, except for completing the three small devices and what you have to do."

"I?"

"Or whoever will activate the device," Kharl said. He stood up and retrieved an object resting on top of the trunk. It was made of metal and was a flat plate about half an inch thick, with a teat-shaped closed tube attached to its bottom. "Some of the material is in here," Kharl said, tapping the teat. He unscrewed the top of the plate. "There is a layer of plastique here, with a threaded hole on top that will admit a detonator." He dropped the teat end into the tube and screwed it tightly into place, then screwed a small metal tube containing the igniter into the top. "Then close this panel"—he pointed—"insert this key"—he held up one like the ones he had seen for the smaller devices—"then tap into the keypad the elapsed time to ignition, up to ten hours, then turn the key to the right. When the digital clock reaches zero, the blasting cap will set off the plastique, which will fire the tube containing a bullet of enriched uranium into the fissionable material at the bottom of the trunk, creating what is known as a critical mass. You must be many, many miles away by that time."

Hamish unrolled a map of Los Angeles and pointed to The Arrington's location with a draftsman's compass. "What sort of damage can we expect from this device?"

Kharl took the compass and placed it on the scale at the bottom of the map, adjusting it to the correct distance. "Each kiloton of explosive force will decimate everything inside a radius of one nautical mile, or about six thousand feet. This device has an explosive power of about two and a half kilotons, and thus, a destructive range of about two and a half nautical miles, or a little over three statute miles." Kharl placed the point of the compass on The Arrington's location and drew a circle around it.

"Now, you see what lies in the path of complete destruction: inside the circle are all of the Bel-Air neighborhood and all of Beverly Hills, to the edges of West Hollywood. To the west, much of the blast will be contained by the Santa Monica Mountains, but there are dense residential neighborhoods within the circle. To the south, complete destruction reaches to about Santa Monica Boulevard, including practically the entire campus of UCLA, and much of Centurion Studios, where movies are made. To the north the mountains will absorb much of the blast, but the dams of both the Stone Canyon upper and lower reservoirs will be breached, allowing something like three and a half billion gallons of water to rush down the mountainside. This will, of course, create its own fairly narrow path of destruction, but it will wash an enormous amount of debris far past Santa Monica Boulevard. You get two catastrophes for the price of one!" Kharl giggled at the thought. "Of course, there will be terrible damage and fires well beyond the three-and-a-half-mile circle of complete destruction, not to mention the deaths caused by radiation poisoning. It will take Los Angeles decades to recover."

Hamish's breath was taken away for a moment; he had not fully comprehended what the device would do.

"Now," Kharl said, "do you understand what you must do?"

Hamish repeated the process to the doctor. "Is that correct?"

"It is perfectly correct," the doctor said. "You may stop the process if you insert the key and turn it to the left." Kharl looked at his wristwatch. "My flight to Dubai departs San Francisco International in three and a half hours," he said. "I must leave immediately." He closed the trunk, locked it, and handed the key to Hamish.

Mo spoke from the doorway. "There is a car waiting downstairs to drive you to the airport, Doctor. Come, I'll take your luggage."

Kharl laid his gloves on the table. "You will not need these," he said. "I will leave it to you to dispose of them." He shook Hamish's hand, then Mo's, then followed Mo and his suitcase out of the apartment.

Hamish put both keys into his pocket and went to breakfast. He was eating his muffin when Mo came back into the flat. Jasmine came out of her room and joined them at the table.

"The doctor is on his way," Mo said. "I am uncertain why you allowed him to go."

"I let him go because we may need him again," Hamish said, sipping his coffee. "There are plans for London being discussed."

When they had eaten, they stacked the three small cases onto a hand truck, along with the two Vuitton cases holding Hamish's clothes, wheeled them downstairs to the building's garage, and stowed them in a rented van, then went back for the trunk. Mo tilted it and got the hand truck under it. "It's surprisingly light, considering its contents," he said.

"Lightweight was one of my specifications," Hamish replied. "The metal parts are of aluminum and titanium—only the material at the bottom is heavy." They took it down in the elevator, muscled the trunk into the van, then Jasmine got behind the wheel, and Hamish got into the passenger seat and rolled down the window. "Our work is done here," he said to Mo. "Pack your things into my empty cases, dispose of your canvas luggage, and get your flight back to London." They shook hands, and Jasmine drove out of the garage.

The Cessna Caravan, a hefty aircraft often used as a flying truck, with fixed landing gear and a single, turboprop engine, was parked on a private ramp at San Jose airport when they arrived. With the help of the pilot, Hamish and Jasmine got all the luggage, including the trunk, loaded into the interior. The pilot was around thirty, with a Mediterranean look about him. "My name is Habib," he said.

Hamish shook his hand. "Have you filed your flight plan?"

"I have, and we are fueled. We can depart immediately," Habib replied.

"Then let's go." Hamish embraced Jasmine, then climbed into the copilot's seat of the airplane and watched carefully as Habib started his engine and ran through his checklists. The airplane had the same Garmin avionics as the Citation Mustang he was accustomed to flying, and he knew he could fly this one if he had to. Habib radioed the tower for his clearance and permission to taxi, and shortly, they were climbing out of San Jose toward the Pacific. At a thousand feet of altitude, Habib switched on the autopilot, and the airplane began to fly its flight plan. Since the aircraft was not pressurized, Habib leveled off at eleven thousand feet and set cruise power.

Three hours later they set down at Santa Monica and, getting instructions from ground control, taxied to the western end of the airfield, around a row of hangars to one facing south. The doors were open, and three men stood outside. Habib shut down the engine, and, without a word, the three unloaded the luggage, stowed it in the hangar, then helped the pilot back the aircraft into the hangar, where Hamish took the pilot aside.

"Here is one-third of your money and some extra for cab fare and a motel room," Hamish said, handing him a thick envelope. "You will receive the other two-thirds when we return north." He gave the man a cell phone. "You are to make no calls on this phone," he said. "I will call you at the appropriate time and tell you when our departure will be. Go to the FBO and ask them to recommend a motel nearby, then take a taxi there. Do not go anywhere out of cell phone range. Do you understand?"

"I understand," Habib said. "I will await your call." He let himself out of the hangar and left.

"Now, gentlemen," Hamish said to the others, "we finally meet face-to-face. You have all done well in seeking and finding employment at The Arrington, but we have much more work to do, so I will give you further instructions." He handed each of them a small case and told them to open it, then he handed each of them a key and instructed them on how to operate the device. "Remember, you will have thirty minutes to clear the area after turning the key to the right. Take the key with you and dispose of it.

"Hans, after I am situated in the hotel, I will call you, and you will return here in one of the Porsche

Cayennes operated by the hotel and load the trunk into it. It will fit if you put the rear seats down. Tell the security people on departing the hotel that you are going for a guest's luggage, then they will be expecting you when you return with it. If anyone wishes to open it, tell them you do not have the key, then bring it to the suite I occupy, which will be on the south side of the grounds, overlooking the amphitheater. I will be there to receive it. Do you understand?"

"Yes," Hans said.

"I will e-mail each of you the time for activating the devices. Please turn the key at exactly that time, then leave the hotel." He handed each of them an envelope. "These are your instructions on leaving the hotel. Do not return to your homes. Follow the instructions exactly. Do not open the envelopes until you are well clear of The Arrington's grounds. Clear?"

The three nodded.

"Any questions?"

The three shook their heads.

"Hans, have you brought a hotel vehicle?"

"Yes, it is outside."

"Get my two cases into it, and we'll go. You others, help him get the car around to the hangar and loaded."

The three went outside with the luggage. Hamish went to one of the devices, opened the case, located a small panel, and with a fingernail, flipped down the first dip switch. With the altered dip switch, he handed Rick the case. "This one's yours." The three came back and collected their small cases.

Hamish locked the hangar and gave Hans the key, then they got into the car. "Don't speed, don't attract attention. You have simply picked up a hotel guest at the Santa Monica Airport, should anyone ask."

Hans nodded and drove out of the airport, headed for Bel-Air and The Arrington.

33

Everyone's luggage was loaded into Stone's and Dino's cars, and they departed for Teterboro. The big Gulfstream 550 was parked outside the Jet Aviation terminal, and the crew supervised the loading of the luggage. Shortly, everyone was seated, and the big cabin gave everyone room for comfort.

The stewardess checked their seat belts and gave them the lecture about the oxygen masks and the life jackets, then the engines were started, and shortly, the airplane began to roll. Runway One was active and their taxi was short. Stone watched as the pilot shoved the throttles forward, and they roared down the runway. For a while they were vectored at low altitude by ATC, until they were clear of the approaches to Newark Airport, then the aircraft climbed to its cruising altitude, and the stewardess brought everyone mimosas, straight orange juice for the kids.

Stone went forward to the cockpit. "Mind if I ride jump seat for a while?" he asked the pilot.

"Sure, make yourself at home. Do you fly?"

Stone sat down and buckled his seat belt. "Yes, I fly a Citation Mustang. I just wanted to see what you have in the way of avionics that I don't have."

The pilot gave him a tour of the G-550's avionics suite. "What do we have that you don't have?"

"Not much, I'm glad to say."

Stone went back to the cabin and sat next to Felicity, who was very quiet. "Are you troubled about something?" he asked.

She shook her head but said nothing.

"Come on, Felicity, you're not yourself. What's bothering you?"

She sighed. "All right, it's Algernon."

"What have you learned?"

"I wanted to wait until we got to the hotel and speak directly with the Secret Service, but I don't suppose it matters if I tell you."

"Then tell me."

"The name Algernon appeared in signals intercepted by our GCHQ facility, which is analogous to your NSA."

"When?"

"A while back," she said, "in July 2005, shortly before the suicide bomber attacks on the London underground."

"Oh, shit," Stone said.

"Well, yes."

"Any more details?"

"The messages were similar to those more recently intercepted," she said.

Stone waved at the stewardess and made telephone motions. She brought him a cordless satphone handset, and Stone dialed the number.

"Mike Freeman."

"Mike, it's Stone."

"Good morning, Stone."

"I have some news you need to get to the Secret Service detail."

"Shoot."

"The Brits at GCHQ intercepted previous messages with the code name 'Algernon.'"

"Yes?"

"They were right before the suicide bombing attacks on the London underground. As I recall, fifty died and hundreds were injured. The messages were much like the ones the NSA intercepted more recently."

"I'll call Agent Rifkin immediately," Mike said.

"I wonder if the president's visit should be canceled?" Stone said.

"Air Force One arrived at LAX at eight this

morning after an overnight flight from Rio to Washington, thence here. The president and his party are probably all asleep by now. The president of Mexico is due in momentarily."

"I see."

"I'll call Rifkin now, and I'll see you later today." Mike hung up.

"Did I hear you say the president's visit should be canceled?" Felicity asked.

"That's what I would do, if I were the Secret Service detail commander, but of course, I'm not. The president arrived early this morning and is in bed asleep. The president of Mexico is due shortly."

"What sort of quarters does the president have?"

"Both presidents are in large cottages that have bulletproof windows and walls, and each has a basement bomb shelter. I'm told there's no place in Los Angeles that is more secure."

Mike Freeman watched as Agent Rifkin talked on a telephone at the other end of the living room. There was a conversation of ten minutes, then Rifkin came back and sat down beside Mike.

"We appreciate the information, Mike, but our director, after consulting the White House, believes we don't have sufficient information to scrub the visit. A huge amount of staff work has gone into the preparations for the talks between President Lee and President Vargas, and the powers that be are unwilling to disrupt their conferences. A major treaty is to be signed at the conclusion of their talks, and there would be a huge flap in the media if we scrubbed it, and that wouldn't be to the benefit of your hotel."

"I understand," Mike said. "Did you rerun the background checks on the list of hotel employees I gave you?"

"Every one of them, and we didn't turn up a single piece of information on anybody that we didn't learn in the first investigation."

"I guess I'm glad to hear that," Mike said. "My people had the same result in their rerun."

"My director has told me that he's putting another fifty agents outside the hotel grounds, patrolling the surrounding neighborhood, so if there's somebody out there with a rocket-launched grenade or two, we'll have a shot at finding him."

"I think that's a smart move," Mike said.

The Gulfstream landed at Burbank, and was met by three Bentleys from the hotel, along with a Porsche Cayenne for the overflow luggage. Half an hour later they drove through the main gate of The Arrington and were immediately shunted into a parking area where they were asked by Secret Service agents to get out of the vehicles.

Stone looked around and saw landscapers unrolling swaths of sod and trimming shrubs. The grounds were very beautiful.

Peter came over. "Vance planted hundreds of specimen trees here," he said, "and they seem to have saved them all."

"I remember the landscape architect mentioning that," Stone said. "The sod looks like the last of their work."

Passports and other ID were examined and checked against the guest list, the luggage was unloaded and the cars thoroughly searched by a swarm of security personnel. Finally, they were all cleared, the cars were reloaded, and they were driven to their cottages up the hill.

They dropped Felicity at her cottage first, then Stone and his party were delivered to the main building, which was formerly the Vance Calder mansion, and across a road from the two presidential cottages. The cars drove around the building to deliver the luggage, but Stone wanted to see the finished reception building.

He took a few steps inside and froze in his tracks. Dead ahead of him stood Arrington.

Peter came and stood beside him. "I remember this well," he said. "It embarrassed Mother, and she took it down."

Stone stared at the portrait, which was life-sized. Arrington was dressed in riding clothes and stood next to a beautiful horse, which seemed to be nibbling at her shoulder. He didn't know who the artist was, but he had caught Arrington perfectly. Her hair was a little windblown, and there was mud on her boots, all of which added a natural quality to the work.

The hotel manager walked up and greeted Stone and his party. "I expect you've seen this before," he said.

"No, I never have," Stone replied, "but it's beautiful."

"We found it stored in a back room of the house, and we decided to hang it here. I hope you approve."

"Yes, I do, and it's the perfect spot," Stone said. "Who was the artist?"

"Jamie Wyeth."

"I know his work, and this is the best thing of his I've ever seen."

"Did you know the car could have delivered you to your cottage?" the man asked.

"Yes, but I wanted to walk through this building."

"I'll give you the tour, then. This way."

After the tour they walked to the new cottage; Stone made the room assignments. He unpacked his clothes in the master suite, then walked around the ground floor, checking out the house. It was impeccable. There were bouquets of fresh flowers everywhere, the bar was fully stocked, and there was a kitchen staff awaiting food orders.

The doorbell rang, and a staffer admitted Mike Freeman. Stone mixed them a drink and they sat down on the rear patio.

"What was the reaction of the Secret Service?" Stone asked.

Mike told him of the steps that had been taken. "Everything that can be done has been done," he said.

"Good."

Perhaps two hundred yards away, Hamish McCallister, who was accredited to the grand opening and the presidential conferences as a correspondent for a London newspaper and a travel magazine, watched a movie on the large-screen television set in the living room of his suite. There was a knock on his door and he answered it. Hans stood there with the Vuitton trunk on a hand cart.

"This way," Hamish said. "Just set it next to the window in the bedroom."

Hans did as he was told.

"Any problems getting through security?" Hamish asked.

"None at all."

"Hide your small case somewhere in your workplace," Hamish said.

"We had all assumed that would be the case."

"Wait for my e-mail message," Hamish told him. That was still a couple of days away. "Soon our work will be done."

34

Late in the afternoon Stone answered the phone in the living room. "Hello?"

"It's Holly."

"Well, hello, there. I heard you got in this morning."

"Yes, the president stopped in D.C. on the way back from a conference in Brazil and picked up the first lady."

"And you."

"And me. Have you settled into your new quarters?" she asked.

"Yes, everyone's here and unpacked."

"The first lady asked me to call you. They'd like to get together for a drink, but there are too many staff and Secret Service here to be having guests."

"We'd be delighted if they'd join us here for drinks," Stone said. "We're just across the road."

"I think she was hoping you'd suggest that. In an hour?"

"That's perfect. They have to be back over here at seven thirty, since President and Mrs. Vargas are coming for dinner."

"We'll see you in an hour." They both hung up.

Stone stood up and clapped his hands. "All right, everybody, go scrub up and change clothes. The president and first lady are coming here for drinks in an hour. Don't overdress, though." He called Felicity and Mike Freeman and invited them.

The group scattered to their own rooms, and Stone went to the kitchen and asked the staff to have canapés ready and to find a bartender, then he went to the master suite, showered, shaved, and changed into a tan linen suit, which didn't seem too formal.

By the time he got back to the living room, there was a team of Secret Service agents checking out the house, upstairs and down. Their work done, they vanished. Mike Freeman and Felicity Devonshire arrived soon, and Stone introduced them. Each pretended it was the first time they had met. Stone knew of their history and said nothing to make either of them uncomfortable.

At the appointed hour the doorbell rang, and Stone answered it himself.

President Will Lee came in first, his hand out-stretched. "Stone, it's good to see you," he said. Then the first lady entered, followed by Holly Barker and a female Secret Service agent. Another agent remained outside the door. Air kisses were exchanged.

Stone led the group into the living room where he introduced Dino's girlfriend, Viv, Ben and his girlfriend, Emma, plus Peter and Hattie. They were acquainted with Felicity, but Mike was new to the Lees.

A bartender and two waiters worked the group quickly, then got out of their way. The first lady, Holly, and Felicity were drawn together, and after some polite chat with the group, the president asked Stone and Mike to show him the patio. The three men walked outside and took seats at a table beside the pool.

"First of all, Stone," Lee said, "I want to thank you again for your and Dino's brilliant assistance when you were in Washington last year."

"We were delighted to be of help, Mr. President."

"Why can't I get you to call me Will when we're alone?"

"Maybe when you've left office," Stone said. "When I try, I become speechless."

"Mike, I'm glad to meet you at last," Lee said. "I've heard nothing but good things about you and your company."

"Thank you, Mr. President."

"I knew Jim Hackett, of course," Lee said, referring to the late founder of Strategic Services. "He was a good man."

"He certainly was."

"I want to thank you both for the way you've worked with Kate, the NSA, and the Secret Service concerning this visit."

"We haven't done much, except listen," Mike said.

"I find it reassuring when all the relevant groups are agreed on the threat and the way to proceed. It makes it easier for me to make decisions. Stone, I'm grateful to you and your partners in the hotel for making the facilities of The Arrington available for this meeting. Our respective staffs have done a great deal already, but President Vargas and I still have a thorny point or two to negotiate, starting at tonight's dinner, and we're both appreciative of the solitude and beauty of this place, not to mention all you've done to make it secure."

"It was the great pleasure of all concerned to do what we could, Mr. President," Stone replied.

Will Lee sat back in his chair and sipped his ginger ale. "Now tell me bluntly—bluntly, please—

what you think is going on with this nursery-rhyme trio," he said.

Stone and Mike looked at each other, and Stone nodded to Mike.

"Mr. President," Mike said, "as you pointed out, all the relevant parties are in agreement on the information we have so far. We think there is an active al Qaeda team in California, probably in Los Angeles, whose mission it is to disrupt your talks with President Vargas."

"And perhaps kill both of us and a great many prominent people, as well," Lee pointed out. "You're going to have an extraordinary grouping of entertainment, business, and media folks gathered in one place, and that has to be an inviting target for them. It was suggested to me that I should cancel the event, but I decided to go ahead for many reasons, not the least of them that to cancel in the face of a mere threat would put our government in a bad light."

"I can't disagree, Mr. President," Mike replied, "and I'm impressed with the way the government agencies are cooperating. Interagency rivalry has been put aside."

"That's something I'm trying to engender all the time," Lee said, "and not always with success."

Stone spoke up. "Felicity Devonshire at MI-6 has been very helpful, too."

"Yes, I understand they've connected one of the

names to the subway bombings in London a few years back. That's very disturbing."

"And that information has caused a redoubling of all our efforts," Mike said.

"My wife and I appreciate that," Lee said. "Has there been anything new while I was sleeping?"

"No, sir," Mike replied.

"Then let's rejoin the others," Lee said. "Since it's a special occasion, I think I'll stand myself to a second ginger ale."

They went back to the living room. "This is a beautiful house," Kate Lee said to Stone.

"Thank you. Arrington worked with the architect on the design until shortly before her death," Stone replied.

"We saw her portrait in the reception area," Kate said. "I loved it."

"I hadn't seen it before today," Stone said, "but I loved it, too. How did the intelligence summit go?" he asked, indicating Felicity and Holly.

"I wish all my intelligence were so smooth and cordial," Kate said, and the others laughed.

A young woman wearing a Secret Service button in her lapel approached. "Mrs. Lee, you asked me to remind you when it was time to return to the residence for dinner."

"Thank you, Agent," Kate said. "Will," she called across the room. "Dinnertime. I hope you haven't had too much ginger ale."

Lee set down his drink and joined his wife. "I'm still steady on my feet," he said. Good-byes were exchanged, and the presidential party left.

"I hope we can all get together before this weekend is over," the president said, as he led his party out of the house.

"Wow!" Peter exclaimed. "I can't believe I just met the president of the United States!"

35

That night Felicity and Mike stayed for dinner, and everyone was in a good mood, in the afterglow of their brush with the president. Almost everyone turned in early, tired from their cross-country travel.

Felicity left by the front door, then, half an hour later, parted the curtains of the master suite and stepped in from the patio.

"Haven't we met somewhere before?" Stone said.

Felicity sat down on the bed, released a silk stocking from her garter belt, and rolled it down her beautiful leg. "Yes, and you know very well that the man you call Mike Freeman and I have met before, too."

"I haven't the slightest idea what you're talking

about," Stone replied, pushing back the covers for her. He was already in bed, naked. "Who else on your side of the pond thinks he may have met Mike before?"

"I believe myself to be the only one. Of course, I've done everything I can to paper over that crack in the history of my service."

Mike Freeman, when younger and under his original name, had been a rising star in MI-6, until an episode in his private life made him a target of people who wanted to see him dead. He built an identity for himself in the United States and was brought into Strategic Services by its founder, Jim Hackett. Stone and Felicity had both been instrumental in seeing that he was not exposed.

"I'll tell Mike that," Stone said.

"Please don't, I'd rather that only you and I shared the details of that episode. There are still people in high places who would feel great resentment toward us, if they knew. Let sleeping dogs snore."

Stone laughed. "My lips are zipped."

Felicity went into the second bathroom with a small bag she had brought. Stone dimmed the lights and waited for her to emerge, naked, and get into bed with him.

She snuggled close. "One of these days I'm going to retire from the service, and when I do you are going to be in big, big trouble," she said.

"I could use some of that kind of trouble," Stone replied, turning to her and slipping a leg between hers, where he found her to be already wet. He kissed her eyes and her face, then bit her softly on a nipple. "I believe this is the start button?"

"Yes, and it's in perfect working order," she breathed. She pulled him on top of her and brought him inside her. "There," she said, "that's where you belong."

And he remained there for some time.

Before dawn, Felicity dressed and slipped out onto the patio, then let herself out of the garden and strolled down the pathway to her nearby cottage, passing a Secret Service agent on the way. He gave her a little salute, but they did not speak.

It was eight hours later in London, so she called her office on her encoded cell phone.

"Aren't you up very early?" her secretary asked.

"I couldn't sleep—jet lag," she lied, "so I thought I'd check in."

"Do you want your messages?"

"Just e-mail them to me. I'd be interested to know, though, if there's anything from GCHQ?"

"Nothing," the woman replied.

"If they should call, get in touch with me without delay," Felicity said. "And now, I'm going to try to get a couple of hours' sleep." She hung up, undressed, and was out as soon as her head hit the pillow.

Stone slept soundly until he heard voices from the living room. He showered and joined them for breakfast. "Everybody sleep well?" Stone asked.

"I was too excited to sleep well," Hattie said. "I get to play on a movie sound track today."

"That's wonderful, Hattie. By the way, I've arranged for a hotel car to take the four of you to Centurion and wait to drive you back. The great bulk of the guests won't arrive until the day after tomorrow, so they won't need the car, and it will be faster to clear security on your return if you're in the vehicle you left in."

"Thanks, Dad," Peter said. "Are you sure you don't want to come with us?"

"No, thank you, Peter, I've had that tour, and I need to speak with my office about some things. I might even get some actual work done."

After breakfast he called Joan. "Good morning from fantasy land," he said to her.

"Is it absolutely wonderful?" she asked.

"Absolutely wonderful. Tomorrow the guests start arriving."

"And the Immi Gotham concert?"

"That's the day after tomorrow."

"I would kill to be there."

"Don't worry, it'll be televised later. Any messages?"

"Bill Eggers and his wife will be with you tomorrow, and Herbie Fisher wants to talk to you. That's it."

"Okay, can you transfer me to Herbie?"

"Hang on." There was a click, and Herbie's secretary answered. "Mr. Fisher's office."

"It's Stone."

"Oh, yes, he wants to talk to you."

Herbie came onto the phone. "Hey, Stone."

"Good morning, Herb."

"I've shunted some work out of the way, so Harp and I are coming out there. I've booked us into the Beverly Hills Hotel."

"Great, Herb. I'll check with the manager and see if there have been any cancellations."

"Thanks, Stone. If you can do anything about the Immi Gotham concert, I'd appreciate that, too."

"That may be one miracle I can't work," Stone said, "but I'll try. What time are you due in?"

"Midafternoon tomorrow."

"I'll get back to you." Stone hung up and called the hotel's executive director, Morton Kaplan. "Good morning, Mort."

"Good morning, Stone. I hope everything is all right with your cottage."

"Everything is absolutely perfect. We had the president and first lady for drinks last evening, and your staff performed beautifully. I wanted to ask a favor, perhaps an impossible one."

"Tell me what you need."

"I have a friend and associate at Woodman & Weld coming out tomorrow. He's booked into the Beverly Hills, but if you should have a cancellation here . . ."

"Hold on a moment and I'll take a look," Kaplan said.

Stone heard the sound of a computer keyboard, then Kaplan came back.

"No cancellations, but we have some smaller rooms that are normally for the use of our guests' air crews or secretaries, and I have one of those available."

"Wonderful! I'm sure that will be just fine. His name is Herbert Fisher, and his companion's name is Harp O'Connor."

"I'll get their names to the Secret Service for checking, but I'm sure there'll be no problem. And if we should have a cancellation, I'll try to improve Mr. Fisher's accommodations."

"One other thing: any chance of concert tickets?"

"We can put a couple more chairs in your box."

"Perfect. Thanks so much, Mort."

"Would you like your friends met at the airport?"

"Yes, they're arriving at midafternoon. I'll get you the flight number."

"That won't be necessary. There'll be a little stand with the hotel's name on it—tell him to go there, and they'll have a car for them."

"Wonderful!" He thanked Kaplan again, then hung up and called Herbie with the news.

"Thank you, Stone," Herbie said. "Now Harp will think I'm a god."

36

Peter, Hattie, Ben, and Emma walked through the hotel reception building and out under the portico, where a white Porsche Cayenne with The Arrington's logo, a gold A on the door, waited, and they got in. Peter took the front passenger seat, and there was plenty of room for the other three in the back.

"Good morning, Mr. Barrington," the driver said. "My name is Hans."

"Good morning, Hans," Peter replied. "Do you know the way to Centurion Studios?"

"Frieda knows the way," Hans replied, starting the navigation system. "Turn left at the main gate," a gentle voice said.

"Ah, Frieda," Peter said, patting the dash. "We are in your hands."

Frieda guided them precisely to the studio's front gate, where the guard stuck a pass to the inside of the windshield, then waved them through.

"We're looking for the executive building," Peter said, pointing at a sign.

They pulled into a parking lot, where a woman holding a cell phone waved them into a guest slot, then spoke briefly on the phone. "Mr. Goldman will be down in thirty seconds," she said.

A stretched electric vehicle pulled into the lot and stopped as Leo Goldman, the chairman and CEO of Centurion, came out of the building. "Good morning, everybody," he said, turning the front passenger seat around so that it faced the rear. "Hop in."

Peter got in facing Leo. "Thank you for greeting us, Leo, but is it a good use of the CEO's time to be a tour guide?"

"Spending time with a major stockholder is always a good use of my time," Leo said, sticking a cigar into his mouth, but not lighting it. "Forgive me. I'm giving these up, and I haven't smoked one for months, but chomping down on it still helps." He turned to the driver, a studio intern. "Let's go to New York," he said.

"Mr. Goldman," Hattie said, "we just came from New York."

"Not *this* New York," Leo said, laughing.

Shortly, they were driving down a composite

big-city street. "This is the largest, most-used standing set on the lot," Leo said. "We can dress it as New York, which is how you see it now, Chicago, or half a dozen European cities. Amazing what the set dressers can do with a little Styrofoam molding and some streetlamps. These are only facades, of course. In a movie, when someone walks through a door we cut to a studio shot on a sound stage."

They turned a corner and emerged from the set, then turned down a row of huge hangarlike buildings. "These are our sound stages: there are eight of them, constantly in use for films and television shows." They pulled to a stop before a large stucco building. "And here we have our music department. Follow me." Goldman led them through a reception area, down a hall, and through a large steel door. They emerged into an audio control room, which had a row of comfortable chairs behind the engineers' stations. "Hattie, you come with me, the rest of you take a seat." He waved at the row of chairs, then led Hattie through another door and into a large room with chairs for an orchestra and a giant movie screen behind them. A man was standing on the podium, leafing through a musical manuscript.

"Good morning, John," Goldman said. "This is your guest artist for the day, Hattie Patrick. Hattie, this is John Greenfield, the studio's musical director."

Greenfield, a tall man with a shaved head, turned and offered Hattie his hand. "It's a pleasure, Hattie. Leo has told me about you. Did you get the music I sent you?"

Hattie handed him a thick brown envelope. "Yes, thank you, Mr. Greenfield."

"Well, you'll need it," he said, trying to hand it back.

"That's all right, I've learned it."

Greenfield paused for a moment, then tossed the envelope onto the podium next to him. "Well, we'll keep it here, in case we need it." Orchestra members began to file into the room and take their places. "Hattie, we're waiting for Andrei Serkinoff to join us to rehearse a piece he's playing at Immi Gotham's concert at The Arrington the day after tomorrow. He's also playing piano on our film's sound track. While we're waiting, would you mind running through what you'll be playing for me? Just cue yourself when you're ready."

Hattie sat down at the Steinway concert grand and, without hesitation, began to play. Greenfield watched with interest, looking slightly puzzled. When she had finished, he took the podium. "All right, everybody, Mr. Serkinoff is late, so let's rehearse the title music with our guest artist, Hattie Patrick. Ready, Hattie?"

She nodded and waited as the conductor gave the orchestra a downbeat, then joined in when she was cued. They played for a little over four minutes by a large clock on the wall while the film's opening titles appeared on the screen behind the orchestra. When they were done, Greenfield turned to Hattie. "That was perfect. If you were a member of the musicians' union, I'd say we'd have that in the can."

"I am a member of the musicians' union," Hattie replied.

That brought Greenfield up short. He turned toward the glass panel separating him from the control booth. "How was that for you, Jerry?"

Jerry's voice came back over a loudspeaker. "Absolutely perfect, John. The time was right on, too."

"Then we have the title music in the can," Greenfield said. "Can you burn a DVD for Ms. Patrick to take home?" He looked at his watch. "Mr. Serkinoff is now forty minutes late," he said, "and I have to rehearse his piece before Immi gets here. Hattie, do you think you can get through a performance of 'Rhapsody in Blue'?"

"Yes, Mr. Greenfield."

"Get me a copy of the piano part, please," Greenfield called to an assistant.

"What arrangement are you using?" Hattie asked.

"The Previn," Greenfield replied.

"I won't need the music, I know it," she said.

He stood, staring at her.

"I recorded it with the Manhattan Youth Orchestra two years ago," Hattie said.

Greenfield turned back to the orchestra and raised his arms. "All right, everybody, this is a rehearsal, but I'm not going to stop. Let's see if you can all get it right the first time." He raised his arms and cued the clarinetist, who played the opening trill, then the glissando, the entire orchestra came in, and Hattie played her first phrases.

At the end of the piece, the orchestra gave Hattie an ovation, and Greenfield simply beamed at her, shaking his head. Then Immi Gotham entered from the control room where she had stood at the rear, listening. She was applauding, too. She hugged Hattie and introduced herself.

Hattie was flushed and smiling. She thanked everyone. "And thank you, Mr. Greenfield, for allowing me to . . ."

But John Greenfield was on his cell phone. He finished his conversation, then hung up. "Ladies and gentlemen," he said to the orchestra, "I've just been told that Andrei Serkinoff was in an automobile accident on the freeway an hour ago, and I'm told he's now in the emergency room at Cedars-Sinai, having a broken left wrist set. We are without a soloist."

There were sympathetic sounds from the orchestra.

"John," Immi Gotham said, "I'm sorry to hear of Mr. Serkinoff's accident, but you are *not* without a soloist."

Greenfield turned to Hattie. "Are you doing anything Saturday evening?" he asked.

37

The group left the music department, Hattie with two DVDs under her arm, and got back into the electric cart to continue their tour. They visited set design and the props warehouse, the motor pool where a collection of vehicles, some of them going back decades, was kept, ready to be used in scenes, and the costume department, where they watched Immi Gotham being fitted for her concert gown.

Finally, they were driven down streets occupied by a mix of small office buildings and cottages, and the cart stopped in front of a traditional California bungalow with a wide front porch and a beautifully tended front garden. Goldman led everyone to the house and opened the front door with a key. "Peter," he said, "this was your father's . . . excuse me, your stepfather's bungalow for more than fifty years. I've left it just as it was the last time he used it. It's sentimental of me, but in fact, no one on the lot has had the courage to ask me for it."

They walked through the bungalow, which contained a living room, dining room, and kitchen, plus three other rooms, several utility rooms, and Vance Calder's office, which opened onto a back porch that offered a good view of the entire lot from a small rise. Nobody said much of anything.

Peter took a chair and waved to the others to gather around a table on the porch. "Leo," he said, "Hattie, Ben, and I have been on an accelerated program at Yale, going to school the year 'round, and we're going to graduate next year."

"What are your plans then, Peter?" Goldman asked. "I know you well enough already to believe that you have some."

"Our plan is to come to L.A. and make pictures for Centurion."

Goldman broke into a wide grin. "I'll tell you the truth, I was hoping you'd say that. Your first film, *Autumn Kill*, has already grossed more than sixty million dollars, and we're about to release it in Europe and Asia, where we project it will earn at least that much more. And a lot of people couldn't understand why I paid so much for it! The quicker we have another film from you, the better."

"Thank you, Leo. Hattie, Ben, and I want to operate as a unit on the lot, drawing on the studio's resources as we need them, and, of course, we'll need a space to work in. Do you think you could keep this bungalow for our use?"

"I'd be delighted to do that, Peter. Of course, you'll want to bring it up to date, but we'll have plenty of time to get it ready for you."

"I think the main things we'll need are sound-proofing, a piano, and recording facilities for Hattie's studio, and an editing suite for Ben and me, and, of course, wiring for computers and wi-fi."

"Tell me which rooms you'd like to use, and I'll get an architect started on some drawings for your approval."

"Let's go take a look," Peter said. They went back into the house, where the three of them discussed their needs in the space and Leo took notes. Half an hour later, they were done. They had a late lunch at the studio commissary, then resumed their tour of the Centurion lot.

Late in the afternoon, after a look around the executive offices, Goldman walked them to the waiting hotel SUV, and they started back to the hotel.

"That was a very exciting day, wasn't it?" Ben said.

"Nobody's more excited than me," Hattie said. "Immi is doing an all-Gershwin program at her concert, and Mr. Greenfield wants me to come back to-morrow and rehearse a number for her with me on piano."

"Wonderful! It was a very satisfying day for me, too," Peter said. "I can see a future for all of us. It's what Dad calls 'severe clear.'"

"What does that mean?" Hattie asked.

"It's a pilot's term, it means a cloudless sky, ceiling and visibility unlimited."

"Severe clear," Ben said. "I like it."

When they arrived back at the hotel the Cayenne was shunted into a parking area again.

"I thought we wouldn't have to go through this another time," Peter said, "coming and going in one of the hotel's cars."

"Something must have happened," Ben said.

After the search of the car had been completed, Hans drove them back to their cottage. They arrived simultaneously with Mike Freeman, who was carrying a briefcase.

Inside, Stone was sitting with another man they hadn't met.

"Hi there, kids," Stone called out. "I don't think you've met Special Agent Rifkin, of the Secret Service." Everybody shook hands.

"Dad," Peter said, "they put us through the big search again at the front gate. Has something happened?"

"No, no," Stone replied. "The security folks are just a little nervous, what with two presidents here and a lot of celebrities to arrive tomorrow. Will you excuse us, please? We have some things to discuss."

"Sure," Peter said. "What about a swim, everybody?"

The others nodded, and they all went to change.

"Let's go into the study," Stone said when they had gone. The three men got up and walked into the next room, and Stone closed the door behind them. "All right, Mike, what's up?" he asked.

Mike sat down. "First of all, Agent Rifkin, I want to apologize to you and the Secret Service."

"For what?" Rifkin asked.

"Late yesterday I got word from the NSA that they had located the geographical point from which the e-mails were sent by our friend Algernon. It was an apartment house in Palo Alto."

"Why didn't you call me at once?" Rifkin asked.

"That's why I'm apologizing," Mike said, "for that and my reason for not calling you."

"Which is?"

"Frankly, I don't think your people are sufficiently trained and experienced to work a scene as well as . . . well, some other agencies. Nor as well as our people at Strategic Services."

Rifkin thought about that, but didn't contradict him. "Go on, what did you find?"

"Not much," Mike said. "The place had been cleaned and wiped down—very professionally, I might add. Except for one thing."

"Come on, Mike," Stone said, "spit it out."

Mike set his briefcase on the coffee table and unlatched the locks. "We found these under a table." He reached into his briefcase and removed a zipped plastic bag containing a pair of heavy gloves.

"I'm sorry," Stone said, "I don't get it. Gloves?"

Mike set the bag on the coffee table. "They're lab gloves," he said. "There's good news and bad news about them."

"Go on, tell us," Stone said.

"The good news is, they're not sufficiently protective for handling plutonium."

"And the bad news?"

"They're sufficient for handling enriched uranium."

"Oh, my dear God," Rifkin said.

38

Mike waited for a moment before continuing. "On the way in here I ordered my people to redouble their efforts to search every vehicle and guest entering the grounds. They're already at work. Agent Rifkin, I suggest you issue the same order to your people."

Rifkin produced a cell phone and pressed a single button. "This is Rifkin," he said, then he gave orders to intensify the search routine.

"Further good news," Mike said when Rifkin had finished, "is that my people checked the gloves with a Geiger counter and got a negative reading, and we are not expecting a rush of guests until tomorrow. Even further good news is that, if a nuclear device is being brought here, it will be too large to easily smuggle in. The suitcase nuclear bomb is a myth—even a small one would be much larger than that. We have to comb the entire hotel and inspect anything that came in a large package— a kitchen appliance, a piece of furniture. The bell captain can tell us by questioning his staff if anything like that was taken into a suite or room by one of his bellmen."

"I know what's coming next," Rifkin said.

"Well, I don't know," Stone said, "so tell me."

Mike spoke up. "What Agent Rifkin means is, if a nuclear device is involved, it won't have to be on the hotel grounds to destroy the place."

"How big an area are we talking about?"

"The Arrington is in a canyon," Mike explained. "Anyone who wanted to destroy the hotel would need to place the device in the canyon, not beyond it, where the landscape would deflect the blast."

"I'm going to have to call my director," Rifkin said, "and ask for more agents and the authority to search every house and building in Stone Canyon."

"I don't think you'll have to search every house," Mike said. "It's enough to talk to the occupants and see if a large package has been delivered to them. Most of them will not be suspicious characters, but we're dealing with a Middle Eastern threat, so anyone with that appearance living locally should have his residence thoroughly searched. Can you get a broad federal search warrant?"

"In the circumstances, yes," Rifkin said. "The

more immediate question is whether to get the two presidents out of here."

"I think it's logical to assume," Mike said, "that such a threat would be carried out at the time when it could do the most damage, and that would be on the night of the grand opening, when the place will be packed. And there's always the concert to think about, too."

Rifkin left the room and walked out onto the patio with his phone.

Stone looked at Mike. "Should I get my people out of here?"

"Not yet," Mike said. "We don't want to start anything until we've searched the place. If we find the package, Rifkin will call in the various bomb squads to deal with it, but we'll evacuate everybody first."

"And the two presidents?"

"One minute after Rifkin's phone call, the president will know, and he will make that decision, presumably in concert with President Vargas."

They were quiet for a moment.

"Stone," Mike said, "you have to remember that we're talking about this because of a pair of gloves. We don't even know if they were used for what we think they were. After all, they're clean of any nuclear material."

Rifkin returned after fifteen minutes. "My director spoke with the president, and since there was no radioactivity associated with the gloves, his decision is to redouble the search of guests and vehicles, but not to canvass the neighborhood. However, he has authorized another one hundred federal agents from various agencies to be on standby, in case further evidence points to a nuclear device." He picked up the gloves and put them into his own briefcase. "In the meantime, I have some people on the way over here with equipment to check the gloves further."

Mike nodded. "I think the response is at the correct level for the moment," he said. He looked at Stone. "If I had a family here—which of course I don't—I would not get them out at this time."

"That's good enough for me," Stone said. "I'll say nothing to my party about this, not even Dino."

Rifkin left by way of the patio, and Mike and Stone returned to the living room. They could hear the kids laughing and splashing in the pool outside.

"I don't think it's too early for a drink," Stone said, going to the bar. "How about you, Mike?"

Mike nodded. "Large scotch, please. Rocks."

39

Hamish McCallister sat in a golf cart with The Arrington's director of public relations, a lovely young woman named Clair Albritton, as she showed him the grounds of the hotel.

"Vance Calder planted more than a thousand specimen trees around the property," she was saying, "and we have preserved every one of them, although we had to move and replant a couple hundred of them."

"They are very beautiful," Hamish said, and he meant it. "This is really an extraordinary property."

"Yes, Vance bought the first of it in the 1940s, and he continued to buy up neighboring plots to the end of his life. After his death his wife, Arrington, bought the final two plots, which he had optioned a year or so before. The total property now runs to twenty acres."

"Even larger than that of the Bel-Air Hotel," Hamish pointed out.

She smiled. "A fine establishment with its own clientele."

"And how many of them do you expect to steal?" Hamish asked.

She laughed. "Oh, I'm sure there will be some, but Los Angeles attracts a worldwide army of regular travelers, and our initial market research indicated to us that there was room for another top-of-the-line property in Bel-Air."

Hamish saw a procession of unmarked white vans come through the front gate without being stopped and proceed up the hill to the reception building. "What are those vans about?" he asked. "They weren't even stopped and searched like every other vehicle entering the property."

"Oh, they're just part of the security for the weekend," Clair said. "Don't worry, their presence makes us all that much safer."

Hamish watched as they drove past the reception area. A couple of dozen men were unloading equipment, some of which appeared to be detectors of some sort. He couldn't be sure if it was for detecting metal or nuclear material. He felt a light sweat break out on his forehead.

Then they were underground. "One of the great

features of the hotel is that we've been able to hide a great many parked vehicles down here. It helps keep the grounds so much more attractive, don't you think?"

"I do," Hamish replied.

"The landscape architects wanted a pastoral feeling about the place."

"They've done a wonderful job."

"I hope room service has been doing a good job of feeding you," Clair said. "Our restaurants won't be opening until lunchtime tomorrow, when our guests begin to arrive."

"How did you manage to get Immi Gotham to perform?" Hamish asked.

"Centurion Studios and The Arrington share some important investors, so Centurion has arranged for most of its stars to be here, either as guests or performers. They've taken a quarter of our accommodations for the opening weekend, and Leo Goldman Junior, their CEO, arranged for Ms. Gotham to appear. I don't think she's ever done a concert like this before, preferring to appear in films and make recordings."

"I'm looking forward to seeing her," Hamish said. "I'm a big fan."

"Who isn't?" Clair said. "I'll certainly be there, if I have to sit in a tree."

Hamish reflected that by the end of the concert, there wouldn't be any trees.

Clair pulled up to his cottage. "Now you've seen it all," she said. "Please give me a call if there's anything else I can do for you, Mr. McCallister, and we look forward to reading your reportage."

Hamish hopped out of the cart. He could think of a number of things she could do for him, but he imagined she was far too busy with her duties to provide them. He let himself into his cottage, went to the bar and poured himself a glass of San Pellegrino from the fridge. He pulled the curtains back in his bedroom and gazed down into the Arrington Bowl, imagining it at capacity for the concert.

It was that concert that would be the cherry on the sundae of the event he had planned. Not only would he take out two presidents, he would cause to vanish virtually the entire roster of stars of one of Hollywood's top studios, all in a single flash. The worldwide media would print and broadcast nothing else for weeks. It would be bigger than 9/11, he reckoned—a much greater loss of life and property in the heart of America's most decadent community, with the possible exception of Las Vegas.

And he would be alive and well to read about it, hear about it, and bask in its afterglow for decades to come. Then there would be London to deal with.

40

Kelli Keane got off a corporate jet at Burbank, followed by the photographer Harry Benson, his four assistants, and their luggage, plus many cases of photographic equipment. A very large van pulled up to the airplane and began stowing their bags, while Kelli and her team climbed into the seats.

When they arrived at The Arrington, the van was waved to a parking area and two men in dark blue jumpsuits approached. "Okay, folks, everything out of the van, we're unloading your luggage," one of them said.

"Wait a minute," Kelli said, holding up a hand. "We're not unloading any of our stuff. We're here from *Vanity Fair* to photograph this event." She held up a letter. "Here's my authorization from the director of public relations."

The man read the letter and handed it back to her. "Very nice," he said, "now here's my authorization." He held up a badge.

Harry leaned over and whispered in Kelli's ear, "They're Secret Service. Shut up, and let's get everything unloaded." Two bellmen appeared in a big cart and began removing luggage, while the two agents opened the black equipment cases and started taking out equipment.

Kelli got on her cell phone.

"Clair Albritton," a voice said.

"Clair, it's Kelli Keane from *Vanity Fair*. I've just arrived with my team, and we're being given a hard time by the Secret Service."

"Kelli, please remember we have two presidents and a lot of other important people in residence. *Everybody* is being given a hard time. Please do as they ask."

Kelli put away her phone and turned to find an agent pawing through her underwear. He closed the bag and started on another. She stood there, sputtering, while Harry relaxed in the van, looking through an *L.A. Times*.

"Take a few deep breaths, Kelli," Harry said, in his Glaswegian accent. "This is a little more than par for the course, but there's nothing you can do to rush it. Just have a seat and relax."

Kelli leaned against the van and longed for a cigarette. She had quit, cold turkey, two years ago, but when she was annoyed about something the urge came back, and she was very annoyed at the moment. Now the agents started closing the cases, and two others began removing the seats from the van. Another one was lying on his back on a creeper, surveying its underside.

"Okay," somebody said finally, "you can reload now." The bellmen got everything back into the van.

"You see," Harry said, "that took only forty minutes. It's not like we have to be somewhere. There's nobody to photograph until tomorrow."

"There's the grounds," Kelli said.

"Somebody else is doing that," Harry said. "I'm not a landscapist."

Kelli finally wilted before the wisdom of one of the world's great photojournalists. "All right," she said, "I'll settle for a cold beer."

The van moved off up the hill and finally stopped in front of the reception building. Clair Albritton was there to meet them. "Hello, Kelli, sorry about security. A warning: if you leave the grounds, you'll have to go through all that again when you return." She spread a map on the hood of the van and gave Kelli and Harry a briefing on the layout of the hotel.

"Where are you going to want to put the lights, Harry?" Kelli asked.

"Lights? We're not going to need any lights that aren't handheld. This place is too big, and there are too many people to do setups. I'm going to be working on the fly. Don't worry about it, dear, it's not my first time."

Everybody got back into the van, and they followed a cart with Clair and the two bellmen down the hill to a two-story building. Clair got out and began instructing the bellmen. "Kelli, you and Harry have the two ground-floor rooms. Your assistants are upstairs in two other rooms."

"We don't have suites?" Kelli asked. She had become accustomed to suites.

"The suites are all reserved for the people you've come here to photograph and interview," Clair said. "We could have let them all three times over."

"It's fine, Kelli," Harry said. "We could be in a motel somewhere, you know."

"What about interiors?" Kelli asked.

"*Architectural Digest* is already here, photographing some suites, the restaurants, and the rest of the grounds," Clair said.

"How many other journalists are here?"

"A dozen or so. A fellow from a London paper is next door to you. Most of them are nearby."

"Why do I feel we're being quarantined?" Kelli asked.

Clair laughed. "Kelli, you have free run of the

grounds and the public buildings. What more do you want?"

"A suite," Kelli muttered. "Where is Stone Barrington staying?"

"He has his own house," Clair replied. "And all the rooms are full."

"Where is it?"

"Through the reception building, out the back door, and around the pool. But don't go up there unless you call first—it's next door to the presidential cottage, and the Secret Service will be all over you." She handed Kelli a thick envelope. "Here are your hotel press passes. You and your people must wear them at all times."

Kelli opened the envelope and found hers, with the word MEDIA emblazoned across it below her photograph. "You're belling the cat, are you?"

"Our guests have the right to know when they're talking to a reporter," Clair said. "Remember, you're to wear that, prominently displayed, at all times, otherwise we'll have a problem."

"Got it," Kelli said. "Thanks for all your help, Clair."

"Your bar is fully stocked," Clair said, "compliments of the house." She got into a cart and drove away. As she did, another cart came down the path, stopped, and a man got out. He was immaculately dressed and quite handsome, even if bald.

"Good afternoon," he said. "If you're bunking

here, I take it you're press." He offered his hand. "I'm Hamish McCallister. I'm just next door." He pointed at the door next to Harry's. "Hello, Harry, how are you?"

"Good grief, Hamish, you came all this way?" They shook hands and embraced.

"Good God, I'm surrounded by Scots!" Kelli said.

"Lucky girl," Hamish replied. "Can I buy anybody a beer?"

"Sold," Kelli said, following the two men into Hamish's quarters. She looked around. "It's a fucking suite," she said. "How'd you do that?"

"Charm," Hamish replied.

"You didn't think of that, did you, Kelli?" Harry asked.

Kelli peeked into the bedroom. "My word!" she said. "You travel with a *steamer trunk?*"

Hamish closed the bedroom door and handed her a drink. "Wardrobe is so important, don't you think?"

Kelli took the beer. "I'd be a happy woman if I could travel with a steamer trunk," she said.

41

Late in the afternoon, Stone and Mike were having a drink in Stone's study, when Special Agent Steve Rifkin appeared.

"The search is still under way," he said. "I've got seventy men combing every nook and cranny of this property." He set his briefcase on the coffee table and took out a stack of paper. "One good thing: the bell captain keeps a log of every piece of luggage that his men have delivered to any suite or room. It's meant to resolve lost luggage issues, but it's a stroke of luck for us."

Stone and Mike each took a sheet from the stack. "And this is accurate?"

"It is, and here's the good news. There's not a single piece of luggage bigger than a large suitcase, and we've checked every one of those so far. There are no large boxes and no trunks, and from this point on, every piece of luggage arriving here will be opened and hand-searched, and if there are any trunks, they'll be subject to radiation checks before they're opened. We have a very well-equipped bomb squad on site, and they'll stay through the entire weekend."

"Well, that's a relief," Stone said.

Rifkin's cell phone rang, playing "The Stars and Stripes Forever." "Special Agent Rifkin." His face drained of expression, and he hung up. "They've found a bomb," he said.

Stone and Mike stood up.

"Not you, me," Rifkin said.

"I'm in charge of hotel security," Mike reminded him, "and Stone is a member of the board. Let's go."

Rifkin shrugged and led the two outside to a cart, and they were driven away.

"Where is the bomb?" Mike asked.

"In a wine and liquor storage area behind the restaurant," he said. After another minute's drive the cart stopped, and Rifkin led the way past a dozen agents into the building, then into a large room with wine racks on three sides and shelving on the other. Thousands of bottles of wine and spirits were in the racks and shelves, and there was a large pile of cardboard boxes in the middle of the floor, all opened. A man in a heavy, helmeted suit was examining a small suitcase on top of a stack of boxes. He did something to it, and the lid fell open, exposing a metal panel.

"Oh, shit," Rifkin said under his breath.

The suited man reached into the case and came out with an object, then he noticed the crowd behind him. "Get the fuck out of here, all of you!" he yelled. His voice was muffled by the helmet. "We've got a couple of pounds of plastique here, and I want every human being at least a hundred yards from this building!"

"Turn on your radio, Jim!" Rifkin yelled, then he started hustling everybody out of the room. He, Stone, and Mike got into the cart and headed back up the hill, where they parked behind the reception building. Rifkin picked up his radio. "Jim? Do you read?"

"Yeah, I read," Jim replied. "I'm going to need a few minutes to go over this thing and try and figure out how to deal with it."

"Is there a timer?"

"Yeah, but it's not running," he replied. "If it starts running, I'm running, too. I'll get back to you."

The three men sat in the cart silently for a couple of minutes. Finally, Mike spoke. "This one isn't nuclear," he said. "Too small."

"I agree," Rifkin replied.

"I hope you both know what you're talking about," Stone said.

Rifkin spoke up. "I did a week's intensive course on bomb making and disposal," he said. "I'll bet I can tell you exactly how this one is put together."

"Okay, shoot," Stone said.

"It's pretty simple: there's a timer attached to a detonator, like a blasting cap, which is shoved into the plastique. Somebody starts the timer, and when it hits zero, the detonator goes off, exploding the plastique. If there's a couple of pounds of the stuff, like Jim says, it will take down that entire building and damage others nearby, and it will kill nearly everybody in the building."

"Nearly everybody?" Stone asked.

"Somebody always gets lucky."

The radio crackled. "Steve?"

"I'm here, Jim."

"Okay, I've isolated the plastique, and the device doesn't seem to be booby-trapped. There's a T-shaped key with a hexagonal tip, like a drill bit, and there are three positions: up, right, and left. I can't tell which position fires it, so I'm going to try them all."

"Jim . . ."

"Don't worry, it's just a blasting cap—the plastique is across the room. Stand by."

A moment later there was a noise like a large firecracker.

Jim came back on the radio. "I found the firing position," he said. "You can come back in now."

They took the cart down the hill again, got out, and went inside. Jim had taken his helmet off, and there was a large black spot covering the chest of his suit. "It's simple," he said, "but very professionally made." He held up the key, then inserted it into a slot. "Neutral position, off," he said, then he turned the key. "Right position, timer." He tapped a keypad, and the timer started to run. Jim turned the key all the way to the left. "Left position, immediate detonation. Suicide."

Rifkin took the key from him and examined it. "I could make this in my home shop," he said.

"You could make the whole device in your home shop," Jim replied. He closed the small case, picked it up, then walked to the cube of plastique and picked it up. "I want to get this back to my shop and take it apart," he said. Then one toe of the heavy suit caught the corner of a box, and he stumbled. The plastique flew from his hand and landed on the tile floor. "Oops," he said. "Don't worry, guys; it needs a detonator to blow."

"That wasn't funny, Jim," Rifkin said.

An agent came over. "Boss," he said, "we've finished our search. The bomb was in a wooden wine crate, and we've opened every other crate or box in the room."

"What about the rest of the hotel?" Rifkin asked.

"We're done—every conceivable hiding place."

"Okay, stand down and tell the crew to go home

but to remain on call. Nobody turns off his cell phone."

"Yes, sir."

Rifkin led Stone and Mike back to the cart, and they started up the hill, then stopped at Stone's cottage.

"Steve, can I offer you a drink?" Stone asked.

"I wish I could, Stone, but I'm not having a drink until this weekend is over and both presidents are on their respective airplanes."

Mike spoke up. "Wynken, Blynken, and Nod," he said.

"What?" Rifkin asked.

"That's only one bomb—there could be two more."

"Maybe," Rifkin said, "but not in this hotel. And if another one shows up, we'll find it."

"I hope you're right," Mike said. They got out of the cart, and Rifkin reached into his pocket. "Here's a present for you," he said, handing the bomb key to Mike, then he drove away.

"I hope he's right, too," Stone said.

42

Holly Barker had been working almost nonstop since her arrival in L.A., assisting Kate Lee during the security discussions with President Vargas and Mexico's head of national intelligence. The only break she had had was drinks at Stone's cottage on the evening of her arrival. Now everybody had initialed the draft of the security agreement, and it was being edited and translated for signing at the closing ceremony. Holly wanted out of the presidential cottage. She called Stone's cell number.

"Yes?"

"It's Holly."

"How are you? I haven't seen you since cocktails."

"I've been working eighteen hours a day, and I am now experiencing an extreme case of cabin fever."

"Sounds like what you need is a change of cabins."

"That and at least one drink, followed by, ah, exercise."

"Is now too soon?"

"Nope."

"Come through the garden gate—it will be open, as will the French doors to my suite."

Stone put down the book he had been trying to read, Chernow's biography of George Washington, and checked the little bar for the proper ingredients, which were a bottle of Knob Creek and ice.

There was a scratch on the French doors, and Holly swept in. "Hallelujah!" she exclaimed. "Free again." She lavished a kiss on Stone for half a minute, then broke. "Bourbon whiskey, please," she said, kicking off her shoes.

Stone poured two and handed her one.

"To the completion of negotiations," she said, raising her glass.

"Congratulations," Stone replied, and they each took a large bite of bourbon. "All done?"

"It's being prepared for signatures as we speak," she said. "I can't say the same for the presidents' discussions, but I understand there are only a couple of sticking points."

"How much time have you got?" he asked, kissing her on the neck and scratching a nipple.

"An hour and three minutes before I have to

attend a video intelligence briefing from Langley with my mistress."

"Then let's not waste any of it," Stone said. Seconds later they were in bed and in each other's arms.

"I'm surprised Felicity Devonshire is over here, sniffing around," Holly said.

"Jealousy? I like that. Don't you like her?"

"She's just a little too perfect," Holly said, feeling for him. "Never a hair out of place."

"An admirable quality," Stone observed, growing in her hand.

"And one that I should cultivate?" Holly asked, archly.

"Nah, I like a hair out of place now and then."

Holly rolled him onto his back and mounted him. "Aaaaah," she breathed, "that's where you belong."

"No argument here," he replied, thrusting. "Have you noticed that each of us still has a glass of bourbon in hand?"

"Then this is a first," she said, taking a gulp.

Stone raised his head and managed to get a swallow down without spilling it. "An historic moment," he said. Stone held his chilly glass against a breast.

"Yipe!"

"Sorry." He raised his head again and warmed the nipple in his mouth.

"That's better." She reached behind her and took his testicles in her glass-chilled hand.

"Wow!" Stone said, and he felt a climax rising. "If you're going to come with me, you'd better do it now."

"I'm with you," she said, then they both experienced the ecstatic paroxysms of orgasm. Finally, she leaned down and kissed him again. "And we didn't spill a drop," she said, polishing off the drink.

Stone finished his and they rolled sideways without separating. "This is good," he said.

"It doesn't get any better," she replied. "Gone are long hours of discussing cross-border intelligence exchanges." She contracted her abdominal muscles, squeezing him.

"Oh! Do that forty or fifty more times."

"I'm afraid I'm spent," she replied.

"I'm well spent," he said. "Normally sex renders me unconscious, but I have the sneaking suspicion that more is going to be expected of me."

"More, more, more," she said.

"Don't I get some recovery time?"

"As I recall, you've never needed much." She squeezed him again.

"I think I'm getting the message," he said.

"Then, like the song says, 'Do it again.'"

And he did.

43

Scarcely a hundred yards away, another couple was locked in an unconscious duplication of Stone's and Holly's actions.

Kelli Keane and Hamish McCallister lay, panting, in his bed. After her departure from Harry, at Hamish's whispered invitation, Kelli had returned. It had taken them less than half an hour to complete the seduction ritual before leaping into bed, and now they were entirely satisfied with each other.

"So," Kelli said, by way of conversation, "who are you reporting for?"

"A London paper and a travel magazine, neither of which you have ever heard."

"And they sprang for a suite?"

"You are obsessed with the idea of a suite, aren't you?"

"I'm obsessed with the idea of not having one."

"Well, now you have half a suite for as long as we can put up with each other. And to answer your question, I have discovered that having private means greatly augments the pleasures of reporting for peanuts."

"A rich journalist? I've never heard of such a thing."

"All it takes is selecting the right parents. It also helps that, when they are inevitably divorced, proper support for the issue of the marriage is cemented into the final agreement."

"Which side of your parentage was the rich one?"

"Both of them."

"You are just sounding luckier and luckier," Kelli said, sighing. "Are you married?"

"Certainly not! My principles would not allow me to be in bed with you, if I were. How about you?"

"Nope. Of course, I've been living with a very nice man in a very nice New York apartment for a year, but he isn't here, is he?"

"Nicely rationalized," Hamish replied.

Kelli smiled. "It was, wasn't it? Is there any more of the champagne?"

Hamish leaned over the side of the bed and came back with half a bottle and their two glasses. "There you are," he said, pouring.

Kelli sipped. "Ah, yes, champagne. I can never seem to get enough of it."

"There are two more bottles in my fridge," Hamish said, "courtesy of the management."

Kelli looked over by the windows. "What happened to your steamer trunk?"

"I unpacked it, and a bellman took it away for storage until my departure."

"What do you travel with that you need a trunk?"

"Habitually, four suits, a dinner jacket, tails on some occasions, a blazer, two tweed jackets, a dozen shirts and a dozen each of socks and underwear, six pairs of shoes, two hats, a jewelry box, a toiletries case, and enough neckties to choke a very large horse. Also, depending on the weather at my destination, a trench coat or an overcoat or both."

"That explains the trunk," Kelli said.

"I believe it does. The simple truth is, you can take as much luggage as you wish, anywhere in the world, as long as you are prepared to pay a baggage overcharge or bribe a ticket agent—and tip well."

"I never thought of it that way," Kelli said. "I'm always just trying to jam my carry-on into the overhead bin."

"Poor darling, you must learn to be more extravagant; you'd be much happier."

"I must learn to earn enough to be extravagant," she replied.

"That is entirely unnecessary," Hamish replied. "You must simply do a better job of choosing men."

"I hate to say it, but you have a point," Kelli said. "Take my present beau: he's handsome, charming, well educated, well housed, and well employed, but he's not rich—not until he comes into his inheritance, anyway—and that might require a wait of some years or, perhaps, murder."

"He does have *most* of the qualifications."

"What else must he have?"

"A generosity of spirit and an absence of parsimony."

"Ah, well. How would you define an absence of parsimony?"

"Before a man can be generous with you, he must first be generous with himself. Then, if he is paying three thousand pounds for a Savile Row suit, two hundred for a Jermyn Street shirt, and two thousand a pair for shoes, he cannot, in good conscience, deprive his woman of similar accoutrements. He cannot travel in first class and expect her to occupy steerage."

"Ah, so I should encourage him to dress more expensively and travel better?"

"Certainly. Then, as the night follows the day . . ."

"You're an eminently sensible man, Hamish."

"And of course, the frequency of and competency in sex must be sustained at a high level."

"No objections there," Kelli said. "More often, my men have been unable to keep up."

Hamish laughed.

"I don't suppose you would care to form a more lasting bond than a one-nighter in a grand hotel?"

"We can talk about that," Hamish replied, swinging his legs over the side of the bed. "Excuse me, call of nature."

Kelli looked around. "Where can I find a robe?"

"Closet," Hamish replied, closing the bathroom door.

Kelli got out of bed and approached the closet, of which there were two. She chose the left and found herself staring at a steamer trunk.

Then there was singing coming from the bathroom, in a language she did not understand.

44

Herbie Fisher and his girl, Harp Connor, got off their airplane at LAX and hoofed it to baggage claim, where they found a small booth emblazoned with the name THE ARRINGTON. Minutes later they were ensconced in a Bentley, headed for the hotel.

Herbie called Stone Barrington's cell number.

"Hello, Herb, welcome to L.A. Where are you?"

"On the way from the airport. Be there in, I don't know, twenty minutes?"

"It's going to take longer than that, pal. Getting through the front gate is going to take a while and may require a cavity search."

"Are you serious?"

"Almost. We've got two presidents in residence. Come for dinner tonight?"

"Love to. How are we dressing?"

"We're doing it New York style—wear a necktie. Oh, and there's a secret guest of honor."

"Who's that?"

"Didn't I just say it's a secret? Drinks at seven. Ask your bellman to show you my cottage on the site map. See ya!" Stone hung up.

"We're invited for dinner, and there's a secret guest of honor," Herbie said to Harp.

"Who?"

"Didn't I just say it's a secret? Listen, Stone managed to get us into the hotel on short notice, but it will be a room, not a suite, and it may be small."

"I can live with that," Harp replied. "I'm a simple woman. All I need is a closet, a bed, a bathtub, and a minibar."

"I expect you'll have all of that, and if there's no minibar, there's always room service. Oh, by the way, security will be severe at the gate, so expect, maybe, a cavity search."

"Promises, promises."

They were received at reception with apologies for the lack of more luxurious accommodations, then driven in an electric cart to their room, which had a very nice view of a stucco wall around someone else's patio.

The bellman handed Herbie the key to the

golf cart. "Compliments of Mr. Barrington," he said.

"Could you give me directions to his house?"

The man unfolded the hotel map and pointed out the Barrington cottage, then he left, having been rewarded with a very good tip.

"Pretty nice," Harp said, looking around.

"It's where they put the help, like corporate pilots," Herbie explained.

Harp unpacked everything and put her things in the closet and chest of drawers provided, then kicked her cases under the bed.

"I'm impressed," Herbie said, looking around.

"This way we have more space," she replied, and Herbie followed suit.

"What should I wear to dinner?" she asked.

"I've been instructed to wear a necktie, and presumably, a suit. An LBD should do."

"An LBD it is," Harp replied, inspecting the minibar and retrieving two tiny bottles of Chivas Regal.

"Are those both for you, or may I have one?" Herbie asked.

Harp poured them into separate glasses and handed him one. They toasted, then she reached behind and unzipped her dress. "Now," she said, "I believe you promised me a cavity search."

Herbie and Harp arrived at Stone's cottage at ten past seven, and were met at the door by their host.

"Come and meet everybody," he said. He led them into the living room. "You know Dino and Viv, of course, but you haven't met my son, Peter, his girl, Hattie, and Dino's son, Ben, and his girl, Emma." Then he turned toward a tall, blond beauty in a knockout dress. "And this is Hattie's guest, Immi Gotham."

Herbie went weak in the knees but managed to shake her hand. Harp was more composed. "Like everybody else, I'm a great admirer of your work," she said.

"Immi is giving a concert tomorrow night," Stone explained, "and Hattie, on piano, is going to open for her, and later, accompany Immi for her encore."

"I can't wait," Herbie said, accepting a scotch from a waiter.

"I understand you're an attorney with Stone's firm in New York," Immi said.

"That is correct," Herbie replied. "Stone was my mentor and role model."

"I'm going to be buying a place in New York soon," Immi said, "and Stone is going to help me with the legal work."

"I'm sure the whole firm will be standing in line to help you," Herbie replied.

"And, Harp," Immi said, "I understand you're a private eye?"

"For lack of a better term," Harp replied.

"I'll let you know if I need any private eyeing," the actress said.

The doorbell rang. "Excuse me, we're quite a crowd tonight. It's going to be a buffet." Stone went to answer the door and came back with Felicity Devonshire, Holly Barker, and the president and first lady.

Herbie and Harp, having been surprised to meet Ms. Gotham, were now stunned and nearly speechless.

"I hope your talks went well," Stone said to Will Lee.

"Indeed they did. We're signing our agreement tomorrow morning, and then I'm on vacation for a couple of days."

"You deserve it," Stone said.

The president and first lady fell into conversation with Immi Gotham, and Holly managed to cut Stone from the herd and get him in a corner.

"I heard about the gloves," she said.

"Yes, that was disturbing."

"Fortunately, the bomb specialist's lab was unable to detect any trace of radiation."

"Let's hope they were being used as oven mitts," Stone said.

"How did this come about?"

"The NSA managed to locate the site, an apartment in Palo Alto, and Mike Freeman's people searched it and found the gloves. This fellow Shazaz had apparently been living there and made some bombs, one of which, as you've probably heard, was found in the wine storage room today."

"Yes, but what was that name again?"

"Shazaz? I think that's it."

Holly blanched. "First name?"

"Mo, for Mohammad." Stone looked at her closely. "Is something wrong?

"Excuse me," Holly said, "I need to talk to the first lady."

45

Holly stood at the edge of the group around Immi Gotham, waiting for a moment to get Kate Lee away from them. Finally, as a waiter invaded the crowd with a tray of canapés, she was able to touch Kate's elbow. The two retreated to a corner.

"Don't look so concerned," Kate said, smiling, "you'll scare everybody."

Holly forced the frown away from her face. "Something disturbing has just arisen," she said, then she told Kate about the name. "Does Hamish have any siblings?" she asked.

Kate's smile had disappeared. "As I recall, after his parents were divorced his father remarried and had a son and a daughter, so they would be some years younger than Hamish. Why don't you call Langley and have them run their names?"

"Apparently, the brother's first name was Mo, short for Mohammad, but I don't know the girl's name."

"Well, see what you can come up with."

Holly excused herself, went into the study, and called Langley. Twenty minutes later, she returned, and the first lady rejoined her.

"There's nothing on them," she said. "There were hits on the father's name, but that's it."

"Did the search produce anyone else at all named Shazaz?"

"No."

"Try to get in touch with Hamish," Kate said. "Ask him for the whereabouts of his brother for the last month. If he can give us that, we'll have something to go on."

"Right," Holly replied. She went back to the study and called the number she had for Hamish. There was a long pause before she was connected.

"Hello?"

"Hamish?"

"Yes."

"Encode."

There was some electronic noise, then Hamish came back. "Is that you, Holly?"

"Yes. Something has come up."

"How can I help?"

"I understand you have a half brother."

"Mo? Yes."

"Do you know where he has been for the past thirty days?"

"Yes, he was at my family's home on the Scottish isle of Murk, south of the Hebrides."

"For the entire period?"

"Until recently."

"Do you know where he is now?"

"Yes, he's at Annabel's, a London nightclub, sitting right across the table from me. Would you like to speak with him?"

"Ah, no. Was there any break between his time in Scotland and tonight?"

"Only travel time. He arrived by train yesterday."

"I see."

"What is your interest in my half brother?" Hamish asked.

"Tell me, is Shazaz a common name?"

"It's not uncommon, at least, not in the Middle East."

"Has your brother ever visited the United States?"

"He attended a boys' school in Virginia for a semester, when he was eight, but he was unhappy there, so he returned to England and completed his education here."

"Is he an observant Muslim?"

"Yes, but not radically so. I mean, at this moment he is consuming a glass of champagne. I would say he is about as observant as I."

Holly couldn't think of anything else to ask. She ended the call and went back to the living room, where people were starting to move into the garden for the buffet dinner, and found the first lady.

Kate listened intently to Holly's report of her conversation with Hamish. "Well," she said, "maybe it's just a coincidence, if the name is not uncommon in the Middle East."

"I remember that Hamish's mother's family has a home—a castle, I think—on a Scottish island," Holly said.

"Yes, that's correct." She was quiet for a moment, looking up at the stars, then she turned back to Holly. "May I borrow your Agency phone?" she asked. She walked away toward the light coming from the living room, dialed a number, and spoke to someone.

"Who was on the phone?" Kelli Keane asked.

"Just an acquaintance."

"Why did you say you were at Annabel's?"

Hamish smiled. "Because she's in L.A., and if she knew I was here, well . . ."

"She would be displacing me in bed?"

Hamish turned toward her and took her in his arms. "No chance of that at all," he said.

Kate came back and handed Holly her phone. "Thank you. I've had Langley track Hamish's phone, and it puts him in Berkeley Square, London."

Hamish went into the bathroom, taking his phone with him. He pressed a speed dial button, and the phone took a moment to connect.

"Yes?"

"It is I. Where are you parked?"

"Just outside Annabel's."

"Wait one hour, then go back to my address and park the car outside the house."

"It will be done."

Hamish flushed the toilet, then went back into the bedroom. "Where were we?" he asked, jumping into bed.

46

Stone took his plate and went to sit by Dino. Viv was in deep conversation with Immi Gotham a few yards away.

"I'm sorry I haven't seen much of you the past couple of days," Stone said.

"Not your fault, pal. I've been pretty busy myself."

"And I don't blame you a bit," Stone said. "Viv is a knockout."

"Okay, so what the fuck is going on around here? What have you and Mike and that Secret Service dick been up to?"

"You got something against the Secret Service?"

"I've got something against all feds," Dino replied. "Every time I've tried to work with them I've gotten fucked."

"Well, there is that."

"You didn't answer my question," Dino pointed out.

"Would you believe me if I told you you wouldn't want to know?"

"Half of what I know I didn't want to know."

"You probably noticed a lot of security around here—I mean, more than when we arrived."

"Yeah, I noticed."

"Well, they searched the whole property, and they found a bomb in a wine storage room adjacent to the main restaurant."

"What kind of bomb?"

"Both simple and sophisticated, the expert said. A kilo or two of plastique."

"Since we're sitting here having dinner with the president, my guess is they disarmed it."

"Right, but there may be two more. Not here, because the place has been ransacked, but somewhere. They may try to get them onto the grounds."

"I hear they're practically strip-searching every arrival."

"That's true, so if the bombs are not here, it's a pretty sure thing that they're not going to be."

Dino nodded. "Is there anything else you want to tell me?"

"Why do you ask?"

"Because you look like you know something you don't want anybody else to know."

"Am I that transparent?"

"Come on, are you kidding me? Should I be running for a flight out of here?"

"I think the answer to your question is right over there," Stone said, nodding in the direction of the president, "eating fried chicken with his fingers."

"I always thought that was the best way," Dino said. "I mean, if you're gonna eat fried chicken. And if he feels safe, so I and mine should feel safe?"

"You see the young man talking to the president?"

"I think I recognize him. He's related to you, isn't he?"

"He is. And if I thought he weren't safe, he would be on a plane back to New York, along with the rest of us."

Peter Barrington sat on the sofa next to the president of the United States and ate his fried chicken with his fingers.

"You know," Will Lee said, "I've got a son—stepson, really—who's a little older than you. His name is Peter, too."

"I heard that," Peter replied. "I heard he slipped up and went to Harvard."

Lee laughed and handed his plate to a passing waiter, then wiped his hands carefully. "Our Peter sent us a copy of your film, *Autumn Kill*. Kate and

I thought it was terrific, and I couldn't believe a student did it."

"Thank you, sir," Peter replied.

"How much of it was true?"

Peter shrugged. "Well, nobody has sued me yet, though I hear it caused quite a stir at my old school. It was based on rumors, really, kind of a legend that gets handed down from class to class. I filled in a lot of blanks, just made up stuff, but the reaction made me think I might have guessed right." Peter wiped his fingers, and a waiter took his plate and the president's napkin.

"You're at Yale Drama, right?"

"That's right. Ben Bacchetti and I are, anyway. Hattie, whom you met, is studying composition at the School of Music."

"I hear she's quite a pianist."

"You'll hear her tomorrow night. She's going to open the concert and do a number with Ms. Gotham, too."

"That will be quite a showcase for her," Lee said. "Don't let her go all Hollywood on you."

Peter laughed. "We're all going to go Hollywood next year. We're going to have a production deal at Centurion Studios and make our own movies. Ben will produce, Hattie will score them, and I'll write and direct. Oh, and I haven't told Dad about it yet, so keep it under your hat, will you?"

"Don't worry, I'm accustomed to keeping secrets," Lee said.

"By the way, congratulations on your agreement with President Vargas. It's already on MSNBC."

"Thank you, Peter. It's just one more box to check off before my term ends."

"What are you going to do then?"

"I'm going to go back to Meriwether County, Georgia, and write my memoirs. I have to—the publishing deal is already done. And by the way, keep that under your hat until you hear about it on the news, which won't be long."

"I'll look forward to reading it," Peter said.

"And I'll look forward to seeing more of your movies."

Dino sidled over and caught Viv by herself for a moment. "How you doing?"

"Just great, thanks. You know, that Immi is quite a nice lady."

"I noticed that for the last twenty years," Dino said.

"What are you doing over here talking to me, when you could be talking to her?" Viv asked.

"I just wanted to tell you something."

"I always like to know something."

"Something might happen here that will come as a surprise."

"Pleasant or unpleasant?"

"I'm pessimistic."

"So what is it?"

"I can't tell you that."

"You said you were going to tell me *something*. That was nothing."

"I can't tell you, because Stone wouldn't tell me."

"Why not?"

"I don't know, but I know Stone well enough to know that if he could've, he would've."

Viv sighed. "Sheesh, you guys!"

47

Holly finished her fried chicken and called Langley again, asking for a position on Hamish McCallister.

"Stand by," the officer said. Then, a moment later, "Got it. Position is now Chelsea, right by the river."

"Do you have a home address for him?" Holly asked.

A brief silence. "Negative, I have nothing. When I run the name a note comes up saying, 'Contact the office of the director.' That's you, isn't it?"

"Right," Holly said. "Thanks." She hung up and went to find Kate Lee.

Kate was standing by the pool, talking to Stone, and Holly gently pulled her aside. "Do you know where Hamish McCallister lives?"

"In London," Kate replied, "when he's not traveling."

"Where in London?"

"He has a house on the Chelsea Embankment—very expensive neighborhood."

"By the River Thames?"

"Good guess. What's going on, Holly?"

"I don't know, exactly. I'm just very concerned to hear that Hamish has a half brother whose name has come up in a search for a bomb factory in this country."

"I agree, that's not happy news. My recollection, though, is that Hamish and his brother are not close, having grown up in different families."

"Is that what Hamish told you?"

"It's what Dick Stone told me."

"I called Hamish after you and I talked earlier. He told me that he was at Annabel's, in London. A position track confirmed that."

"Good."

"But when I asked him about the whereabouts of his brother, Mohammad, he told me that Mo was sitting across the table from him, drinking champagne, and that Mo had spent the past month at the McCallister place on the Isle of Murk, having just arrived from there by train yesterday. That raises the question: if they're not close and were raised by different families, why is Mo spending a month at a time on Murk with a family that is not his?"

Kate frowned. "I can't come up with even a hypothetical answer to that question. Call London and have them investigate the whereabouts of Mo."

"Yes, ma'am," Holly said. She went back to the study and called the CIA station at the American Embassy in London.

A woman answered. "Please state your business."

"This is Assistant Director Holly Barker. What time is it in London?"

"Seven a.m.," the woman replied.

"Is the station chief in his office at this hour?"

"He gets in at seven. I'll connect you." There was a click, then a pause.

"Good morning, Holly, this is Tom Riley."

"Good morning, Tom. Scramble, please."

There was some noise on the line, then, "We're scrambled."

"I'm calling from Los Angeles, where the director is traveling with her husband, and we need a position check on somebody, stat. His name is Mohammad Shazaz, known as Mo." She spelled it for him. "He was alleged to have been at Annabel's an hour or two ago, and for the month before that, visiting a prominent family called McCallister, on the Scottish isle of Murk."

"Got it," Riley said. "Do we know him?"

"We know his half brother, Hamish McCallister, who is our asset, reporting directly to the director's office."

"The director has an asset in the U.K. that's reporting not to me but directly to her?"

"That is correct. It was approved by Dick Stone. I'd also like a position check on Mr. McCallister. His Agency phone locator puts him currently at his house on the Chelsea Embankment, London. If that is correct, Mr. Shazaz may be staying with him."

"We'll start there," Riley said, having apparently gotten over the fact that his boss had bypassed him in running an asset.

"Thank you. Are you reading my cell number?"

"Yes, I've got it."

"It's eleven p.m. in L.A. Call me, no matter how late it is."

"Will do." Riley hung up.

There was a knock at the door, and Felicity Devonshire poked her head in. "Are you receiving company?"

"Sure," Holly said, "come on in." Felicity took a seat next to her on the sofa. "I think there's some brandy over there," Holly said, nodding toward a bookcase. "Can I get you one?"

"A small one, please," Felicity replied.

Holly walked across the room and poked around a row of books until a panel came down, revealing a fully stocked bar. She returned to the sofa with a bottle of Rémy Martin and two snifters. She set them on the table. "You decide what a small one is."

Felicity poured herself a stiff cognac, and Holly followed suit. "There's something in the air," Felicity said. "Anything I can help with?"

Holly took a sip of her brandy. "Now that you mention it, yes. Can you call your service and see what, if anything, you have on a Mohammad Shazaz, called Mo?"

"Certainly," Felicity said, reaching into her handbag for her phone. "Just give me a moment." She pressed a button. "Architect here," she said. "Director of records, please." After issuing instructions, she hung up. "There. Shouldn't take long."

"We haven't had much of a chance to talk," Holly said.

"Busy, busy, both of us."

"I was looking forward to a little R and R when the agreement was signed, but now I don't know."

"I suspect you're talking about the discovery of the bomb earlier today, and about Wynken, Blynken, and Nod."

Holly nodded. "My best guess is that one of them is connected to the bomb and that the other two are lurking somewhere nearby."

"That seems a logical conclusion," Felicity said. "But after today's search of the property, it would seem that they haven't got the other two on the property. Yet."

"You think they're going to try?"

"One would suppose."

"Your people at GCHQ picked up some of the same e-mails as NSA did, didn't they?"

"That is so."

"You know what bothers me about that?"

"Tell me."

"It's too easy."

Felicity took a sip of brandy. "How so?"

"I mean, if you were running three operatives in a foreign location, would you pick easily connected names for them? Say, Tom, Dick, and Harry?"

"Or Wynken, Blynken, and Nod? That would be rather poor tradecraft, wouldn't it?"

"It's so stupid, it would have to be deliberate," Holly said.

48

Holly and Felicity had nearly finished their cognac when Felicity's phone rang. "Yes?" She listened intently. "You've checked every database? Thank you." She hung up and turned to Holly. "We don't know him."

Holly sighed. "How has this person, who we know exists, eluded both our services' attention until the past couple of weeks?"

"Holly, there are zillions of people on earth that we have no record of. Maybe in the next century or two we'll know everything about everybody, but not yet."

Holly's phone rang. "Barker."

"It's Tom Riley. Scramble." They both scrambled.

"Okay, shoot," Holly said, putting her phone on speaker so Felicity could hear.

"A Bentley Mulsanne registered to Hamish McCallister is parked outside a house on the Chelsea Embankment, with a neighborhood parking permit stuck to the windshield, also registered to McCallister. A housemaid entered and a couple of tradespeople have been seen to come and go. We sent two operatives to the front door, posing as Mormon missionaries. The door was answered by a uniformed butler who said that Mr. McCallister was not at home, which in butlerese means he might be there but isn't receiving callers. Our 'missionaries' tried to engage the butler further, but he closed the door in their faces."

"So we don't know who's in the house, besides a butler and a housemaid?"

"We called the house, which has an unlisted number, posing as alumni relations from Christchurch College, Oxford, and asked for Hamish. The butler said he was not at home. That's it. If we want to know, fast, who's in the house, nothing short of phoning in a false fire alarm is available, and that might get more of Mr. McCallister's attention than we want."

"Anything on the presence of Mo on the Isle of Murk?"

"One of our people phoned the post office on the isle, posing as a Ministry of Posts and Telegraphs official, and inquired about mail deliveries to the house. The postmistress said that the post delivered had seemed routine for the past month, nothing addressed to a Shazaz. The most interesting delivery to the house was a package from Paxton & Whitfield, a well-known London cheese shop, marked 'Perishables enclosed. Kindly deliver without delay.' The evidence will probably have been consumed by now."

"So we don't know if Mo was there or if he wasn't?"

"Correct."

"Did you find out anything at all about the man?"

"A birth certificate, records of graduation from Eton and Oxford, a British driving license, no photograph. His address is the same as his brother's, no employer stated on his tax returns, so he must have a private income. We haven't been able to locate a photograph since he left Eton—none at Oxford—and he's never made the papers or been arrested, except for two speeding tickets on the M4 motorway, four and seven years ago, both promptly paid. He's a member of Annabel's, Mark's Club, Harry's Bar, and George, all founded by Mark Burley, deceased, now owned by his heirs. He has charge accounts at Harrods, Fortnum & Mason, Kilgour, French & Stanbury tailors, Turnbull & Asser shirtmakers, and John Lobb bootmakers. Clean credit record. All this adds up to an overprivileged upper-class twit, except that his father was Syrian and his mother Egyptian, both deceased."

"Good job, Tom, thank you. Please stay on locating Mo and call with any news."

"Will do." He hung up.

Holly pressed the end button. "I'm surprised your people didn't have any of that," she said to Felicity.

"You asked what we had, not what we could find out," Felicity replied archly. "Still, your people did very well in the course of a single brandy."

"They did, didn't they? I'm pleased."

"You should be—that would have taken my lot half a day."

"Algernon," Holly said.

"What?"

"The signer of the e-mails. He's running Wynken, Blynken, and Nod, and he doesn't care if we find them, as long as it takes our eye off the ball— off him, Algernon."

"In that case, you're unlikely to find the trio alive."

"Are you thinking suicide bombs?"

Felicity shook her head. "The only suiciders al Qaeda has used in the States are the 9/11 hijackers. I think it's more likely that Algernon will erase the three himself when he's done with them. If caught, they might identify him."

"It bothers me that we haven't found out who brought in the bomb found in the wine storage room."

"I expect the Secret Service are working that very hard. They'll be interviewing the restaurant and kitchen staff."

"I suppose it could have been brought onto the premises by somebody delivering wine or booze," Holly said. "Which will make him harder to find."

"I don't know," Felicity said, "I think it might more likely be an inside person, who brought the item in and hid it. Otherwise, some worker might have stumbled on it while unpacking bottles."

At that moment, Special Agent Steve Rifkin was sitting in The Arrington's main restaurant with two of his agents and a list of food and beverage staff. "And you've interviewed all of these?" he asked, holding up the list.

"Every one," an agent replied.

"How did you classify them?"

"We didn't. We just talked to everyone, in alphabetical order."

"Let's take another look at this," Rifkin said. "I think that whoever brought the device in is more likely to be in a supervisory position, because he knew where to put the bomb where it wouldn't be found before he needed it."

"I guess that makes sense."

"All right, then," Rifkin said, handing the man back his list, "eliminate all the waiters, bartenders, busboys, dishwashers, and cooks from your list, and let's see who we have left."

The two men divided the list between them and went to work, crossing out names. After a few minutes, they handed back the list to Rifkin. "We're down to a dozen," one of them said.

"Now, let's eliminate everyone who does not deal directly with wines and spirits."

That took another minute. "In this building, three," he said. "The restaurant manager, the head-waiter, and the chief bartender, who oversees all the bars."

"Read me a profile of each of them," Rifkin said.

"All right," an agent said, consulting his notes. "Restaurant manager, Enzo Pagani, born Naples, fifty-six years ago, came to New York at eighteen, worked his way up from busboy to maître d' over twenty-odd years, worked two years in that position at a Las Vegas casino, promoted to restaurant manager, then hired out of there by The Arrington."

"Did he apply?"

The agent looked at his notes. "No, they approached him."

"He's not our guy," Rifkin said. "How about the headwaiter?"

"Pierre du Bois, born Marseilles, forty-nine

years ago, came to U.S. as a child, to New Orleans, long career in restaurants there, then hired from Commander's Palace by The Arrington."

"Not our guy," Rifkin said. "Who is the other one?"

"Chief bartender, Michael Gennaro. Born U.S. of Italian parents thirty-eight years ago, worked in his family's restaurant in Studio City since childhood, doing pretty much everything. Applied to the Beverly Hills Hotel eight years ago for a bartender's job, then came to The Arrington, answered an ad in a restaurant trade magazine for a bartender's job, got hired as chief bartender."

"That's interesting," Rifkin said, "that he got hired for a bigger job than they advertised for. I don't think he's our guy, either, but find out more about him fast. Start with the guy who hired him. And find out what his religion is."

"How are we going to do that?" an agent asked. "They can't ask for that information on an employment application."

"Ask Michael Gennaro," Rifkin said.

The two agents got up and left the room. Rifkin looked at his watch; he was hungry. He got up and went in search of food.

49

Steve Rifkin had already talked to the food and beverage manager; now he was staring across the table at Michael Gennaro, the chief bartender. Rifkin looked for trembling, rapid respiration, sweat on the brow or lip, and rapid blinking. Nothing: cool, calm, and collected. He gave Gennaro a little smile. "Good morning," he said.

Gennaro returned the little smile. "Good morning."

"My name is Steve Rifkin. May I call you Michael?"

"Sure."

"Your boss has given you a glowing report," Rifkin said. "First, he liked the way your job interview went, then he liked the way you've done the job he gave you."

"I've hardly done it yet," Gennaro said. "Our

first guests are just arriving, and nobody's asked for a drink, so far."

"I guess not," Rifkin said, chuckling appreciatively. He looked at Gennaro's employment application. "I guess you know just about everything about restaurants, don't you?"

"I guess you could say that."

"Why did you leave the family business?"

"I had two older brothers who wouldn't go first."

"No room at the top, huh?"

"And my father is still running the place."

"No room at even nearly the top."

"You got it. A friend of mine introduced me to the Beverly Hills Hotel operation, and it worked."

"But not in the restaurant end?"

"The bar is in the restaurant end," Gennaro replied.

"What would your next logical promotion there have been?"

"Maybe maître d', but I'd have had to wait for the owner of that position to die—he would never have retired."

"So you applied for a bartender's job at The Arrington?"

"Not really. I was aiming for a managerial job."

"So you invented one for yourself."

"I showed them how I could be more useful in a supervisory position."

"So what's your next promotion possibility here?"

"Maître d', if the owner of that job dies. He's only fifty-six."

"Nothing else?"

"Sure, food and beverage manager. I mean, my boss isn't going anywhere, but in a new hotel, things are fluid. He might get promoted."

"An astute observation. You have access to the wine and spirits storage room, don't you?"

"I'm in charge of it," Gennaro replied. "Word is, you found something illegal in there."

"You might say that," Rifkin replied. "Any idea what it was?"

"I heard a guy came out of there in what looked like a diving suit. Lobsters?"

Rifkin laughed. "I'll bet you know what that suit was."

Gennaro shrugged. "I go to the movies, I watch TV."

"Tell me, Michael, you're a bright guy—speculate for me how whatever he found in there got in there."

Gennaro tilted his head back and stared at the ceiling, then he looked back at Rifkin. "How big was it?"

Rifkin held his hands out to demonstrate.

"No bigger than a case of wine, then? My guess would be that a supplier's delivery man brought it

in there on a hand truck with several cases of wine
or liquor."

"Any idea of which supplier?"

"We buy from four suppliers: I give them a list
of what we want, and they bid. I always take the
lowest price for, say, a case of Absolut Vodka or
Knob Creek bourbon."

"Same for the wines?"

"Yes, but if we specify a wine and a vintage, all
four might not have it. If I don't get a low enough
bid, then I go to the Internet before I accept, then
the delivery would be made by UPS."

"What else do you do on the Internet, Michael?"

Gennaro tilted his head to one side in thought.
"Shopping for clothes, shoes, sex toys, household
appliances. I use Google to look for stuff."

"E-mail?"

"Yeah, but not so much."

"Why not?"

"I guess I don't have all that many friends. In
this business you work nights. It doesn't lead to an
athletic social life. The cell phone works better for
me."

"How many cell phones do you have?"

A flick of an eyebrow. "Ah, just one, an iPhone."

"Like it?"

"Yeah, it does a lot more than I know how to do
with it."

Rifkin closed the file in front of him. "Well, I

guess that's about it. Thanks for your time, and I hope the job goes well for you here." Rifkin held out his hand.

Gennaro shook it, then got up and took a step toward the door.

"Oh, Michael?"

Gennaro stopped and turned around. "Yeah?"

"What's your religion?" Rifkin saw Gennaro's jaw tighten.

"Catholic," he replied.

"Thanks, Michael." He gave the man a little wave and watched him go. Just before he closed the door he looked back.

Rifkin turned to his two agents, who were sitting at a nearby table. "I want a membership list of every mosque in L.A., starting with Studio City and spreading out from there. I don't care how you get them."

50

Stone and Dino had breakfast on the patio beside the pool. "I don't know what to do with myself today," Stone said. "It's the first time since we arrived that my mind hasn't been full of what I have to do today."

"That sounds like a complaint," Dino said.

"No, just an observation. I don't really want to leave the house today. All the guests are checking in, and it's going to be chaos out there."

"Why chaos? People check into hotels all the time."

"Yes, but not all on the same day and with as much security."

"You have a point."

"The concert tonight will be great," Stone said.

"Viv and I are looking forward to it."

Peter and Ben appeared and joined them.

"Where's Hattie?" Stone asked.

"I couldn't get her up. I think she's nervous about her performance tonight, and sleep postpones having to think about it."

"Hasn't she done a lot of performing?"

"Sure, but this is her first appearance in a professional setting. Before, it was all student stuff."

"I guess that makes sense."

"Dad, Dino, Ben and I have some good news."

"Good news I can always use," Dino said. "Pardon the rhyme."

"You're pardoned, Pop," Ben said.

"So what's the news?" Stone asked.

"The three of us are going to have a production deal at Centurion," Peter said.

Stone looked alarmed. "When?"

"Don't worry, Dad, it's for after we all graduate."

Stone relaxed a little. "What's the deal?"

"We haven't worked that out yet," Peter said, "so I'll want your help on structuring the contract."

"You're going to need showbiz help," Stone said. "Let me talk to Bill Eggers about somebody in the L.A. office who does entertainment law. Leo Goldman is a nice guy, but he's going to be a tough negotiator."

"See? That's just the kind of advice we need."

"So, Ben," Dino said, "you're going to produce?"

"Executive-produce," Ben replied.

"What's the difference?"

"There are often several producers on films, even several executive producers, but that's mostly a billing argument. We're going to run a leaner operation, but I'll still want an experienced line producer to do the day-to-day production work."

"Sounds good."

"And, Peter," Stone said, "you'll write or direct?"

"Both," the boy replied, "though I can see just directing, if somebody comes to us with a good script already written."

"Sounds good."

"What's really good is, Leo showed us Vance's old bungalow, which has been empty since his death, and he's going to redo it for us, to our specifications."

"That sounds wonderful!"

"Yeah, but I don't have any experience with that kind of space planning."

"Why don't you talk to James Rutledge? He was trained as an architect, then he was with *Architectural Digest*, and now he does just the sort of thing you need. You were at the High Cotton Ideas party—did you like that place?"

"Oh, wow, did I!"

"Well, Jim was the designer on that. Get Leo to send you the plans, then send them to Jim for a look."

"He's sending them over today, so I'll call Jim as soon as we're back."

"Can't hurt to start early."

Hattie wandered onto the patio, looking sleepy, and sat down.

"Good morning," Stone said.

"Is it?" Hattie asked, looking at the sky and squinting. "I can't tell."

Stone laughed. "Trust me, it is. Are you all ready for your performance tonight?"

Hattie looked alarmed. "I forgot about that. Don't remind me."

"Relax, you'll do fine."

A waiter appeared and took everybody's breakfast order.

Steve Rifkin had not slept well. He had doubled his crew for the overnight search of The Arrington's theater, where the two presidents would hold their joint signing and press conference at ten a.m., and now he was up early and walking around The Arrington's theater, having a final look for himself.

His search detail leader approached. "Don't worry, boss," he said, "this place is clean."

"We're missing two bombs," Rifkin said.

"I understand that, but I don't think the other two even made it onto the property."

Rifkin looked around. "All right, seal this place—nobody in here that isn't essential to the press conference. There's a list—stick to it."

"Right, boss." The man went away to do his work.

Hamish McCallister arrived at the theater, along with at least a hundred other reporters, each with his credentials hung around his neck. He found a seat in the fourth row of the theater, which was a structure half-embedded in the landscape on the north side of the hotel's grounds. He stood in front of his seat and looked around the big room as his colleagues, many of them recognizable from television, filed into the theater. This, he reflected, would have made a wonderful target for one of his three small bombs, killing the two presidents and most of the media representatives present.

But that was not a worry for Hamish. He didn't need the other two bombs now, and the Secret Service had the other one. The device in the Vuitton steamer trunk would do the work of a thousand of the smaller bombs.

Secret Service agents, a dozen of them with sniffer dogs, wandered the room, making a final check. The dogs hadn't helped find the missing bombs because one was concealed in a place no one would ever look, and the other was in a vehicle that had already been searched several times.

Half the reporters in the room were on their cell phones; the other half were scribbling in their notebooks. Hamish watched them, feeling relaxed and content. His plans were made, and they would be carried out. He took out his throwaway cell phone and sent messages to Wynken and Blynken. He had already made his travel arrangements. He would not need the Cessna Caravan; it was now his backup escape plan. He sent a text to the pilot, instructing him to be ready for takeoff at three p.m.

Then a hush fell over the room as the president of the United States, accompanied by the president of Mexico, entered the theater from stage right and took their seats at a table at the center of the stage.

51

Stone and Dino were sitting with Mike Free-man, watching the presidents' statements, when Steve Rifkin came in, mopping his brow.

"Everything all right?" Mike asked.

"So far, so good. I had to get out of that theater. Standing around waiting for something terrible to happen was just too much."

"Relax," Mike said. "Those two bombs are not on the premises. I think we've satisfied ourselves of that. How's it going down at the front gate?"

"Nobody was supposed to arrive before noon, but they're lined up, waiting to have themselves and their vehicles searched. Pretty soon, they're going to start blowing their horns. What's the president saying?"

"This is good stuff," Stone said. "The Mexicans

have agreed to create a new border guard unit in their army that will patrol their side of the fence, and that will mean a doubling of the number of people looking for illegal crossings."

"Very good," Steve said.

Holly Barker came into the room. "How's it going?" she asked.

Stone brought her up to date.

"May I use the study for a moment?" she asked.

"Help yourself."

Holly went into the study, called the Agency's London station, got Tom Riley on the line, and scrambled. "Anything new?" she asked.

"We got a guy into the McCallister house posing as a gas worker looking for a leak in the neighborhood, but they wouldn't allow him above the ground floor."

"Swell, so we still don't know if Hamish and Mo are in the house?"

"Our man did see the cook put a breakfast tray in the dumbwaiter and send it up."

"A tray for one or two?"

"He thinks for one."

"So one of them isn't in the house?"

"Or one of them doesn't eat breakfast. Take your pick."

"Tom, do a search of everything for the name Algernon." She spelled it for him.

"In what context?"

"In any context at all. We've got an al Qaeda operative calling himself Algernon."

"Okay."

"Call me when you've got something." She hung up and went back into the living room.

"The president has finished, and now Vargas is having his say," Stone said. "You look a little stressed. How come?"

Holly turned and walked out onto the patio without replying. Stone got up and followed her.

"What's going on, Holly?"

"I'm missing something, that's what's going on," she said.

"I don't understand."

"Do you understand that we're under siege here in this hotel? There are at least two bombers out there, determined to do their worst, and nothing we've been able to do about finding them has worked."

"You sound like Steve Rifkin," Stone said. "Leave it to the Secret Service, they're the experts here, not you."

"I've got a contact in London who I think is lying to me, but I can't prove it."

"I should think you'd get lied to a lot, in your business," Stone said.

"I feel out of my depth," Holly said. "I'm accustomed to playing offense, not defense."

"I wish I could help," Stone said. "Why don't you talk with Felicity? Maybe she can help."

"We had a long chat last evening," Holly said, "and she's working her side of the pond."

"Have you done everything you can do?"

"I've done everything I can think of, which may not be the same thing." Her phone rang. "Excuse me," she said, and walked away a few yards.

"It's Tom. Scramble."

Holly scrambled. "Shoot."

"We haven't got much: There's a hotel in South London by that name, could be a drop. There's Algernon Moncrieff, a character in *The Importance of Being Earnest*, Oscar Wilde, and there's a short story and then a novel called *Flowers for Algernon*, made into a movie called *Charly* that starred Cliff Robertson. He got an Academy Award for his performance. That's it. Nobody here can think of anything in either work that would relate to al Qaeda or spying or anything else."

"Okay, Tom."

"We'll keep at it."

"Sure, call me." Holly hung up and went back to where Stone had sat down.

"Anything new?"

"Absolutely nothing."

52

Hamish opened the closet door and took the key to the steamer trunk from his pocket, opened it, and swung open the door. The finely machined panel glowed in the light from the overhead bulb.

Hamish inserted his T-key into the slot at the top of the panel and turned it ninety degrees to the right. With a click, the clock was powered, displaying a row of zeros. Hamish checked his wristwatch, added the number of hours until eight thirty p.m., then carefully tapped the hours and minutes into the keypad. He took a deep breath and let it out, then he pressed the enter button, and the clock began its downward march to zero.

The concert would begin at seven p.m., perhaps a few minutes later. It was scheduled to run until eight-thirty, so the device would detonate at about the time of the last number in the concert, or, perhaps, during an encore. Even if the detonation came late there would still be fifteen hundred people in the Arrington Bowl, among them the presidents of the United States and Mexico. All the others—movie moguls, movie stars, entertainers of various skills, the cream of Los Angeles society, business leaders—would simply be cannon fodder for the greatest lethal attack on the United States ever recorded. Upward of a million people would die in an instant—many more of their injuries or radiation sickness in the months and years to come.

The loss of the great Osama bin Laden would be avenged. Any evidence of the perpetrators would be vaporized in the initial blast, so no one would ever know who had caused it, until the announcement was made worldwide on the Internet. Neither he nor Mo nor Jasmine nor any of the people who had helped them would ever be known to the authorities. Wynken, Blynken, and Nod would be dead.

Hamish checked his watch again: he would leave The Arrington at three p.m.; his flight from LAX would depart at five p.m. and arrive in London after a nonstop flight at midmorning the following day. He would drop off his luggage at his house, then have lunch at his club.

He closed the trunk and locked it, then put the

two keys into his pocket. He would have time for a nice lunch at the patio restaurant; he had already booked the table, late, for two p.m.

He packed his two Vuitton cases with his clothes and set them near the front door for collection by Hans, then he showered, shaved, and began to dress for lunch.

Holly Barker returned to the presidential cottage with the president and the first lady after the press conference. The president seemed in a particularly good mood, and so did the first lady.

"Lunch in half an hour," Kate Lee said, and at that moment, Holly's phone rang.

"Holly Barker."

"It's Tom Riley: scramble."

She scrambled. "Yes, Tom?"

"I don't know why we took this long," Riley said sheepishly. "We should have had it last night."

"What, Tom?"

"Algernon."

"Yes?"

"When we ran the search on Mo, we got his birth certificate; we got Hamish's, too, in his birth name of Ari Shazaz. What we didn't pick up on was the deed poll."

"Tom, what the hell is a deed poll?"

"It's the legal procedure used when the name of a British subject is changed. Ari Shazaz's name was changed at the age of nine, after his parents' divorce. His full name became Hamish Algernon Mc-Callister."

Holly's knees went weak, and she sank into a chair. "Tom," she said.

"Yes, Holly?"

"Phone in a fire alarm on the house on the Chelsea Embankment. Put some smoke on the roof, if you can, for verisimilitude. When the fire brigade arrives, send your people in with them and detain both Hamish and Mo. Get them to a quiet place quickly and start interrogating them. No nice chat—use whatever you have to use to find out what they did in Palo Alto. No police department, no intelligence service is to be brought into this. When you have everything you can get from the two men, get them out of the country to Gitmo. Is that clearly understood?"

"It's understood, Holly, but I'm going to have to hear it from the director, in person, before I can do any of that."

"Stand by, Tom, don't hang up." Holly went into the next room and looked for the first lady; she was nowhere in sight. Clutching her phone, she ran up the stairs to the second floor where the first couple's bedroom was. A Secret Service agent stood at the top of the stairs.

"Yes, ma'am?" the man said, blocking her way. "How may I help you?"

"I must see the first lady immediately, priority one."

"And your name, ma'am?"

"Oh, God, you're new, aren't you?" Holly asked.

"Yes, ma'am."

"I'm Holly Barker, assistant director of intelligence. I'm Mrs. Lee's number two."

"May I see identification to that effect, please?"

Holly smote her forehead. "It's in my handbag downstairs."

"I'll wait while you get it, ma'am."

"I don't have time for this. Go and tell the first lady I'm waiting. I'll be right here. It's a matter of life and death."

"I think I'd better call my supervisor," the man said, producing a handheld radio. "Just a moment."

"I don't have a moment," Holly said.

But the man was already speaking into the radio; he wasn't moving, and he was too big for Holly to move. "This is Special Agent Jack Shorstein," he said into the radio. "Chief of detail, please, priority." He took the radio away from his lips. "This will take just a moment."

Holly began to take deep breaths, trying to bring her rate of respiration down. She raised her phone. "You still there, Tom?"

"Yes, Holly. I can hear you having difficulties."

"Just hang on."

The agent's radio crackled, and he put it to his hear. "Yes? Special Agent Shorstein, sir. A woman who says her name is Holly Barker is demanding to see the first lady. She has no ID. Yes, sir." He handed the radio to Holly. "Special Agent Rifkin wishes to speak with you."

Holly snatched the radio from him. "Steve? It's Holly. I've got to see the first lady *right now*."

"Holly, give the radio back to my agent."

She handed him the radio and waited while he listened, then put the radio back on his belt. "You're cleared to see the first lady, ma'am," he said, stepping aside.

Holly ran down the hall to the master bedroom and knocked on the door. It was answered by a maid.

"Yes, ma'am?"

"I'd like to see the first lady at once," Holly said.

"I'm sorry, ma'am, but she's in the bath."

Holly shoved the woman aside and went for the bath. She opened the door without knocking, stepped into the bathroom, and saw, clearly, the president of the United States and the first lady in the shower together.

"I apologize for the intrusion," Holly shouted over the noise of the running water, "but this can't wait!"

53

Kate Lee sat in a terry-cloth hotel robe and listened to Holly's story. "Hamish's middle name is Algernon," Holly said.

Kate looked stunned. "This doesn't seem possible."

"Ma'am, Hamish recruited—or at least, assigned—Wynken, Blynken, and Nod. All the e-mails the NSA and the Brits intercepted originated from him. We've *got* to interrogate him at once." Holly held out the cell phone to her.

Kate took the phone. "Tom? It's Kate Lee."

Nothing.

"The phone's dead," Kate said.

Holly took it from her and redialed the number. "Tom Riley."

"Tom, we got cut off. Here's the director." She handed the phone back to Kate.

"Tom, it's Kate Lee. You recognize my voice?"

"Yes, Director."

"Carry out Holly's instructions and report back to her at every stage of the operation. Get the two men to that air force base in the Midlands and on an airplane to Guantanamo. The brothers are to be isolated from each other and everyone else. Am I clear?"

"Absolutely clear, ma'am."

"Good-bye. Let us hear from you."

"Yes, ma'am." Riley hung up.

Kate handed back the phone to Holly. "I hope this is productive," she said, "because, believe me, this is going to come back and bite me on the ass. Probably the president, too."

"You can always blame me," Holly said. "I've still got my army pension."

"I hope you won't need it," Kate said. "Can my husband and I get dressed now?"

Holly turned red. "I'm so sorry, ma'am."

"What do you want to bet this makes his memoirs?"

"Oh, God, I hope not."

"You can hope."

Holly ran for the door, then downstairs to her room and installed a fresh battery in her cell phone. Almost immediately, it rang. "Hello?"

"It's Stone. Want to have some lunch?"

"Yes, please, I need to think about something else."

"Something else than what?"

"I can't tell you."

"Meet me at the patio restaurant in ten minutes," Stone said. "I've got a table."

"See you there." Holly ran into the bathroom, checked her makeup, then hurried out of the presidential cottage. She hopped into her electric cart and barreled down the cart path toward the restaurant.

Stone was sitting at a table, drinking iced tea. Holly joined him.

"This," she said, "is the first time I've ever been able to see three movie stars in one place, live."

"I know," Stone replied, "the place is infested with them." He waved at someone behind Holly.

"Who are you waving at?"

"Charlene Joiner."

"Another movie star? How do you know *her*?"

"Don't ask."

"She's the one who had an affair with Will Lee when he was still a senator, right?"

"I think it was more of a one-nighter, and they were both single at the time. I've heard some opinions expressed that when the news of that incident broke, he picked up half a million votes."

Holly laughed. "America wanted a stud president?"

"I guess so. Now, what were you so discom-bobulated about when I called?"

"Well, I barged into Kate Lee's bathroom with-out knocking and caught her in the shower with her husband."

Stone burst out laughing. "No kidding?"

"I kid you not. She says the incident will prob-ably make his memoirs."

"It's nice to know they still have that kind of relationship."

"I guess so."

"What was so important that you went into her bathroom without knocking?"

Holly sighed. "I wish I could tell you."

"Are you forgetting that I'm still under contract to the Agency as a consultant and that I have the highest security clearance?"

"That's right—you do, don't you? All right, here's what's happened." She told him everything from her phone call to Hamish at Annabel's the day before.

"Who the hell is Hamish?"

"He's an asset of the Agency who reports only to Kate and me."

"How did that come about?"

"Your cousin, Dick Stone, was running him when he was still station chief in London, and when he left London he handed Hamish off to Kate, who kept him. I think she found it entertaining that she had her own asset that nobody else knew about."

"I hope that relationship doesn't come back to bite her on the ass," Stone said.

"Funny, that's what she said."

A waiter brought them each a huge lobster salad.

"I hope you don't mind my ordering for you," Stone said.

"Not a bit if it's lobster salad."

"I understand the lobsters here are flown in from Ireland."

"Ireland? Whatever happened to Maine?"

"The Irish lobsters have a very high reputation, but nearly all of them are sold to the French. It's just one of those little touches that makes The Arrington The Arrington."

Holly dug into her salad. "God, this is good. Maybe they have a point about the Irish lobsters."

"Would you like a glass of wine?"

"I'd love that, but I have to remain stone-cold sober for the rest of the day. Iced tea will do nicely."

Stone ordered her an iced tea. "Do you have any time off coming?" he asked.

"I've got about two years of vacation I haven't used," she replied.

"Tell you what, why don't you fly back to New York with us and spend a few days there with me?"

"That's very tempting," Holly replied. "Let me

talk to Kate—maybe we'll have a bit of a lull when this business here is all over."

"You do that."

They finished lunch and chatted for a while. Holly checked her phone to be sure she hadn't missed a call. "I've got to get back," she said, "there's too much going on."

Stone signed the check and stood up with her. "Call me when you know if you can fly back with us."

"I'll do that."

They headed off in different directions, Holly toward where she had parked her cart.

"Holly? Is that you?" a voice from a table behind her said. A familiar voice.

She turned and looked over her shoulder. He sat there, sipping an espresso, beautifully turned out in a white linen suit. *"Hamish?!"*

"Good afternoon," Hamish said, rising to greet her.

"But I spoke to you in London yesterday. What are you doing here?"

"I caught a ride on a friend's corporate jet. We landed this morning. I wanted to stay here, but of course that was impossible, so I'm at the Beverly Hills."

Holly's cell phone buzzed at her belt. She grabbed it. "Excuse me a moment," she said to Hamish, then walked a few paces away for privacy. "Hello?"

"It's Tom Riley: scramble."

She scrambled. "Okay, what?"

"We went into the house this morning, but it was empty, except for staff."

"That doesn't surprise me, since Hamish is sitting at a table in The Arrington's garden restaurant, sipping espresso, just a few yards away from me."

"It begins to make sense," Tom said. "We checked out the car phone on the Bentley and found an Agency GPS card in it. We checked with the doorman at Annabel's—the car was parked out front all evening, but Hamish and Mo were not in the club. We've been chasing our own tails."

"Well, I'm sorry about that," Holly said defensively. "Now I've got to go and wrap this up. Bye." She hung up and turned back to where Hamish sat. He was gone.

Hamish walked quickly through the back of the garden and got into the white Cayenne at the curb with Hans at the wheel. "Did you pick up my two bags?"

"Yes, in the back."

"How about your device?"

"In the spare tire well, under the trunk."

"Drive normally and get us out of here."

54

Holly darted around the restaurant, looking for Hamish. She opened the men's room door and shouted his name. A man elbowed past her. "Sorry, wrong guy."

"Is there anyone else in there?" she shouted at him.

"Not a soul, lady." He hurried away.

Holly got on her phone. She had to look up Steve Rifkin's number, which took a minute. Finally, she had it ringing.

"Rifkin," he said.

"It's Holly Barker."

"I'm going to have to call you back," Rifkin said.

"No, no!" But he had already hung up. She looked up Mike Freeman's number and tried that.

"Freeman," he said.

"Mike, it's Holly Barker."

"How are you, Holly?"

"Listen, Hamish McCallister is on the hotel grounds."

"Who?"

"Algernon!"

"How do you know that?"

"I just had a conversation with him in the garden restaurant, but I lost him. Can you alert your security people? It's vital that we interrogate him."

"Is he registered at The Arrington?"

"No, at the Beverly Hills Hotel."

"Description?"

"Five-nine, bald with a dark fringe of hair, one-sixty, tanned."

"Any particular place we should look?"

"Everywhere!"

"Did you call Steve Rifkin?"

"I did, but he couldn't talk and hung up on me."

"We're on it."

"Call me when you find him." But Mike had already hung up.

The white Cayenne approached the main gate and slowed; the uniformed guard, recognizing the car and driver, waved them through.

"Turn left," Hamish said. "LAX, British Airways."

"You're leaving the country?" Hans asked.

"No, but I want certain people to think so."

Traffic was moderately light at that time of day, and half an hour later, the car stopped at the curb.

"Stay in the car," Hamish said. "I'll deal with the luggage. Here are your instructions: drive to Santa Monica Airport and go to the hangar where the Cessna Caravan is stored. The pilot will be waiting there. Drive the car inside the hangar. I'm going to check my bags through to London, then I'll take a cab to Santa Monica, and we'll fly north from there."

"What about the device?"

"Leave it alone. I'll deal with it when I arrive."

"Got it."

Hamish got out of the car, and Hans pressed the button to open the hatch. Hamish allowed a porter to take the two bags. "London," he said, "first class." Then he opened the spare tire well, opened the device case, inserted his key into the lock, turned it clockwise ninety degrees, then set the timer for forty-five minutes. He closed the case, closed the lid, and pressed the button to close the hatch. He slapped the car twice on the fender, and Hans drove away.

Hamish followed the porter to the first-class ticket counter, checked his bags, cleared security, and went to the first-class lounge. He was sitting at a table by the window with a drink, looking north, when the device detonated at Santa Monica Airport. A crowd gathered at the window, staring at the towering smoke and flames five miles to the north.

Hamish had seen all he needed to. He got out his throwaway cell phone and sent a text to Wynken. *At 8:20 p.m. sharp set device for thirty minutes and leave the area.* Wynken would get quite a surprise when he turned the key in the device.

Then Hamish relaxed, finished his drink, and ordered another.

Holly went to Stone's cottage and hammered on the door. Stone opened it and took one look at her. "What's going on?"

Holly went into the house, dialing Mike Freeman's number.

"Freeman."

"It's Holly. Have you found him?"

"He's in none of the obvious places," Mike replied. "We're searching the grounds, and Steve Rifkin's people are helping, and Steve has sent a team to the Beverly Hills Hotel."

"When you find him, bring him to Stone's house in handcuffs." She hung up.

"Bring who here?" Stone said. "And why in handcuffs?"

"Algernon. Hamish McCallister. He was sitting a few tables away from us at the restaurant."

"I thought you said he was in London."

"I was wrong." She dialed Kate Lee.

"Yes?"

"Director, we've had a surprise. Hamish McCallister is here, on the hotel grounds."

"But I thought . . ."

"Yes, ma'am, but we were wrong. He took the GPS tracking device out of his phone and put it in his car phone. He told me he hitched a ride in a corporate jet to Burbank, landing this morning, said he's staying at the Beverly Hills. The Secret Service is looking for him there."

"I thought you said he was here."

"He disappeared."

"Well, at least we don't have to send him to Gitmo in order to interrogate him. Keep me posted." She hung up.

The doorbell rang, and Special Agent Steve Rifkin entered the house. "Nothing yet," he said.

"Steve, we've got to do the search for a bomb all over again," Holly said.

"You think he brought something onto the hotel grounds? That's impossible—he would never have gotten through security."

"Steve is right," Stone said, "and if we start a new search with all of the guests arriving, we'll be all over CNN in five minutes. I don't think we want that."

"This is my call, Holly," Steve said. "No new search."

Holly threw up her hands. "Well, what are we going to do?"

"Nothing," Steve said. "Sometimes nothing is the best thing to do. It won't help us to alarm the arriving guests." His cell phone rang. "Rifkin." He listened for a moment. "I don't see how that can be anything to do with us. Keep me posted on the investigation." He hung up.

"What happened?" Holly asked.

"There was a huge explosion five minutes ago at Santa Monica Airport."

Stone switched on the TV. A local channel was on with a banner saying, "Breaking News." "We now have footage from chopper five on that explosion at Santa Monica Airport. Five hangars are in flames, some of them with aircraft inside." The camera moved along a row of burning hangars.

"I think that may have been one of the two bombs we were looking for," Stone said.

"I hope it was," Holly replied. "And I hope Hamish was standing next to it when it went off."

"One to go," Stone said.

55

Kelli Keane left her room and went next door to Hamish McCallister's suite. There was a "Do Not Disturb" sign on the doorknob, and when she rang the bell no one answered.

Where the hell had he gone? Lunch, maybe? She drove her cart down the hill to the garden restaurant and walked through the tables, noting celebrities for her piece and looking for Hamish, but he was nowhere to be found. She got out her cell phone and called The Arrington's front desk.

"Good afternoon, The Arrington. How may I help you?"

"Please ring the suite of Mr. Hamish McCallister, and please stay on the line if he doesn't answer."

"Of course," the woman said. The number began ringing. "I'm sorry, there's no answer from that suite."

"Has Mr. McCallister checked out?"

"One moment . . . No, he's not due to check out until tomorrow."

"Thank you." Kelli hung up and immediately her cell phone rang. "Hello?"

"Hi, it's Hamish. I've been looking for you."

"Same here. Where are you?"

"On my way to London, I'm afraid. Why don't you join me? You'll have to hurry, though, my flight leaves in forty minutes."

"I'd love to, but I can't. I've got to work the concert tonight with the photographers. It's important to my piece, and I'm going to want more work from this magazine."

"I understand. Kelli, I have to give you some serious advice, but what I'm going to tell you is completely confidential. Is that agreed?"

"Agreed."

"There is very likely going to be a serious disruption at the hotel sometime this evening. Skip the concert and get the next flight back to New York. Do you understand?"

"No, not really."

"Leave the hotel. Got it?"

"I've got it, I guess."

"I'll call you from London next week, and we'll reschedule. Good-bye, love."

"Good-bye." Kelli hung up. What the hell was he talking about?

Holly sat nervously with Stone, Mike, and Steve Rifkin, waiting for the results of the search. Rifkin's phone rang.

"Steve Rifkin." He listened for a moment, then hung up. "Nothing," he said. "No Hamish McCallister."

Holly thought for a moment. "Do an airline search for his name," she said. "All flights departing for Europe."

Mike Freeman spoke up. "I can do that faster than you can, Steve." He made a call. "I'm on hold while they check," he said. "Yes? Thank you very much." He hung up.

"There's a Hamish McCallister traveling to London on BA 106, nonstop to London Heathrow. Departed eight minutes ago."

"Shit!" Holly said.

"You've got ten hours to arrange a reception committee for Mr. McCallister at Heathrow."

"I don't want him in London, we'd have to deal with the Home Office bureaucracy."

Mike turned to Steve. "You must know somebody who can divert that flight to an American airport," he said. "And you'd better get it done before that aircraft crosses the Canadian border," Mike pointed out.

Steve got out his cell phone and called his director in Washington. He explained himself as quickly as he could, then asked that the flight be diverted to JFK on the excuse of mechanical trouble. There was some back-and-forth, then he hung up and put away his phone. "He's going to get the flight diverted," Steve said. "The only problem is, we've got to get the FBI involved."

"Too bad," Stone said. "That's always a complication."

"Yes," Rifkin replied. "I hate it, but it's a jurisdictional thing."

Stone turned to Holly. "What are you going to do with him when you have him?"

"Good question," Holly said. "I'll need to talk with my director." She left Stone's cottage and went next door to the presidential cottage. She found the first lady in the living room talking to Felicity Devonshire.

"Oh, Holly," Kate Lee said, "I was about to call you. Sit down with us, and let's talk about Hamish McCallister."

Holly sat down. "Hamish is on a flight from LAX to London as we speak."

"Then I'd better mobilize my people," Felicity said.

"No, that won't be necessary. The Secret Service

is arranging to have the flight diverted to JFK on some maintenance excuse. The FBI will pick him up there."

"You've been busy," Kate said.

"Yes, ma'am. I'm sorry we couldn't detain him here, it would have been easier. The question now is, once the FBI has him in New York, what do we do with him?"

"The same thing we were going to do with him before," Kate said.

"With the FBI involved?"

Kate stood up. "Excuse me a moment, I think I know somebody who can get the FBI uninvolved." She left them and went upstairs.

Felicity sighed. "This would have been a lot easier if you had just kidnapped him in London."

Holly laughed. "Would that have been your preference?"

"I'd have been happy to have him off our hands," Felicity said.

Ten minutes later, Kate returned. "All right," she said, "the FBI is off the case. Holly, you call Langley and get a crew out to JFK to greet the gentleman. Have them remove him to our East Side facility in the city and locked down, no conversation with anybody. I'll have further instructions for them when they have him secured there."

Holly excused herself, went into the study, and called Lance Cabot.

"Yes?"

"It's Holly."

"Good day, Holly. I trust you're enjoying the California sunshine. Everyone here hates you for being there."

"Thanks so much. The director asked me to call you with some instructions."

"I'm listening."

"There's a passenger aboard British Airways Flight 106 from LAX to Heathrow, departed LAX about twenty minutes ago. The flight is going to be diverted to JFK, and the director would like for you to assemble a team and transportation and meet that flight. There's a passenger named Hamish McCallister aboard."

"Wait a minute, I know that name from when I was at the London station. Man-about-town, and all that."

"He's our asset, reporting directly to the director."

"*What?*"

"Don't get your knickers in a twist, Lance. All will be explained later. You are to remove McCallister to our East Side facility in the city and isolate him pending further instructions. He's suspected of being the ringleader in a plot to bomb The Arrington."

"Hamish McCallister? That fop? He's harmless!"

"He's real trouble, Lance. You have less than three hours to put this together, and I suggest that once you've given the orders, you chopper to New York and take charge."

"All right, tell the director it shall be done. Anything else?"

"Call me when he's in hand."

"Certainly." Lance hung up.

56

Kelli Keane dressed for the Immi Gotham concert. She had been saving her best dress for the event, and she thought she looked sensational, while remaining entirely professional. The image in the mirror was very reassuring.

What was not reassuring, however, was Hamish's advice to her on the phone earlier. He wanted her to leave the hotel because of a likely disturbance to come; he had already left the hotel—left the country, in fact, and without checking out. This didn't make any sense.

He had not actually used the word "terrorist," but "disturbance" sounded to her like British understatement. She needed to tell somebody about this, she reckoned, but she didn't fancy walking up to some security guard and trying to explain to him, or his boss, that a slight acquaintance had warned her to leave the hotel because of a possible "disturbance."

She checked her makeup one last time. Stone Barrington: he was plugged into everything at the hotel; he'd know what to do with this information.

She grabbed her clutch bag, left her room, and got into her electric cart, then drove to the reception building and walked to the building behind it that she understood to be Stone's cottage. She rang the doorbell and waited, then rang it again.

A man in a white-jacketed uniform finally answered the door. "Yes, may I help you?"

"Yes, I'm Kelli Keane, from *Vanity Fair* magazine, and I'd like to speak to Stone Barrington."

"I'm afraid Mr. Barrington isn't in right now," the man said.

"When do you expect him?"

"Probably not until later tonight, certainly not until after the concert. He's having drinks at the presidential cottage right now, and they're all going to the concert together."

"That's just across the street, behind this house?"

"Yes, ma'am, but you're not going to get in there without an invitation. The Secret Service will see to that."

"Thanks very much," Kelli said, and left the cottage. She walked around to the street behind and looked at the presidential cottage. Two men in dark suits stood at the door.

She went back to the cart. She wasn't about to get into it with the Secret Service; maybe she'd see Stone at the concert. Perhaps she should just go straight there now; it was getting dark, and her press pass didn't give her reserved seating.

She drove down to the Arrington Bowl and found a parking spot, then wandered in with the crowd, which was streaming in in great numbers, all in formal dress. The place was beautiful, spread out in a fan shape with a lovely band shell as if from some gigantic scallop.

The orchestra was beginning to take their seats, now, and a concert grand piano stood at center stage. Tune-up sounds wafted from the pit. Kelli looked at her watch: seven p.m. They would be starting any minute.

She looked over her shoulder and up to a private box near the top of the seating area. The president and first lady were entering and finding seats, while a file of others followed them. She saw Stone among them.

She ran up the stairs to the top of the Bowl and around the seats toward the presidential box. She could already see a man and a woman with pins in their lapels moving to head her off.

Kelli stopped. "My name is Kelli Keane, I'm from *Vanity Fair* magazine."

"Yes?" the man said.

"It's extremely important that I speak to Mr. Stone Barrington, who is sitting in the presidential box."

The man and the woman exchanged a glance. "Will you come this way, please?" the woman said, slipping her hand under Kelli's arm. They led her to one side of the box and out of its view. "Now," the man said, "please let me see your press pass."

Kelli dug the pass from her bag and handed it over.

"And who was it you wanted to see?"

"Mr. Stone Barrington."

"What is the nature of your business?"

Another man joined them from the direction of the box, then just stood and listened.

"It's a personal matter," Kelli said. "If you could please just ask Mr. Barrington to step over here for a moment."

Then the other man spoke. "You're from the press, aren't you?"

"Yes, I'm Kelli Keane, from *Vanity Fair.*"

"Thank you," the man said to the Secret Service duo. "It's all right, I'll deal with this." The two nodded and stepped away.

"Thank you," Kelli said. "I was beginning to have visions of being taken away in handcuffs."

"I'm Michael Freeman," the man said, "from

Strategic Services. We're in charge of security here. You seem very concerned. What's the problem?"

"Well, I wanted to tell Stone, because he could tell the right people, but I guess you'll do."

Mike smiled. "I'll do. What is it?"

"Well, there was a man from London at the hotel named Hamish McCallister. He called me from the airport this afternoon and said I should leave the hotel before the concert, that there would be some sort of disturbance."

The audience burst into applause as the conductor strode to the podium and bowed, then a disembodied voice rumbled through the crowd. "And now, ladies and gentlemen, our special guest, Miss Hattie Patrick, of the Yale School of Music, who will perform our opening number with the Los Angeles Philharmonic."

A pretty young girl walked onto the stage, bowed once to the audience, and sat down at the piano.

"Wait right here," Mike said to Kelli. "Don't move."

A clarinetist began the opening trill to "Rhapsody in Blue" and the orchestra joined in, followed by the guest pianist.

For a moment, Kelli forgot her anxiety and just let the music wash over her.

A moment later, Mike Freeman was back with Stone and two other men. Mike led them up a flight of stairs to an exit, and they stopped on the lawn.

"Kelli, what is this about Hamish McCallister?" Stone asked.

"I had dinner with him the other night, and we got along very well. Then, this afternoon, he called me from the airport and asked me to fly to London with him. I said I couldn't, I had to cover the concert, and he told me, in a very serious manner, that I should avoid the concert and leave the hotel and go back to New York."

"Did he say why?"

"He said there would be a serious disturbance at the hotel tonight."

"At the concert?"

"No, he said at the hotel. Or, at least, that's what I inferred."

"Kelli, this is my friend Lieutenant Dino Bacchetti from the NYPD, and this is Special Agent Steve Rifkin, who is in command of the Secret Service presidential detail."

"How do you do?" Kelli said to the two men.

"Thank you for letting us know about this," Stone said. "We're aware of Mr. McCallister and that he's on a plane to London."

"How did you know that?" Kelli asked, ever the reporter.

"We got word," Stone replied. "The airplane will make an unscheduled stop in New York, and

Mr. McCallister will be removed from the flight."

Steve Rifkin spoke up. "It would be helpful if you could make yourself available for further interviewing after we have Mr. McCallister in custody."

"What do you suspect him of?" Kelli asked.

"There's nothing specific at the moment," Rifkin replied. A radio on his belt crackled, and Rifkin answered it. "Tell the chief of the bomb squad to meet me at the top of the Bowl right now." He replaced the radio on his belt.

"Bomb squad?" Kelli asked. "Is there a bomb somewhere around here?"

"The grounds have been thoroughly searched," Rifkin replied, "and security has been very strict with anyone entering the grounds. It's very unlikely that anyone could have smuggled a bomb in. Anything large enough to hold a significant bomb would have been searched immediately."

"I'm so relieved to hear that," Kelli said. "Tell me, would a steamer trunk be large enough?"

Everyone turned and stared at her.

57

The group moved up the hill from the Bowl, and Mike Freeman saw four of his men in their Strategic Services shirts standing on the grass, listening to the concert. He broke off from the group he was with.

"Good evening," he said to the men.

They suddenly looked sheepish.

"What are you doing out here? You're supposed to be manning the surveillance center, aren't you?"

One of the men spoke up. "It's very quiet around the hotel, because everybody's at the concert," he said. "Our supervisor said that we could come upstairs and listen for a while, he'd cover us and he'd radio if anything came up."

"Who is your supervisor tonight?" Mike asked.

"Rick," the man said.

"And he's down there by himself?"

"Yes, sir, like I said, there's nothing going on."

Mike's mind was spinning backward to his earlier conversation with Steve Rifkin about the screening of his men. "Did the Secret Service search our bunker?" he asked.

The men looked at each other. "No, sir," one of them said. "Not on my shift. I mean, we're security; why would they search us?"

"Follow me," Mike said, "but stay well back behind me." He strode up to the entrance of the half-underground bunker, tapped in the security code, and quietly opened the door. He had a terrible, terrible feeling, and he was beginning to sweat. He unholstered his Glock and let himself into the bunker, then walked down the flight of stairs into a vestibule. The door to the surveillance room was closed. He tried the knob: locked from the inside. He switched the pistol to his left hand and fumbled for his key ring, finally found the right key, and inserted it into the lock, turning it slowly to avoid a loud click. He pushed the door open slowly and stepped into the room.

Rick was standing at the end of a workbench, inspecting something in front of him. He snapped open the locks of a case and folded down the lid.

Mike could see just enough of it to recognize the case as identical to the one the search had turned up in the wine storage room.

Rick rooted around in a pocket and came up

with a T-shaped key. He inserted it into a slot at the top of the metal panel.

"If you turn that key, I'll kill you where you stand," Mike said quietly but firmly. He racked the slide on the pistol for emphasis.

Rick froze but said nothing. Mike walked forward, pressed the Glock to Rick's head, and pushed him aside with his elbow. Mike's left hand closed over his on the key. "Let it go right now," he said, nuzzling Rick's head with the barrel of the pistol.

Mike could feel him trying to turn it, but he held tightly to the younger man's hand, pulling until the key left the slot. Mike took the key from him. "On your knees, back to me," he said. He took the key from his hand as he went down and put it into his jacket pocket.

"Mr. Freeman," a voice behind him said, "is everything all right?"

"Get me a pair of handcuffs from the equipment locker and get over here," Mike said, holding his left hand out behind him. He heard the locker open, then the cuffs were placed in his hand. "Hands on top of your head, fingers interlaced," he said to Rick, who complied. He cuffed the man, then put his foot between his shoulder blades and pushed him onto his belly. Then he turned toward the four waiting men.

"Get a manacle set from the equipment locker and secure this man hand and foot, then search him thoroughly. Then I want him on the floor under guard until the Secret Service comes for him." He closed the case on the workbench. "Give them this case when they come. Now get back to your consoles."

Mike walked up the stairs holstering his weapon and came out into the cool night air. His shirt was sticking to his body. He looked around. Now where did everybody go?

Applause rippled from the Bowl; cheering and whistling and the stamping of feet were heard. "Encore!" the crowd was shouting. Then the noise died, and Immi Gotham said, "Seventy-five years ago, very near this place, George Gershwin was at the piano working on the last song he ever wrote. A few days later, he was dead at the age of thirty-eight. This is the song he wrote."

A piano introduction could be heard, then Gotham began to sing "Our Love Is Here to Stay."

Stone sat beside Kelli Keane as she drove her electric cart rapidly along a path toward a row of cottages. Another cart followed, driven by the chief bomb technician. "His place is next door to mine," she said, finally slowing to a halt. "Right there." She pointed at a door. A "Do Not Disturb" sign hung on the knob.

A bellman cruised past them, and Steve Rifkin signaled for him to stop. He flashed his ID. "Secret Service," he said. "Give me your pass card."

"Yes, sir." The bellman retrieved the card from his shirt pocket.

Rifkin slid the card into the door lock; a green light came on, and he pushed the door open.

Kelli spoke up. "The trunk was in a bedroom closet, to your left." Stone, Dino, Rifkin, and the two bomb men filed into the suite, and she followed them.

Stone found the closet first. "Here we are," he said. He turned the knob. "Locked."

The bomb chief took the pass card from Steve Rifkin, inserted it into the door lock, and opened the door.

The trunk stood there: elegant, with the patina of age and travel.

"Locked," the chief said. "Bob, I need a jimmy, please."

The other bomb man set down the case he was carrying, opened it, and handed his chief a small crowbar. The chief made short work of the lock.

"Do you think it might be booby-trapped?" Bob asked.

"I don't think we have time to worry about that," the chief replied, swinging open the trunk door. He stepped back, so that everyone could see the titanium panel with a slot and a digital clock at the top. The clock was counting down: forty-one, forty, thirty-nine . . .

58

Hamish McCallister lounged comfortably in his first-class berth, sipping his second mimosa, reading a magazine, and listening to Haydn over his headset. The music popped off and the pilot's English-accented voice replaced it.

"Good evening, ladies and gentlemen, and welcome aboard our flight. As you know, we are nonstop to London, but we are encountering strong headwinds, and that is going to make it necessary for us to make a fuel stop at Kennedy Airport in New York. I apologize for the inconvenience, but it will add only less than an hour flight time, and with the extra fuel, we may be able to cut that down by flying at a higher power setting. We will be landing at Kennedy at eleven p.m., New York time, and in order to be back in the air as quickly as possible, we ask that you remain in your seats during our brief stop. Thank you so much for your patience."

Hamish sighed, but the music resumed and he returned to his magazine. Then he stopped reading. His flight, he recalled, had pushed back at five minutes past five p.m., L.A. time. That would have been eight p.m., New York time, and the New York landing time of eleven p.m. would make their flight across the USA a four-hour one. Since a normal flight from LAX to JFK would take at least five hours, they were experiencing a strong tailwind, not a headwind. Something was wrong. He buzzed for the flight attendant.

"Yes, may I help you?" the young woman asked.

"Yes. Since we're stopping in New York, I'd like to have a prescription medication delivered to me there, something I need but forgot to bring. Can you find out our gate number for me?"

"Of course," she replied. She went forward, spoke over the intercom to the cockpit, then returned. "We will be refueling at gate ten," she said, "and I've asked our gate agent to be on the lookout for your delivery."

"Thank you so much," Hamish said. When she had left he picked up his seat's remote control, which was also a satphone, and called a New York number.

"Yes?" His brother Mo's voice.

"It is I," he said. "Listen carefully. Do we have a friend at Kennedy Airport?"

A brief silence. "Yes, a—"

"No further information, please."

"I'm sorry. What do you need?"

"My aircraft is making an unscheduled stop at Kennedy. Ask our friend to arrange for an airport vehicle, appropriately lighted, to meet me at the foot of gate ten, flight BA 106. There may not be stairs. Our ETA is eleven p.m. Do you understand?"

"Yes."

"We will be leaving the airport area immediately. Please make arrangements for our departure from the airport and for secure accommodations."

"It will be done."

"See you soon. Good-bye." Hamish broke the connection. They would arrive before the device in L.A. detonated, so there was time for a clean getaway.

Mike Freeman flagged a bellman with a cart and began looking for Stone, Dino, and Rifkin.

"Will they be in a cart, sir?" the bellman asked.

"Very probably."

"I gave my pass card to a Secret Service agent at cottage 202. Is that who you're looking for?"

"It is. Hurry, please."

The man put his foot down.

Stone watched the clock count down. His mouth was dry, and his hands were sweating. Thirty-seven, thirty-six . . .

"Can you stop it?" Rifkin asked the bomb crew chief.

"Unlikely," the man said, "but I can try." He found a screwdriver and began removing screws from the panel.

"This isn't going to happen fast enough," Dino said under his breath.

Twenty-five, twenty-four, twenty-three . . . "Give me the jimmy," the chief said. He accepted the crowbar, placed its edge under the rim of the front panel, and with great force, pried it open. He took hold of the top edge of the panel and put all his weight into bending it down to the perpendicular. Now some of the inner workings were exposed, including the wiring. The chief began sorting through a bundle of wires. "Most of these do nothing," he said. "They're camouflage for the active wires."

Ten, nine, eight . . .

Stone was salivating, now, and he swallowed hard. He thought of his son, Hattie, and Ben. Everyone he loved would die in six seconds. "Dino," he said, "give me your gun."

Dino handed over a snub-nosed .38. "If you're going to shoot yourself, shoot me first."

Stone raised the revolver. "Out of the way, Chief," he said, and cocked it for emphasis.

The chief turned and stared at him. "You can't—"

Stone fired twice at the rapidly changing numbers.

"—do that," the chief continued. The clock stopped at four seconds. "It might still blow."

Then a voice came from the doorway. "I've got the key."

Mike shoved the chief out of the way, inserted the T-shaped key he had taken from Rick into the slot, and turned it left, ninety degrees.

Three seconds remained on the clock. The numbers went dark.

"Okay," the chief said, "one of those actions worked—I'm not sure which one."

Stone handed Dino's revolver back to him. "Thanks." He looked around the room for a wastebasket, found one and threw up into it.

Kelli Keane's knees gave way, and she fell onto the carpet, out.

A few minutes later the chief had disconnected everything inside the trunk, and he began to give his audience a tutorial on the device:

"There's maybe three kilos of fissionable material," he was saying. "That would have caused an explosion that would have leveled everything and killed everyone within a two- or three-mile radius. It would also probably have brought the Stone Canyon reservoirs above us down the canyon."

"How many dead?" Steve Rifkin asked.

"A million, maybe two—lots more over a period of weeks and months. It's simply but ingeniously designed. The builder would have sent drawings of various machined parts to several suppliers, who wouldn't know the purpose of their work. Then they would have assembled the device in a safe house somewhere. They could have brought it here in a van, a station wagon, even, or a light airplane." He looked around the room. "Unless we find these people, they could do it again in a matter of weeks."

Hamish McCallister's aircraft stopped at the gate. His briefcase was already in his lap, and the moment the flight attendant opened the door he got up, strode forward, and walked into the boarding tunnel, and looked for the door. It was dead ahead, at the first turn. He opened it and looked outside; no stairs, but a white van with a yellow flashing light on top was parked immediately below. To his right, people with guns were running down the tunnel. Hamish took a deep breath and jumped, landing on top of the van and rolling off onto the tarmac. He got up, opened the passenger door, and got inside.

Mo was at the wheel, and he drove away quickly. "There's a gate about a quarter of a mile away," he said.

"Are you armed?" Hamish asked.

"Yes." He handed Hamish a pistol. "Here's one for you."

"If necessary, shoot anyone who impedes our progress."

Mo drove on. A gate loomed ahead, one man in a small guard booth.

Mo stopped and flashed some sort of ID card. The guard nodded, and the gate slid open slowly.

"Not too fast," Hamish said.

"Right."

"Where do we exchange cars?"

"A couple of miles, at a rest stop on the Van Wyck."

"Good."

Lance Cabot jumped from the boarding ramp onto the tarmac below, spraining an ankle. He raised his gun to fire, but the van had disappeared behind another airplane. Lance grabbed at the radio on his belt. "Seal the airport," he said. "Intercept a white van with a yellow flashing light. I need transport at gate ten right now!"

59

Lance leaped into the front passenger seat of the black SUV. "Nearest exit gate!" he yelled. Two more of his people, carrying submachine guns, jumped into the backseat.

"Got it," the driver replied, stomping on the accelerator.

"Lights!" Lance yelled, and the car lit up.

"Gate dead ahead," the driver said.

"If that jerk in the booth doesn't open it, knock the fucking thing down!"

The driver increased his speed, and the gate rolled open just in time for him to miss it. He screeched to a halt. "Which way?"

"Van Wyck! They've gotta be headed for the city."

The driver made the turn and accelerated. "Do we want the NYPD?" he asked.

"No," Lance replied, sounding calm but determined. "This guy is ours." He pointed ahead. "Half a mile up there," he said. "Flashing yellow light. Turn off our lights."

The driver did so.

"Try not to kill any innocent bystanders," Lance said, "but I don't give a shit what you do to the guys in the van."

"Look, they're pulling over," his driver said.

"Car switch. Block it!"

"Got it!" the driver shouted back. The white van had pulled into a rest area behind a black Mercedes. He drove around both vehicles and slid to a halt in front of the Merc. The inside lights were on, revealing two men.

Lance yanked open his door. "Fire at will!" he shouted, and he hit the pavement with his .45 semiautomatic pistol up and firing at the Mercedes. His two colleagues opened up with their submachine guns, and the black car's windshield evaporated. The two men inside were jumping like puppets on a wire.

"Cease fire!" Lance yelled. It took a moment, but his two men stopped firing. Lance walked forward, his gun held out, ready for any twitch. His two men yanked open both front doors and inspected the two bloody forms.

"No pulse or respiration here," one man said. "Pupils blown."

"Same here," the other man replied.

Lance raised his radio to his lips. "This is number one. Cleanup crew to the first rest stop on the Van Wyck, flatbed to the same location to take away a black Mercedes. Move it!" Then he leaned against the car and took deep breaths.

Finally, he got control of himself and produced his cell phone, pressing a speed dial number.

"Yes?"

"Number one. Status there?"

"Pending, estimate six minutes."

"Report back." He ended the connection.

In Dubai, a gala was under way at the Burj Al Arab, the huge, sail-shaped hotel on a bridge-accessed island off the city.

A Rolls-Royce glided up to the main doors, and a uniformed doorman opened the rear door.

Dr. Kharl, dressed in a tuxedo and blinking in the camera lights, put a foot onto the red carpet. As he did so, he was momentarily blinded by an intense red flash, and in the following second his head exploded.

Lance watched as the bodies were put into a van, and the Mercedes loaded onto a flatbed recovery vehicle.

"I want the bodies and the car minutely examined for any relevant evidence," he said. "Get it done." As he spoke, his cell phone rang. "Number one," he said.

"Status report, Dubai," a voice said.

"Go ahead."

"Subject is down and permanently out. Our executive has left the scene, headed for his departure point."

"Let me know when he's in the air," Lance said, then hung up. He pressed another speed dial button.

"Holly Barker."

"Scramble," he said.

"Scrambled."

"The situation is finalized," Lance said. "Two down and out in New York, bodies being taken to our morgue for postmortems. One down and out in Dubai, our man on his way out of the country."

"That sounds like a clean sweep," Holly said.

"It doesn't get any cleaner than this," Lance replied.

"Will you call Tom Riley in London and let him know the search for Hamish and Mo is canceled, though I'd still like to have any information about them that he can turn up."

"Will do."

"The director will be very pleased, Lance. I think you just got a leg up on replacing her."

"That would be nice," Lance said. "Good night."

"Good night."

Holly hung up, walked across the room, and whispered in Kate Lee's ear. "It's done," she said. "A clean sweep in both New York and Dubai."

"And the aftermath?"

"The bodies in New York are en route to our morgue for postmortem, our man in Dubai is clear."

"You know," Kate said, "I think that this is the most exciting night of my life that I'll never be able to talk about. I'll tell the president. You go thank everybody for me."

"Yes, ma'am," Holly said, and left the cottage.

60

Stone Barrington sat in the study of his cottage at The Arrington, a brandy snifter in his hand. Kelli Keane sat in the chair opposite him; there was a snifter in her hand, too.

"How are you feeling?" Stone asked.

"Much better, thanks. You're going to ask me not to write about this, aren't you?"

"I'm going to ask you not to breathe it to a living soul, magazine, news service, publisher, or TV news station for as long as you live. If you can't accept that, then others will ask you, and less politely."

Kelli held up a hand. "I know, I know. Can I ask some questions?"

"I don't have all the answers," Stone replied, "but I'll do the best I can."

"When did you—and those other people, the Secret Service and all—know about the nuclear thing?"

"Not until the moment you mentioned the trunk," Stone said. "There had been some very slight indications that something was afoot, but not enough to alter what was happening here for the past couple of days. A thorough search for something as big as a trunk had been conducted, but it seems that the trunk was brought from an airport to The Arrington in a hotel vehicle and deposited in McCallister's suite without the knowledge of the bell captain, who keeps a log of every piece of luggage brought into the hotel."

"Did the explosion at Santa Monica Airport have anything to do with this?"

"Yes. There were indications of three bombs: one was found by Rifkin's people in a liquor storage room yesterday. The chief bartender has been arrested in connection with that. A second was found by Mike Freeman in the Strategic Services security monitoring room, and one of his people arrested. The police found a car door at Santa Monica Airport, a hundred yards from the scene of the explosion, that had an Arrington logo painted on it. A hotel employee had checked out the car, and it's thought that he detonated the third bomb, perhaps accidentally."

"What happened to Hamish McCallister?"

"His flight was directed to land at Kennedy, ostensibly for refueling because of headwinds, but Hamish must have become suspicious, because he ran from the airplane to a waiting car driven by his brother. It's my understanding that they escaped the airport but were caught nearby and didn't survive the encounter. Something similar happened to the man who built the bombs."

"So all the bad guys are dead?"

"All except the two who were arrested, Wynken and Nod."

"And they're in jail?"

"Sort of," Stone said.

"What does that mean?"

"I believe they're en route to a secure facility. And that's all I know about this."

"Just one more question," she said. "What made you shoot at the device with Dino's gun?"

"I reasoned that if the clock would set off the device, maybe disabling it would stop it from going off."

"And that worked?"

"While you were still . . . indisposed, I asked the bomb chief about that, and he said the chances were about fifty-fifty that it worked."

"So you might have made it go off early?"

"Four seconds early. Fortunately, Mike Freeman arrived with a key from the bomb found in his surveillance room, and that worked, too."

"All right," she said, "I promise never to communicate what happened here to anybody, ever."

"That would be best for you," Stone said. "No one would corroborate your story. As far as the rest of the world is concerned, the presidents of the United States and Mexico had a highly successful conference, resulting in a comprehensive new security treaty between the two countries, and The Arrington had a hugely successful opening that went incredibly smooth, without a single hiccup. The concert, too. Be sure and mention in your piece how much you enjoyed Immi Gotham's encore with Hattie Patrick at the piano."

The following morning, Stone sat in the jump seat of the Gulfstream 550 and watched the takeoff. Twenty minutes later they were at forty thousand feet, headed east with a hundred-knot tailwind.

Stone looked out through the windshield at the clearly etched landscape of the Mojave Desert, dead ahead. "Severe clear," he heard the captain say. "I love that."

I love that, too, Stone said to himself, then he got up and went back to join his friends for brunch and champagne. He took a seat next to Holly Barker.

"Congratulations on a successful opening," she said. "I'm sure the hotel will do well."

"Mort, the executive director, told me they're sold out for months ahead," Stone said. "I think that you and I can both take some pleasure in the fact that your people and mine did a fine job."

"I saw the president and the first lady this morning, before they left for the airport," she said, "and both of them expressed their extreme satisfaction with how things went. They asked me to thank you for your part in it."

"Sometimes everything goes right," Stone said.

AUTHOR'S NOTE

I am happy to hear from readers, but you should know that if you write to me in care of my publisher, three to six months will pass before I receive your letter, and when it finally arrives it will be one among many, and I will not be able to reply.

However, if you have access to the Internet, you may visit my website at www.stuartwoods.com, where there is a button for sending me e-mail. So far, I have been able to reply to all my e-mail, and I will continue to try to do so.

If you send me an e-mail and do not receive a reply, it is probably because you are among an alarming number of people who have entered their e-mail address incorrectly in their mail software. I have many of my replies returned as undeliverable.

Remember: e-mail, reply; snail mail, no reply.

When you e-mail, please do not send attachments, as I never open these. They can take twenty minutes to download, and they often contain viruses.

Please do not place me on your mailing lists for funny stories, prayers, political causes, charitable fund-raising, petitions, or sentimental claptrap. I get enough of that from people I already know. Generally speaking, when I get e-mail addressed to a large number of people, I immediately delete it without reading it.

Please do not send me your ideas for a book, as I have a policy of writing only what I myself invent. If you send me story ideas, I will immediately delete them without reading them. If you have a good idea for a book, write it yourself, but I will not be able to advise you on how to get it published. Buy a copy of *Writer's Market* at any bookstore; that will tell you how.

Anyone with a request concerning events or appearances may e-mail it to me or send it to: Publicity Department, Penguin Group (USA) LLC, 375 Hudson Street, New York, NY 10014.

Those ambitious folk who wish to buy film, dramatic, or television rights to my books should contact Matthew Snyder, Creative Artists Agency, 9830 Wilshire Boulevard, Beverly Hills, CA 98212-1825.

Those who wish to make offers for rights of a literary nature should contact Anne Sibbald, Janklow & Nesbit, 445 Park Avenue, New York, NY 10022. (Note: This is not an invitation for you to send her your manuscript or to solicit her to be your agent.)

If you want to know if I will be signing books in your city, please visit my website, www.stuartwoods .com, where the tour schedule will be published a month or so in advance. If you wish me to do a book signing in your locality, ask your favorite bookseller to contact his Penguin representative or the Penguin publicity department with the request.

If you find typographical or editorial errors in my book and feel an irresistible urge to tell someone, please write to Sara Minnich at Penguin's address above. Do not e-mail your discoveries to me, as I will already have learned about them from others.

A list of my published works appears in the front of this book and on my website. All the novels are still in print in paperback and can be found at or ordered from any bookstore. If you wish to obtain hardcover copies of earlier novels or of the two nonfiction books, a good used-book store or one of the online bookstores can help you find them. Otherwise, you will have to go to a great many garage sales.

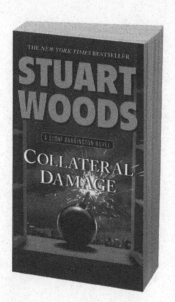

1

Elaine's, late.

Stone Barrington opened the taxi door. "Wait for me," he said. "I won't be long." He got out of the cab and looked around. The yellow awning was gone, but "Elaine's" was still painted on the darkened windows. A film of soap obscured the interior, but Stone found a bare spot and put his hands up to shield from the glare. What he saw was, in short, nothing.

The book jackets, photographs, and posters that had adorned the walls for forty-seven years were gone. The bar and mirrors behind it were still there, but there were no stools. The dining room contained no tables or chairs and no blue-checkered tablecloths. The two old pay phones still hung on the wall near the cashier's stand at the bar; they had always been the only phones in the place.

For a tiny moment Stone could hear the babble of a crowded room, chairs scraping, people calling the length of the room to say hello to a friend. Then a passing bus obliterated the sounds and returned Stone to the present. He got back into the cab and gave the driver his home address.

His cell phone buzzed at his belt. "Hello?"

"It's Dino. Where are you?"

"At Elaine's."

A brief silence, then: "You shouldn't do that."

"You're right," Stone said. "The memory is better than the reality. Have you had dinner?"

"I was just thinking about it."

"Where's Viv?"

"She's working."

"Come over and I'll make you some pasta."

"You, yourself?"

"Me, myself. I can cook, you know."

"There was a rumor, but I never believed it."

"Fifteen minutes."

"Okay. Oh, how are we dressing?"

"Unarmed," Stone said.

"I'm always armed."

"Then you can check your gun at the door."

"Whatever you say."

"How late is Viv working?"

"Until ten."

"Tell her to come over after, and I'll save her something."

"I'll see if she's brave enough."

"See ya." Stone hung up.

At home, he shucked off his jacket in the kitchen and checked the fridge. It was stuffed, as usual. Helene was an overshopper, and she liked to be ready for anything.

Stone found some Italian sausages, some mushrooms, some broccoli rabe, and some garlic. He sliced the sausages and tossed them into a skillet with a little olive oil, and they began to sizzle. He ran some water into a pot and put it on to boil for the pasta. He found some ziti in a cupboard and tossed it into the boiling water, then he chopped some onion and the garlic and tossed them into the pan with the sausages, followed by the mushrooms and rabe.

Dino came into the kitchen and tossed his coat on a chair. "Jesus, that smells pretty good," he admitted.

"Be ready in ten, fifteen minutes," Stone said. "Pour us a drink."

Dino went to the kitchen bar, filled a pair of glasses with ice, then filled one with his usual

Johnnie Walker Black scotch and the other with Stone's Knob Creek bourbon, then handed it to Stone. "Okay, what was the place like?"

"Bereft of all humankind and Elaine. Bereft of everything, come to that." The contents of the place had been sold at auction, along with Elaine's personal effects. Stone had bid on some books but didn't get them.

"You know," Dino said, taking a bite of his scotch, "I think she'd be happy that we can't find a new place."

"She wasn't that mean-spirited," Stone pointed out.

"She was about other joints. I'm still afraid to go to Elio's." Elio was a former Elaine's head-waiter who had opened his own restaurant a couple of blocks down Second Avenue.

"Yeah, me too. I only went once, just to say hello to Elio, but I never let her find out. She would have stabbed me with a fork."

"Or worse."

Stone found a hunk of Parmigianino-Reggiano in the fridge and dug the grater out of a drawer. He drained the pasta, forked some onto two plates, dumped some sausage onto the plates and grated a lot of the cheese over them, then he set them on the table and got a bottle of

Amarone out of the wine closet and opened it. "Sit yourself down," he said.

Dino did, and they both ate hungrily.

When Viv showed up, they hadn't even cleared the table; they were just sitting there, drinking and talking.

"Just like Elaine's," Viv said. "Without Elaine."

STUART WOODS

"Addictive . . . Pick it up at your peril.
You can get hooked."
—*Lincoln Journal Star*

For a complete list of titles and to sign up for our
newsletter, please visit prh.com/StuartWoods